Book 3 of the Treasured Lives

tangled lives

endorsements

Heartwarming characters, emotionally gripping, a five-star read.
—**June Foster**, author, the best-selling *Cranberry Cove* series

Carol McClain's latest book is filled with intriguing characters whose tangled lives will keep you flipping pages to discover what happens next. Always the unexpected. Keeps you reading late into the night.
—**Anne Greene**, author, *Trail of Tears: The Story of John Ross*

Carol McClain weaves a complex story about three characters dealing with desires for love, misplaced identity, sibling rivalry, and lust. These are off-the-page human characters, and Carol McClain deftly navigates the worlds of physical disabilities, insecurity, backsliding, trauma, music, and photography. You cannot find a richer set of characters!
—**Claire O'Sullivan**, author, *Romance Under Wraps* and *Rules of Engagement*.

Another good read by Carol McClain. True to life. As this story confirms, our pasts are always with us. Yet faith will untangle those hard places. You will laugh, cry, and cheer as the characters struggle to make the right choices ... for each other and for what faith demands.

—**Linda Wood Rondeau**, author, *Ghosts of Trumball Mansion*

The three Snow girls have grown up, but that doesn't mean life has become easier. Education and careers clash, love and emotions flair, and lives still seem to become tangled. Another great novel from author Carol McClain.

—**Susan Kite**, author of the Mendel Experiment trilogy, *Zorro's Pacific Odyssey*, *Realms of the Cat*

Meredith's girls are all grown up, and you won't want to miss finding out how their tangled lives have turned out.

—**Tilmer Wright Jr.**, author of *Motes* and *The Bit Dance*.

As always, there is a sort of poetic cadence to McClain's writing. I am immediately drawn in. Her characters grab hold by the heartstrings and create an ache that compels me to read on. *Tangled Lives* is a satisfying conclusion to the Treasured Lives series, and I highly recommend the book to lovers of women's fiction as a story that will stay with you long after you turn the final page.

—**Naomi Musch**, author, *Season of My Enemy* (2023 FHLCW Reader's Choice Finalist) and *Lumberjacks & Ladies* (2023 ACFW Carol Award Finalist).

Book 3 of the Treasured Lives

tangled lives

Carol McClain

A Christian Company
ElkLakePublishingInc.com

copyright notice

Cover and Interior Design:
Editor(s): Peggy Ellis, Cristel Phelps, Deb Haggerty

PUBLISHED BY: Elk Lake Publishing, Inc., 35 Dogwood Drive, Plymouth, MA 02360, 2022

Library Cataloging Data
Names: McClain, Carol (Carol McClain)
Tangled Lives / Carol McClain

328 p. 23cm × 15cm (9in × 6 in.)
ISBN-13: 978-1-64949-967-7 (paperback) | 978-1-64949-968-4 (trade hardcover) | 978-1-64949-969-1 (trade paperback) | 978-1-64949-970-7 (e-book)
Key Words: Coming of age novel; Romance novels; Christian women's fiction novels; Sister novels; Southern fiction; Sibling Rivalry, Redemption

Library of Congress Control Number: 2023xxxxxx Fiction

dedication

To Luciana, the youngest grandchild, who inspired
Crystal Joy with her love for people and her optimism.

acknowledgments

No writer has all the right words for a novel. Ideas must be tweaked and fleshed out. Grammar and formatting need correcting. Left to myself, I'd be offering you a mess you wouldn't want to read.

Always, the first person to thank is the Lord Jesus Christ. When writing becomes too hard or heartbreaking, he always shows up with encouragement or inspiration and enables me to complete what I couldn't by myself.

My husband allows the house to be dirty and dinner to be leftovers, so I can write. His love is a physical and human manifestation of Christ's perfect love.

My critique partners June Foster and Anne Greene refuse to let sloppy writing slip by. Peggy Ellis, my editor, adds the final polish.

Maranatha Masterminds help brainstorm and is a rich source of learning materials.

Tilmer Wright, Cyn Taylor and Susan Kite always help with promotion. Tilmer, especially, finds the last of my errors.

I thank Elk Lake for believing in me and Linda Rondeau for recommending me to Deb Haggerty.

prologue

Childhood behaves like the morning mist. Children dance and delight, then grow and vanish into the light of their days. So many nights, I wished my girls would mature, would give me grandchildren, would give me a moment to myself. First, of course, go to college.

When the time arrived, and they left me, they took their magic. Without magic, the scent of childhood wafted away in the morning fog. How could I have understood, all those years ago, the bedraggled waifs I fostered would steal my heart? In my reluctance to mother the abandoned children, I never fathomed the temporary fostering would turn into everlasting love when I adopted them.

Once more, I bit back tears as Crystal Joy, my youngest girl, climbed into her car. Last week, we outfitted the Honda with hand controls, so she could drive despite her spina bifida. Parker and I watched as she drove away to the University of Tennessee to join her sister.

I imagined I heard her singing. Never was Crystal without a song even as a child. Back then she hammered on pots and Tupperware to make music. Her alto, always on pitch. Her fingers twitched on guitar strings or dulcimers. In the end, my youngest daughter settled on the violin. Never did the spina bifida slow Crystal down or make her feel inferior. Could a mother call one child perfect?

The dust from the road settled, and I stood next to Parker like the day Lisa Simpson tried to adopt Crystal's sister.

Roxie.

Always the most sensitive. Perhaps the proverbial middle child. Sweet, insecure Roxie. Too independent and too needy. Her biological parents died of drug overdoses. Roxie had been old enough to understand abandonment, too young to realize her parents' issues had nothing to do with her worth. Roxie's oldest sister's grandfather adopted Pearl when she was eight. The hole bored through my heart. It compounded sweet Roxie's belief in her lack of worth. Roxie believed I loved everyone more than her.

Parker looped his arm around me.

His closeness soothed. Always.

"Meredith, the girls will be home before you realize they moved out. Now's the time for them to heal, live their passions, and find themselves." He kissed the top of my head. "They'll be okay."

In Parker's eyes, I hoped to see the truth of his words. This time, I didn't run away and hide. I let God take my fears and prayed the sins of my daughters' parents would no longer descend on their innocent offspring. I prayed the love of adoptive parents and a heavenly Father would redeem.

chapter 1

Two Years Later

Sworn to obedience. Promising to obey. Crystal heard her parents' warning. As a rule, she tried to please them. Today though? With humid air and the smell of chlorine drifting around her, she had to shake off the shackles of obedience even as she shook off her braces on the lounge behind her.

Her legs, free of constraints, dangled in the deep end of the motel's indoor pool. She savored the warm water on her skin while her head in the clouds bobbed to the melody playing in her mind. The water begged her, 'Come on. You swim like a mermaid. Jump.' She surveyed the pool room. Empty. Her family attended her oldest sister's wedding rehearsal.

Crystal closed her eyes imagining the warm water caressing her body. Swimming created real freedom of movement. Whether in the company of friends or alone, the water always made her feel normal. Parents and rules would be obeyed tomorrow when Pearl married.

Today, Florida's warmth, the cool water, and the melody humming in her head said, 'Jump.'

With a deep breath of air, Crystal leaned forward. Before she could dive, hands shoved against her back.

Water covered her as she sank, her eyes wide. Water and shock suppressed the scream lodged in her lungs. Down, down, down she plummeted until buoyancy lifted her. Before breaking the surface, warm arms encircled her. Lips whispered in her ear, so close they felt like a kiss. The voice masculine and familiar. The sound warming her body. *No. I can't feel this way.*

"Crissy-sissy, I expected you to be immersed in water without my help. Why were you sitting on the pool's edge?" Jesse Maxwell's breath tickled her ear and forced Crystal closer. Too close. He released his hold.

They tread water inches from each other, and her heart pounded. With eyes focused on his lips, a deep inhale forced her heart to still. After forever, she glanced away from his tempting mouth. "Mama and Daddy made me promise not to swim alone while they were at Pearl's wedding rehearsal. They like to believe I have absolutely no use of my legs." She giggled. "Or arms. Or brain. You know my folks and their stupid rules."

"Since when do you obey rules? Isn't rule-following Roxie's purview?"

The name of Crystal's sister uttered by Jesse Maxwell froze her soul. After an everlasting forever, she exhaled and relaxed.

"I'll race you to the shallow end." With a flip turn, Jesse kicked off the side of the pool and swam like a seal. Water glistened on the muscles of his back. Each breaststroke defined their curves.

Crystal held onto the pool's edge and watched as Jesse swam across the motel's pool.

After reaching the shallow end, Jesse stood and turned. "Hey, lazy, weren't we racing?" His sharp, downward nod beckoned her to join him.

How she wanted to obey, but she needed to keep her distance. Crystal shook her head.

tangled lives

With languid strokes, her sister's boyfriend swam back to her.

Strong hands gripped her waist and helped her to the pool's edge. Water sloshed over him as her weight pushed him down. Like a bobber, Jesse popped to the surface once more.

"I wasn't finished swimming, Mr. Maxwell." She winked. A shudder rippled down her spine. Crystal grabbed her towel. Rubbing the terrycloth over her face hid her angst. *Why am I flirting? Again.*

"I didn't see any swimming. Bobbing? Yes. Swimming?" One smooth move hoisted him from the water. Droplets fell from dark hair curling from the wet. He slanted toward her.

Desire taunted her. Begged her to lean into him and feel those full lips on hers. For four years, Roxie and Jesse dated. For four years, Crystal loved him.

Brown eyes peered into hers. Long, dark lashes, so lush they should've been on a girl, veiled the irises.

His eyes begged her to kiss him or, at least, lured her in to him. *Say something, Crystal. Jesse belongs to Roxie. You cannot give in to this.* "I can't believe on New Year's Eve we're swimming in a motel in Kissimmee. If heaven's like this, I'm ready to go." Still unnerved, she didn't look at him. "Since noon hasn't arrived, what would we call the day? Without a doubt, the daytime isn't an eve. Eve's day. New Year's Eve's Noon?" *I'm rambling. Maybe he didn't notice.*

"I'd call the day perfect."

He didn't notice my—

"Why are you nervous?"

Heat rose to Crystal's face. Fair skin cursed her. By now, her face had to resemble a ripe strawberry. "I'm not—"

"Your blush ... and the rambling ... say otherwise."

5

"You noticed?"

"Too cute not to." He leaned close. Too close.

Crystal threw him a smile. *If only Roxie knew how lucky she was.*

Jesse's voice lost its playful tone. "Can I ask you a question?"

Her throat constricted. She nodded.

"What do you think about having me as a brother-in-law? I'm going to propose to Roxie tonight after the fireworks at Disney."

Propose to Roxie? Crystal opened her mouth. *Shut up, Crystal. Don't say any—* "Not a good idea."

"Why?" Jesse frowned.

Her face heated once more, and she wanted to run, but her braces and crutches lay on the lounge several feet behind her. No way would she wriggle like an inch worm in front of Jesse to strap on her hardware. Instead of physically running, she twisted her head away.

Jesse's fingers tugged her chin. "Look at me."

Crystal shook her head. Blinked back rebellious tears.

Still, Jesse's fingers coaxed her to focus on him.

"Roxie and I have loved each other for four years. We'll graduate this semester, and she's all I ever dreamed about. Everything I want in a woman. Her every action says she loves me."

"Does she tell you?"

"Of course."

Crystal licked her lips. She had to speak the truth. "I'd guess she says the words after you tell her how much you love her."

Jesse's silence confirmed her belief. The silence grew awkward.

"If you propose, my sister will panic. In her fear, she'll dump you." Crystal bit her lip to keep from saying more.

Too much truth lacked wisdom. Still, Jesse had to realize if a man loved Roxie, her sister would panic.

"What do you mean 'Dump me'?"

Crystal had no escape. Jesse deserved to understand reality. "She has dated you longer than any other guy, but my sister hasn't changed. In the end, Roxie always finds something wrong with her man and runs away."

"The other fellows were high school kids—obviously wrong for her."

"Roxie thinks so. The truth about my sister is she never believes she's good enough. If someone loves her, then the fellow is flawed. The last guy, Mark—tailor-made for her." Crystal stiffened. "I'm not implying you aren't."

Jesse smiled his signature grin. "We're ideal. Go on."

"Mark loved the woods and animals. Good-looking. Intelligent. Perfect?" She shook her head. "Nope. My sister found something undefinably wrong. Before Mark, she ditched—"

"Stop." Jesse stood. "Roxie was in high school when she dated Mark and the others. Adolescent crushes last a month. Tops." He grabbed a towel.

Crystal shivered as the air blew cold around her.

"I'm catching a shower for my date. Tonight, I'll prove you wrong." He scrubbed his hair with his towel as he strode out of the pool room.

Crystal watched him go. Longing seized her soul. Jesse teased her. Flirted. Enjoyed her company. In the end, he saw her as the little sister. She was the ally Jesse needed to win Roxie.

She was cursed.

Roxie lowered her camera as her folks and the kids left the rehearsal.

"Hey, Sis, let's finish this up," Pearl called, her eyes still focused on her fiancé. "My man's hungry."

"He's always hungry." Larry, Pearl's useless father, smacked Malachi's stomach. The two men laughed.

"Go stand in the light, please. I don't know how I'm supposed to get a good exposure." Roxie slapped her head in fake frustration as she herded Pearl's wedding party toward the light filtering through the stained-glass window. "Why couldn't y'all have matching flesh tones?"

"Because Violet's daddy spoiled the gene pool." Malachi Moore winked at his sister, Pearl's best friend since rehab. "His white, pallid genes scrubbed away the beautiful ebony of our mutual mama. Not my daddy. Pure onyx."

"If you believe this," Violet said, "why are you marrying a woman whose skin matches her name. Little Miss Pearl White."

Pearl rolled her eyes. "You two! Shut up or neither of you will be invited to my wedding. How many times am I going to hear this stale joke?"

In Pearl's laughter, Roxie heard the love. Pearl's words held no edge. They spoke affection.

Malachi kissed the top of Pearl's head. "Love you too." He glanced at Roxie as he rubbed his well-endowed stomach. "Rehearsal lunch time. Your folks and the kids ain't gonna wait long for us."

Pearl swatted him. "If you're so hungry, listen to my sister, or she'll have us standing around until the day after our wedding."

"Worse," Roxie winked. "I'll quit. Where else could you find this quality of photography at my price?"

"Me? Lose my free photographer? I'll shut up." Malachi's laugh made Roxie smile. His good nature always did. A good-looking man—a head taller than her sister.

Large, dark chocolate eyes. Dreads tied up on top of his head. Broad shoulders. He'd be a dreamboat if he weren't so heavy.

Pearl too had put on weight since she rehabbed from her addiction and returned to Florida eight years ago for culinary school.

What she thought about their weight didn't matter, though. By the way Pearl gazed at Malachi, his size didn't bother her.

Malachi peered down at Pearl. The light in his eyes …

Roxie hit the shutter. She dropped to her knees, took a few more shots. Adjusted the lens as the couple leaned into each other. The kiss? Straight out of Hallmark.

How'd Pearl manage to find such a perfect man?

Jesse's face came to mind. *I did too, I guess.* "Go stand in the light before you consummate the marriage."

Violet, Malachi, his best man, along with Pearl and her father arrayed themselves in front of the stained-glass window. A rainbow of colors splayed assorted skin tones. After a few more pictures, Roxie found the perfect exposure and noted them on her phone. If no rain showed up tomorrow, they'd have wedding photographs to cherish.

"Okay, everyone. Let's go eat." Roxie called as twisted her 200 mm lens.

The wedding party sprinted toward the door as though they were a hoard of locusts who spied a wheat field.

When they reached the door, Malachi wrapped her sister in his arms. They lingered, side lit by the noontime, Florida sun. No sexual intent, no obligatory hug. They held each other in unadulterated love.

Roxie grabbed the shot. Another. In the lens, she saw the life she longed for. Why couldn't she find her dream?

chapter 2

Back in the hotel at one, Roxie threw herself on the bed next to Crystal and kissed her cheek.

"You have your own bed, you know?" Instead of shoving Roxie away, Crystal tossed her book aside and nestled next to her sister.

"Another horror story?" Roxie dipped her head toward the novel.

Crystal nodded. "How'd the rehearsal go?"

"Good, though I can't figure out why Pearl wants her biological dad to walk her down—"

"Larry's changed."

"We heard that before."

Crystal shifted. Her pretty blue eyes gazed at Roxie. "If we can't accept Larry, we can't accept Pearl."

"How can you spew such nonsense?"

"Pearl also used drugs. Was sexually active. An alcoholic. She's been clean for seven years, but she still wrestles with her addictions."

"She's been clean for eight—and never struggles."

"Life's kept you too busy, Rox. Pearl slipped once after she returned to Florida. Until Malachi came into the picture, she called Mama every time temptation overwhelmed her."

Roxie studied the ceiling. *How did I not know?*

"What are you thinking?"

"There's a lot I don't understand." Roxie still stared toward the ceiling. "You should've been the violinist for the wedding. You play better than the one she hired."

"Mama said Harv is one of their best friends. I play the fiddle—"

"You nailed Franz Schubert's Serenade No. 4 in your UT audition—"

"I prefer my mountain band. Girls from the Hollow doesn't fit Pearl's wedding theme. Besides, she and I don't know each other well. How old was I when she split for Florida?"

"Twelve? Thirteen?" Roxie said.

"Pearl had moved home for only a few years before going back to Florida. Most I know about her is what Mama and Daddy tell me."

"Daddy." Roxie's heart squeezed. Words wouldn't form.

"What about him?" Crystal asked.

"Why does he get shunted aside for Larry?"

"Daddy doesn't mind. Aside from Larry and the violinist, is everything going to be gorgeous tomorrow?"

Roxie propped up on her elbow. "Wait until you eat the food Malachi and Pearl's bakery is making for the reception. Oh my … delish."

"Anything's better than hotel breakfasts. I'm hungry."

"The restaurant across the road's good. A yuppie-retro site. Better than the decor, the food is edible. In fact, quite good. Jesse and I had their eggs benedict this morning. Yum." Roxie lay back down and stared at the ceiling once more. "Pearl's wedding party is worse than herding goats. Crazy. What'd you do while we were gone. Without your violin—"

"Fiddle."

"A violin by any other name is still a violin."

"I swam."

"Alone?" Roxie gazed at her sister.

"Jesse pushed me in. I had no choice."

"He's a brat. I told him to watch out for you, not drown you."

"I'm not a baby, you know."

"You're my baby sister, and I love you." Roxie made kissy faces. "We're going to Disney tonight to see in the New Year. Want to come?"

Seconds ticked away. The time elapse seemed longer than the question warranted.

Crystal sighed. "Midnight's too late for me. Wedding's at ten tomorrow."

"Is something wrong?"

"No."

Did Crystal hesitate? Roxie studied her sister as the adrenaline of the photo session drained. "You know, someday the man who adores you will come along."

"Hasn't happened yet."

"I know." Roxie stroked her sister's hair. "You're beautiful."

"Beauty—"

"I'm enumerating your gifts least to best." Roxie chuckled. "Going to take a long time to recite the list of your talents. You have plenty. Beauty, smarts, talent, kindness—and you're the most positive and joyful person who's ever been created. Your man's out there."

"Tell me about the rehearsal," Crystal said.

Crystal waited for Roxie's answer. Soft breathing said her sister dozed. Crystal nestled a bit closer, loving the proximity. Roxie doted on her. Was her best friend. Crystal picked up her Dean Koontz novel once more and read for fifteen minutes.

Roxie tossed and moaned. Her nightmares had lessened since childhood—still they showed up whenever they willed. The dreams startled the whole house awake, and heaven help the victim who woke her up. Flailing arms never failed to beat the unfortunate person. Night terrors were called not for what they did to the dreamer, but for those who woke her.

"Roxie," Crystal whispered.

Roxie moaned louder. She lifted an arm as though to ward off something. She waved it in front of open eyes.

From experience, Crystal knew Roxie still slept. She tapped her sister's arm while keeping a distance. Moving too close would get her smacked. Hard. One time Roxie had given her a black eye. She shifted off the side of the bed and tapped Roxie's arm. "Wake up. Nightmare again."

Roxie screamed. She bolted upright.

Crystal leaned further away. If Roxie was still asleep, terror would make her flail. "Rox?"

Her sister blinked, and her moan would've terrified Koontz himself. Slowly, Roxie turned her head toward Crystal. "I can't ... breathe." Roxie gulped air as though her lungs clogged, as though she'd need a respirator.

"Take slow breaths. Breathe in."

Roxie followed Crystal's direction.

"Hold. Now breathe out." Crystal hummed tunes from their favorite childhood Disney movie, *Frozen*, until her sister's breathing steadied.

"Sorry." Roxie gasped the word as breathing returned to normal.

"The same dream?"

Roxie nodded. "One of the variations. I can smell the cell penning me in. Do you ever smell your dreams?"

"Nope." Crystal eased herself against the headboard and a little closer to her sister. "I'm not psychotic like you."

"Hey." Roxie grinned and playfully smacked her. "Not even a shrink would know what being locked in a tiny cell as a giant head eyeballs me means. The *thing* wants to eat me but can't. The necrotic mouth bites but only nibbles bits of my skin. And the hair! Not a spot is free from the gray, wiry bush. I wish the dream would quit."

"You don't have them so often anymore."

"Praise God. I'm going to wash the stench of this nightmare from me." Roxie leaned over and pecked Crystal's cheek. She headed into the shower.

Crystal lifted her book. Her sister's nightmare infiltrated the words of Koontz's gore. She shuddered. "I'm going for a walk," she called.

Water sounds garbled Roxie's response.

Crystal stuffed her book into her messenger bag and slung it around her shoulders. She grabbed her crutches. The hotel's powdered eggs and stale pastries offered in their so-called free breakfast left her hungry, and lunchtime long since passed. She'd try the restaurant across the road. Nabbing a decent meal sounded good.

After the warm January air outside, the restaurant's cool air chilled Crystal. She shivered as she waited for the hostess. She'd rub her arms, but she needed them on her crutches. Falling over didn't sound fun. Crystal wished she'd brought a sweater. Who thought you'd need air conditioning on New Year's Eve? The seventy-degree temps outside didn't warrant air.

Crystal studied her surroundings as she waited. The high ceilings and exposed pipes made the dining room resemble an industrial loft. Brick walls lined one side of the diner. Stainless steel tables dotted the space.

"Are you waiting for anyone?"

The hostess's question startled Crystal.

"Sorry," the hostess said. "Didn't mean to sneak up on you.

"This place is cool."

The hostess tipped her head. "Very trendy. A table for one?"

Crystal nodded.

"Table or booth?"

"Table." Crystal bit back the need to explain her crutches and braces made booths uncomfortable and crowded. She followed the perky hostess, who seemed to trot ahead of her.

Alone again. This wedding trip to Florida with the whole Crabtree family should've kept her surrounded by people. Not even Pearl's son, Journey, or her brothers, Boone and Grant, hung out around her. Seems Pearl's condo had more to offer the eight-year-old cousins. Eating alone always made Crystal self-conscious. In movies, when a character sat by himself, she found herself aching for his loneliness. Heaven help her if the fellow was murdered while eating. Those scenes always made her stomach clench. She focused on following the hostess, not surveying the eyes of happy diners in crowded tables.

"Crystal. Join me."

She stiffened. *Alone with Jesse again.*

She smiled in his direction.

Jesse patted the table across from him. "We've got to stop meeting like this. Roxie's going to be jealous."

His smile set her heart pattering. *This had to be God. Roxie will ditch him the moment he proposes. Running into him is a sign. We're meant for each other. Not my sister and him.* She'd hope in faith. She'd make him love her before Roxie discarded him. Crystal sat.

Jesse took her crutches. His fingers grazed hers.

Their warmth made her want to clutch his hand. *Lord, help me.*

Jesse leaned her crutches against the side of their table. Her braced legs hid beneath the surface.

If only he'd see past her affliction and accept Roxie's track record.

A half-eaten burger and fries lay on the platter before Jesse.

Crystal nodded toward the dish. "Working on a heart attack?"

"Yep. When Roxie turns me down, I won't have the courage to kill myself. I'll let my ticker snuff me out."

Did his voice sound judgmental? Did he hold a grudge from this morning?

"Sorry. Sitting here's a mistake." Crystal stood, her hands pressed against the table top for balance. She bumped into the waitress bringing the menu.

"Good afternoon, I'm April. I'll be your server. Can I get you something to drink?"

"I'm leaving." She reached for her crutches.

Jesse nabbed Crystal's hand. No signs of anger showed on his face. His brown eyes, so serious, though. Was he annoyed? He glanced at the waitress. "She'll have a hot tea. Crystal likes honey and lemon too. Thank you."

The waitress left.

"Sit. Why are you bolting? I thought you said Roxie was the one to—"

Crystal pulled away. "Your attitude's the reason." *Not my crush on you.* "No need for anger."

"I'm not mad. His voice softened. "Sit."

She obeyed.

"Because we're family—or as good as family—I don't hide my bad temper too well. Forgive me for my attitude?"

Family? Crystal's heart sank. He'd propose tonight. The proposal would terrify Roxie, so in a matter of days, she'd dump him, and Crystal would never see Jesse again.

"Don't be so quiet. Talk to me."

Crystal fingered the menu.

"You're never ill-tempered. All you Snows are good natured—natural born *and* adopted Snows never hold grudges. What's wrong?"

Crystal stared at the menu. If she occupied herself, she wouldn't have to answer. "Think I'll have—"

Jesse pushed the menu away from Crystal's face. He laid his forearms on the table and leaned across. "You're wrong about Roxie."

Crystal caught herself as she shook her head. No use beating this fact to death. Jesse will do what he will do, and the rest remained in God's hands.

"You have to love me now because I'm going to be your brother-in-law." All harshness vanished from his tone

"Jesse—"

"Shh." Jesse laid a finger against her lips.

The touch. So warm and tender and intimate.

His finger lingered a bit too long before he dropped his hand. "You have to love me."

Crystal straightened. She focused on the menu again as though studying the print to determine which standard restaurant fare she most desired. Jesse would think she contemplated the selections, but tears blurred her eyes.

"Loving your future brother-in-law means talking. Tell me what's eating you."

No way.

The waitress returned carrying a small silver pitcher of hot water and a choice of tea bags. "Are you ready to order."

"Give me a minute." Crystal kept her eyes glued to the menu.

The waitress left.

When she lifted her head, Jesse was fiddling with his fries. Without eye contact, courage resurrected. "I'm sorry I said those things about my sister. People grow and change."

"You're right. Tonight, I'm proposing as planned." Jesse lifted his Coke. "Here's to you becoming my sister."

Crystal's hand trembled as she lifted her tea mug. "To you as my brother." Her throat dried so much she couldn't sip.

Fireworks flared overhead. Jesse looped his arm around Roxie as the two lay on the pavement in Epcot and watched the light display.

Roxie gasped, then huddled closer.

He smelled her fresh scent—outdoorsy like crisp air and cleansing rain. She opted for fragrance free everything because animals would smell perfume. Fragrance ruined her wildlife research/photography/viewing. Good thing she didn't roll in elk pee to get a better advantage over the rutting creatures. Instead of watching the firework display, he studied his girl as he pulled her closer. Her warmth. Her smell. Her being. Everything made his heart beat a steady, hard rhythm—so hard that Crystal would be able to hear and play the rhythm on her fiddle.

Roxie wriggled as another round of explosives shot into the sky. "Have you ever seen anything so amazing?"

Now was his chance. He held his breath. He fingered her jaw. "Yes."

Roxie turned to face him.

In the ambient lights, he saw a question in her narrowed eyes and brows.

"Stop, Jesse."

"Stop what?"

"What you're doing? Don't. Please." Every muscle in her body stiffened beside him.

"Has Crystal—?"

"What does Crystal have to do—"

"Roxie. I want—"

"Don't ruin this moment." She shifted away. "Don't destroy our relationship."

Jesse held tight. "I love you, Roxie."

She softened, but her focus seemed centered on the display of lights.

Moments ticked by as he waited for her to respond. This was the first time since they'd dated she hadn't said I love you back to him.

He studied his girl. Beautiful. Talented. Crystal was right, though. Roxie never spontaneously told him she loved him.

Could he change her mind?

chapter 3

Today. Her sister's wedding. Crystal's heart beat as fast as Pearl's must be hammering.

For years, Pearl had made mistakes, egregious errors.

Malachi's love covered them all. His love though, was no match for the Creator's.

Someday, someone like Malachi would see beyond Crystal's braces and crutches and love her.

Guests thronged the church's foyer as ushers directed them to their seats. A large chandelier hung in the center splaying rainbow light over the deep blue carpet. The back wall sported stained-glass windows shedding kaleidoscopic colors across the rich oak reception desk and upholstered chairs. The homey anteroom would beg congregants to linger.

"Ready?" Jesse held out his hand.

Crystal froze. Pearl had ordered her to use Jesse as a crutch, rather than her awkward gear. *Can't I sit out here?*

Jesse crooked his arm.

Crystal linked hers in his. Balanced against him, they inched down the aisle. Around them, guests chatted. The quartet on the stage played romantic melodies. No one would notice how the crutch under her left arm canted her toward him. She, alone, would feel his body heat warming her—in more ways than temperature. The stiffness in his muscles said he was as uncomfortable as she.

How often had she dreamed of this scenario? For four years, the idea of walking down the aisle with Jesse had haunted her, but never like this. Not as an unwanted burden. In her dreams, Jesse desired to be her husband. She lifted her head. Why couldn't he be gazing into her eyes?

No. Roxie and he loved each other. Anyone could see this. Why did her sister not realize the truth, see Jesse's worth, his beauty, his faith? More than anything, Jesse and Roxie deserved to be happy—with or without each other.

"Jesse?" she whispered.

"Shh." Jesse focused straight ahead.

After forever, Crystal slipped into her seat, her back straight, and her eyes focused on the altar. Time to celebrate Pearl.

Jesse sat a foot away. His head turned from her toward the aisle.

If she weren't lame. No. Not lame. Disabled? Differently abled? Why didn't the world see her as a human who had potential. A blue-eyed blond who fiddled better than Tennessee McMaster.

Why couldn't the world see she was a woman abled?

Except in the lack of boyfriends, her spina bifida never bothered her unless she couldn't do something the other kids did like pole vault or clog or ... date.

Her friends in elementary school envied her wheelchair. They especially loved the twinkling tires. Her best friend in third grade made construction paper braces for herself and hobbled around on the crutches her older brother had used when he'd broken his leg playing football.

Crystal grew up. Friends found other friends. She found solace in her violin. Found freedom in fiddling.

Maybe Jesse saw her as handicapped.

No man wanted a semi-paralyzed wife, despite Daddy's reassurances to the contrary.

Franz Schubert's "Serenade no. 4" drew her attention to the front of the church. The violin dominated. With eyes closed, Crystal fingered the notes and felt the rhythm. How often had she played this piece? This music nailed her place in UT's music business program. She'd minored in performance. Should've majored, but her folks thought she'd have a career in the business end.

Think of music, not people's lack of faith.

Music connected Crystal to God. When she and Mama sat on the roof watching the sunrise, Mama begged her to play the classics. She said Crystal's jigs were too dangerous to dance to on the roof. Crystal grinned remembering their standard joke.

The melody neared the end. She opened her eyes.

Malachi and his best man walked from a door behind the altar and took their places. They wore matching rust-colored brocade jackets and bow ties. The deep-cut satin lapel shimmered in the light. The dark brown hue of the lapels accented the crisp white shirts.

Uncle Blake, now a full-time minister, stood to Malachi's left. The three men looked toward the back of the church. Malachi almost bounced on his toes and smiled as though Santa would walk through the door in a moment bearing the one gift he wanted. How lucky Pearl was to find this man. A big man in height and weight. Strong. Smart. A fantastic baker. Yet endearing like a little boy or a comfy teddy bear. A man to hug. A man who protected.

Crystal closed her eyes. *Lord, bless him. Please—*

The music changed to Pachelbel's "Canon in D."

Crystal opened her eyes and twisted in her seat. Her heart strummed.

Violet, Pearl's roommate, and her soon-to-be sister-in-law, appeared. She wore a thin-strapped, empire-waist dress. The material sported a slit from floor to knee. The beige silk gown accented her caramel skin. Her bouquet of rust and cinnamon flowers in the colors of the men's jackets created an elegant picture. Violet and Malachi had the same untamed hair, but for the wedding, Violet wore long, braided extensions tied on top of her head. Bronze-colored pearls matching her dress's color adorned her hair. She resembled a fairy tale princess.

Crystal's breath hitched. If Violet was stunning, what would Pearl look like?

Jesse fixed his eyes on Roxie, who knelt in front of the altar focusing her camera on Violet.

Behind the lens, his girl said she saw nothing but her subject. Roxie forgot the world. With her camera, she fell headlong into her scene. Here, the lives of bear or deer or fox became hers. Sunrises hinted of heaven. Sunsets settled her nerves. Next to biology, photography made her world sing.

Such grace. The filmy material of her skirt-like pants, topped by a satiny, flared shirt threatening to expose skin, made longing rise to his throat as he imagined ... no, imagining what he wanted would lead him into trouble. Big time. Last night made things clear. Roxie cutting him off when he attempted a proposal confirmed Crystal's prediction.

He glanced at Crystal whose gaze slanted toward the wedding party. He'd prove her wrong about Roxie. They would graduate in a little over four months. By May, he'd eliminate all the fears buried deep inside sweet Roxie. He'd eradicate them *if* she ever let him know what frightened her so much about commitment. He turned as Crystal shifted beside him.

Crystal's thick, blond hair flowed down her back. The flowers in a hairband holding the strands off her heart-shaped face, reminded him of an elf-queen. Had she been older when first they met? No. Back then, the gawky sixteen-year-old only hinted about the beauty she'd become.

Besides, Roxie captured his love before he met her sister.

The music changed to Mendelssohn's iconic tune. Roxie crept toward the back of the church. Center aisle, focused on the door.

It swung wide.

Pearl.

With a swish of clothing and a gasp from the guests, everyone rose. Silence confirmed that Pearl's elegance stunned the guests. Her dress matched Violet's except for a train and a translucent bolero. Rust-colored flowers held back hair the color of sand at the water line. Her smile. Pure love.

Roxie pressed the shutter button. Multiple shots fired. One photo would catch the bride's radiance.

Larry, escorting Pearl, peered down at his daughter.

Roxie's breath hitched. *His eyes? Nothing but love. Had he changed?* The camera clicked again and again silencing her thoughts.

Roxie crept backward toward the front of the church. Nothing existed but the world in her viewfinder. From the sidelines, she found her seat in the front pew. At last, her heart stilled. The hard part of her job ended.

As muscles unwound, she turned her head. Jesse settled next to Crystal. He leaned in and whispered something.

Crystal frowned. Her lips moved in answer. Since she explored the restaurant across from the hotel yesterday, her sister had acted strange. Quiet, aloof. Her trademark smile had vanished. Something bothered her.

Wait.

No.

Crystal's school-girl crush was more than infatuation. She loved Jesse too.

The minx.

Roxie would make sure Crystal understood, Jesse was the real deal. *Her* real deal.

All awkwardness vanished as Crystal surveyed the name plates on the table in the entry to the reception hall. She picked up hers. The design was so typical of Pearl—understated paper the color of the wedding gowns printed in bronze ink. Table two.

If luck showed mercy, Jesse sat elsewhere. During the ceremony, he made their awkward conversation from the restaurant worse. As her sister walked down the aisle, Jesse had leaned into her. He said, "Roxie may not be ready to marry today, but I'll prove you wrong. Wait and see." Worse than this, Jesse had asked if she was jealous of Roxie.

Jealous? No. Her heart stuttered.

Crystal headed toward table two. Three seats remained untaken. She slipped into the chair next to her cousin, who threw her a smile.

Crystal leaned toward her to chat about the wedding ceremony as her cousin turned to her sister.

Her grandparents, sitting across from her were lost in conversation. Grandma Cora turned from Grandpa and gave a small wave and a big smile.

tangled lives

Crystal scooted back her chair to move closer to Grandma when Jesse plopped down next to Grandma Cora. Before Jesse settled into his seat, the two were gabbing like they hadn't seen each other a half an hour before.

Awkward.

Crystal, bookended by two people engaged with others, could do nothing but survey the room. Guests gathered in clusters or filled tables. She picked up a truffle and untied the ribbon containing the wedding favor.

"You'll ruin your appetite." Roxie slipped into the remaining chair and grabbed her water glass.

The awkwardness of being alone vanished. All tension leached away. "How're the photos going?"

Roxie opened her mouth, but Jesse turned toward her. She smiled at her man. They said something Crystal didn't hear. Kissed.

She leaned back in her chair, and the silence immersed her into her world. Her fingers tapped her thighs to the rhythm of "Barefoot in the Hollow," the song she and Danica Vaughn, the lead singer of Girls from the Hollow, composed. Her happy place cocooned her. In music, she studied her emotions. Life dumped difficulties onto everyone's lap. Her violin soothed them over. Roxie's insecurity. Pearl's addiction battles. Mama's loss of her first husband and little girl a few months before Mama found her and her sisters. Daddy had been left at the altar by his fiancé Lily. All the blessings of their lives wouldn't be here today without trials. Sort of like riding a roller coaster. Without the world dropping out from under you on the first downhill slide, the exhilaration of the rest of the ride wouldn't arrive.

She'd never marry Jesse, but someone else waited for her. She couldn't move well, but her paralysis was only partial. Below the knee, she felt pressure—little else. Even if paralyzed completely, she had her fiddle. Even if her fingers no longer moved, every note resounded inside her head.

As Malachi's best man stood to offer a toast, Roxie took off once more, camera in hand. If only Crystal had something other than her imagination to soothe her now.

Roxie's stomach groaned. She'd had nothing to eat since last night. With toasts completed and the bridal party engaged in dinner, she returned to her assigned table and stowed her camera under her seat. She had the best spot in the house seated between Crystal and Jesse. She pecked him on the cheek and stole a glance at her sister who seemed lost in another world. Everyone's plates held crumbs from the first round of food. A waiter, refilling empty dishes, slipped another platter of elegant finger foods onto the table—Beef Wellington, mini shrimp rolls, croissants. She turned to Jesse. "The food looks fabulous." Roxie reached for a shrimp roll as the rest of the table chatted. All but Crystal. Not usual for her cheerful sister. Did Crystal still harbor her adolescent infatuation over Jesse? Roxie edged closer to him.

Crystal shifted her chair back.

"Leaving?" Roxie took a bite of her shrimp roll. "I just got here." She wiped a crumb from her lips.

"I'm full. I need to talk to Mama and Daddy." Crystal shuffled toward the parents' table.

Roxie relaxed and moved away from Jesse as the music began. She reached for a mini beef Wellington. No sooner had she bit, than the MC announced the bridal dances. She groaned. "Jesse, fill my plate, and don't let the waiter take my food." Grabbing her Nikon once more, she resumed her job.

tangled lives

The father-daughter dance began.

Roxie smiled. Daddy danced better than Patrick Swayze. She chuckled as she pictured Daddy doing Swayze's moves. He'd reached fifty last year. Too old to be sexy. Still, his dance steps rocked—providing he didn't try to sing. Or shake his booty like Justin Timberlake.

Larry took Pearl in his arms.

Roxie lowered the camera. *Larry? How?* This was so wrong. He'd walked Pearl down the aisle and now ...

Pearl's face took on an angel-like expression—shining eyes, lips curved in a demure smile. She glowed as though haloed in a radiant light.

Camera! Roxie snapped a shot. *Saw love through the lens.*

Pearl's eyes shimmered.

What an angel. No view of Larry in this one.

The couple turned. Larry faced Roxie. His face filled the viewfinder.

Heaven help. Larry. Again.

As though God heeded her grumbling, Pearl leaned back in her father's arms.

Roxie shot. Once more she angled Larry out of the photograph.

Pearl would want pictures of her father.

Roxie maneuvered around the dance floor. She didn't have to savor these photos. This shindig was her sister's. Her sister ... Roxie peered through the viewfinder, saw a father and daughter, experienced their love, lived in their lives. She became the couple floating to the strains of "Daddy" by Beyoncé. Became the bride held by her own father.

Someone moved into her line of vision.

Daddy.

Larry placed Pearl's hand into Daddy's. Larry nodded. What was in Larry's eyes? She focused and snapped.

After a few more choruses, and the mother-son dance—or in Malachi's case—the grandmother-son dance—the DJ called the rest of the guests to join the bride and groom on the floor.

Roxie stepped aside and scrolled through her photos. She came to one showing a face from the bridge of the nose up. Crystal-clear, beautiful focus. Blue eyes lined by age shimmered as though holding unshed tears. Their downward slant told the story of love even without seeing Pearl in the picture. This one, this shot of Larry, was magazine worthy. What was she missing in Pearl's love of her wayward father?

"So. you have time for me." Jesse kissed Roxie's lips and smothered the words she'd utter. *I always ... Don't you know I have a job? ... Quit nagging.* He deepened the kiss to silence her protests. Felt her body respond as muscles softened against his, and he relaxed.

She nestled into his arms, as he drew her onto the dance floor. Roxie pulled so close he felt every curve, each muscle, and his own longing. How could he convince her to marry him?

"I love you, Jesse." Roxie peered into his eyes. Hers sparkled. The softness in their gaze spoke of the honesty of her words. "I love you more than you can imagine."

She said the words first.

Jesse closed his arms around her and tightened his hug. The music changed to "Music Sounds Better with You." Although he smiled at the prophetic title of Stardust's tune, the rhythm would shift her out of his arms.

She twirled away.

Pearl and Violet joined her. Crystal maneuvered into the group of girls. The quartet danced.

Jesse stepped away, pulled up a chair, and watched.

Crystal used her upper body to dance while the crutches steadied her. No awkwardness manifested in her movements. Her rhythm was perfect, and graceful. What he would expect from a music major. Every move illustrated her tremendous musical gift.

The three sisters—artists. Pearl's culinary skills amazed everyone. Rumors said she baked the wedding cake—a four-tiered confection sporting hand-piped seashells and corals climbing the layers frosted to resemble the gentle roll of the ocean.

Roxie's photography made her an animal-oriented Annie Leibovitz.

Crystal? Poetry in motion. Music even when she didn't play her violin.

He couldn't pull his eyes away from the trio.

The dance tune ended, and the women separated. He searched for Roxie in the crowd, found Crystal instead. With a straight back, she worked her way through the throng. Her entire body defied her disability.

"What're you staring at?" Roxie plopped into a chair next to him, her cheek against his.

I'm not an idiot, not gonna tell Roxie her sister entranced me.

The crowd parted like the Red Sea revealing Crystal and Larry talking.

"My sister?" Indignation laced Roxie's voice. "You're ogling Crystal?"

Jesse looped his arm around her shoulder and pulled her stiffened body close. "I'm looking at the guests. Their chatter. The good time."

"Sorry." Roxie's words sounded like a kindergartener whose teacher forced her to apologize.

"Don't sound sorry."

Roxie shot to her feet. "I'm going to chat with Crystal. If I'm standing by her, you'll have no choice but to watch me." She stormed off, not in Crystal's direction but out of the reception hall.

Jesse watched her stride out of the room. *Won't marry me but won't set me free.* He rose to find someone who offered more pleasant company.

In the ladies' room, Crystal splashed water over her hot face.

A stall opened. Roxie.

"Larry and I had a wonderful chat. Did you know he's been sober for four years?"

Her sister scowled and washed her hands two sinks down.

"Are you okay?"

Roxie glared. "Okay? You have no right to feign concern about me."

Crystal opened her mouth, but words choked in her throat.

"When I worked the rehearsal, you had the gall to tell Jesse I won't settle down?"

"I never ..." The lie soured her stomach.

Roxie's eyes narrowed, and she leaned toward Crystal. "He's the real deal. *You* don't get to decide who I'll marry or not. Forget your foolish crush, and keep out of my love life." She strode out of the restroom.

chapter 4

The next morning, the Snows headed home. Crystal was crowded in the back with her twin brothers. She stared at the back of Roxie's head. A frigid silence filled the front seat as Jesse drove his Mitsubishi innumerable hours through Georgia toward their Tennessee home.

Roxie sat ramrod straight. Her head faced the windshield, her hands clasped in her lap. Who knew who angered Crystal's sister this time? Jesse? Her? Jostling brothers who whined for an hour about having to go home and go to school?

Her brothers bumped and butted Crystal.

"My turn for the window." Boone elbowed Grant and shoved into Crystal.

"No. I only had it for an hour."

"There's a hump on the floor in the middle. My knees are in my nose." Boone's leg kicked against Crystal's. His elbow drove into Grant's side.

"I can't move now. We're driving like a hundred miles an hour—"

"Shut up!" Roxie turned and glared at the twins.

The reprimand didn't faze them. With lowered voices, the boys continued their argument and jostling.

Too bad Mama and Daddy were taking a Caribbean cruise. They would've driven their sons home. Or taken her. Or all three. Had she been in another vehicle, she wouldn't have to endure Roxie and Jesse's pique. When the duo fought, the whole world suffered. Crystal turned her head and studied the flat countryside whizzing by.

For another hour, they drove through Georgia and around the roadwork clogging the highway. Signs for a closure of the right lane didn't slow Jesse or make him shift to the left.

They exited Route 75.

"What?" Roxie hissed. "Can't you read? Lane closed. We have one road from Florida to Tennessee. No exits." She crossed her arms and leaned back.

"I need gas." Jesse hummed as he maneuvered his car a quarter mile down the road and pulled into a Shell station.

Roxie flung open her door. "I'm getting a Mtn Dew. Anybody want something?"

"I'll go—"

Roxie stormed toward the minimart.

Crystal shivered as anger coursed down her spine. She wriggled out of the back seat. Roxie asked a question, then didn't listen for anyone's answer. *What does she think I am?*

"Crys, get us chips. I'm going to the bathroom." Boone bounded out of the back seat and scurried into the shop.

"I want Skittles." Grant dashed after Boone, never one to be left behind his twin.

Weather as warm as Florida's wrapped around Crystal as she leaned against the car. She stripped off her sweater and tossed it into the back seat with her purse. After fishing out her wallet, she trudged into the station.

Jesse lifted the nozzle and unscrewed the gas cap. Never once did he look Crystal's way or speak a word.

As Crystal reached the minimart, Roxie strode past her toward the car with a bottle of soda clutched in her hand.

tangled lives

Grow up, Rox. Sometimes Crystal wanted to slap her sister. Then she grinned and looked at her crutches. Her hands held her upright. She couldn't hit the girl. *Trip her with a crutch?* A suppressed chuckle caused her to snort.

Inside the shop, Crystal gathered chips, Skittles, a soda, and an apple, then waited in line behind three other customers.

The first lady couldn't decide which scratch-offs to buy. She chose two of one but changed her mind. The lady had the clerk put one back and asked for the ticket sporting logos of groundhogs. Crystal rolled her eyes. Whether the lotto had a snowman, or a mammal printed on the ticket, the result remained the same.

The guy next in line had no ID for his beer and argued with the cashier. He pointed at his face. "Do I look like a twenty-year-old?"

"I need an ID." The clerk waved to someone behind the line. "Phil, this fellow—"

"Never mind." The man shoved his twenty-four-count box of beer toward the young man and stormed out of the minimart.

The next man paid for gas. Thankfully, he strode out of the store without hesitation.

After her ten-minute wait, Crystal paid and stepped outside.

No car sat by the pumps. She scanned the parking lot. No Jesse. No Roxie. No twins.

Where did they go? She fished in her jeans for her phone. She had tossed the cell into the back seat. Who'd ever think her sister and Jesse would drive off without her?

Her shoulders sank and she leaned on her crutches. Dejection weighted her shoulders, as she slunk against her crutches. The despair, though, shifted. Anger oozed through the pores of her skin and shook her muscles. Her lungs expanded with fury. "How can you do this to me?" She screamed into the sultry air.

Angry tears leaked into her eyes. What to do? Few choices existed. Crystal could stand in the Georgia sun and hope they realized she wasn't in the car before they reached Tennessee. She could walk to a hotel—or home. If the action wouldn't ruin her fingers, she'd punch the gas pumps. She slanted her eyes toward heaven. *Why, God?* Roxie complained often about how she was the forgotten one. No one ever left Roxie in the Southern sunlight baking in Georgia with no means of communication.

Her fingers tightened around her crutches until her hands cramped. She scanned the area, saw no name for the village, nor any returning Mitsubishi. *Where am I?* No way could she stand here like a cur tossed out of the car. She could ask someone inside, but she'd sound stupid—*ah, duh, where am I? Hey, my family forgot their worthless member.*

Only in action did she ever find relief. Jesse had only one way to return, so walking toward the highway would work off her anger.

A few minutes into her trek, a grin eased a bit of Crystal's stress. She stopped her hike and let a smile lighten her spirit.

Every Christmas her family watched a movie where parents left their eight-year-old son home by mistake when they flew off to Paris. Mama always said the boy's high jinks reminded her of Pearl. Then she'd kiss Roxie and her and say her two angels never caused a lick of trouble.

Things like this didn't happen only in the movies. When Jesus was twelve, his family observed Passover in Jerusalem. When they left, they assumed he traveled somewhere in their caravan. He didn't. They forgot to take care of the Son of God.

tangled lives

Even though she wasn't important like Jesus, her sister would soon realize she left the baby sister stranded in Someplace, Georgia. If not her sister, then Jesse. The twins would remain oblivious, though. Crystal surveyed the flat countryside. She started to walk as she hummed "Life in Tennessee," another tune—her favorite—composed by her band because the melody showcased her fiddle. She didn't care if she starred in their performance. Anyone but Danica in the lead would result in a nuclear meltdown. Good thing Danica couldn't bow a fiddle … her group's signature instrument. "Life in Tennessee" or 'Barefoot in the Hollow' would nab them a recording contract.

Crystal adored Roxie, and most of the time, she understood this middle sister's motivations. One thing Crystal couldn't fathom about Roxie was her love of moose. She'd be running off to Maine in the fall to earn a master's degree. Once she left Maine, she'd live in Alaska. Fairbanks, Nome, Barrows. Someplace freezing.

Too cold and too many bugs.

Worse than mosquitoes and no-see-ums, no concerts in the boreal forests. Fewer on the tundra.

Jesse's red sedan sped toward her. Passed her. Skidded to a stop on the side of the road. The engine roared as he backed up, careening toward her at an alarming speed.

She hopped aside. If he didn't slow, she'd be roadkill.

The car skidded to a stop, and Roxie opened the door. "For heaven's sake. Get in.'

Mad at me? Crystal took a slow step.

"Come on, Crystal. We had to backtrack for you."

"And *I* had to jog after you!" Crystal lifted a crutch. *Roxie's in one fine mood.* "Remember, mobility issues." She took another deliberate step. Paused. Hobbled again.

Roxie threw her head against the headrest.

You want a reason to be angry? Try being ditched.

As she reached the back door, Boone hopped out. "Your turn to sit in the middle."

"I can't. I have nowhere to put my legs."

"Come on, Crys." Boone whined like Roxie when she felt overlooked. "We'll never get to Tennessee if you don't quit dilly-dallying."

Listen to the boys bicker or ride in silence? Crystal climbed into the middle of the back seat and splayed her legs over the transmission hump.

Roxie stared out the front window. "Jesse turned around at one of those U-turn-thingies you're not allowed to use, so we could retrieve you. Good thing no cop saw us, or you'd be paying the ticket."

"Me? You were—"

Boone interrupted his sister. "They wouldn't listen—"

"We tolded them you was missin'." Grant spoke over his brother. "They don't never listen."

Everyone bickered at once. The anger in the car crackled down Crystal's spine. How could she ditch her ride and still get home? Only one way. She fished out her earbuds and cranked up Tennessee McMaster's latest album.

Leaving rubber on the roadway, Jesse U-turned and sped back to the highway. Once on the I-75, he turned his head. "Sorry, Crystal. The boys fought and talked over each other. Your sister ..." He glanced toward Roxie. "Anyway, I didn't look around because ... Let's leave my lame excuse at *because*. Someone said we were set to go, and ..." He glanced at Roxie once more, then shook his head.

"Right. Blame someone else." Roxie's hiss showed her anger.

Mad at what? Me? "Shut up and drive. At least you remembered me." Crystal glared out the window. *Before you hit Tennessee.*

Jesse faced forward. "I have no excuse."

No. You do not. Crystal ground her teeth and wrapped her arms across her body. She itched to slap the childish adults in the front seat.

The argument between Jesse and Roxie refused to die. Never had they been so bad. Maybe now Jesse would believe her. He and her sister were toxic.

Crystal closed her eyes and leaned back. Music would take her to another world. One where family wouldn't forget you in a strange Georgia town. Music brought a girl to a place where she did things for herself. As the strains of McMaster's melody filled Crystal's ears, she smiled and laid her head against the headrest. Her sister. Sometimes she was the most thoughtful person on the planet. Other times? Crystal lectured her sister in her head—she was smart enough to not confront Roxie while she was cantankerous even though no one had ever ditched her at a truck stop. Give Rox an hour, and they'd laugh about this. First, Roxie and Jesse needed to quit fighting about ... whatever.

Music soothed even as Crystal tapped her fingers to the frenetic rhythm McMaster employed. Soon she slept. When she woke, her brothers were snoring, and the sky had darkened. Roxie and Jesse spoke, his voice intimate and low, their hands clasped on the console. Crystal inhaled. Things felt normal—if she could judge by held hands and sleeping brothers.

Peace remained until they pulled into Jesse's folks' home in Townsend.

Crystal shook the twins. Boone lay against her left side, Grant on her right. "Rise and shine." They had to move. Now.

Scooting into the cold January air, Crystal shivered and stretched. How wonderful to move her body and straighten her legs. Another minute wedged between the twins and straddling the hump, she would've begged to be dropped on the roadside to walk home. She inhaled crisp air and arched her back. The temperature had to be about twenty-five degrees. After the overheated car, the weather felt divine.

"Howdy." Arlo Maxwell sat under the light on the front porch. He lifted a can to his lips. Jesse didn't talk about his dad's drinking much, but Crystal was sure he was an alcoholic. "Pretty wedding?"

"Sure was, Dad." Jesse's voice sounded cold, like he didn't want to start a conversation with his father. He opened the door to Roxie's beat-up Hyundai and called over his shoulder to his father. "Be there in a minute."

Crystal scooted into the front seat. She leaned back and stretched her legs. The boys huddled in the back seat and complained about the cold. Jesse and Roxie smooched in the dark, backlit by Arlo's light.

Crystal turned her head to see out the window better and studied her sister.

Jesse's right arm pulled her close. His left hand cradled her neck.

Maybe all couples fought like wildfires. Flaring today, burned out tomorrow. She wouldn't know ... probably never would. Roxie and her beaux and her folks summed up her knowledge of love. Although Mama and Daddy never fought.

Five minutes later, her sister climbed into her Hyundai and stuck her key into the ignition. "Sorry. My car is freezing. I should've had you start the car and get the heat cranking."

"Nice for Jesse's dad to wait up for him in the cold."

"Not waiting up." Roxie lifted a shoulder. "He's not feeling the cold either if you get my drift. Darkness, cold temps, and the front porch make him think he's fooling

Joyce about his drinking. Jesse's begged his mother to leave his father, but Joyce won't. Love is weird. Who can understand it?"

Pulling out of the driveway, Roxie navigated the backroads and onto the highway. Without speaking, they started the last ninety minutes of their trip. The silence didn't hold any tension now. The boys listened to their phones or played games—their ears plugged with ear buds.

Roxie leaned against her seat. "Sorry about Georgia."

"You remembered me." Bile rose in Crystal's throat. "Eventually."

Roxie slanted a look toward Crystal. "Mad at me?"

"What do you think?" She stared out the window as though she could see Little River flying by outside the car. If she said more, she'd scream at Roxie or cry.

Roxie's hand gripped Crystal's.

Shallow breaths shuddered Crystal's lungs as though she'd been abandoned a few minutes ago. She shook off Roxie's hand. "Watch the road."

"I'm super-sorry." Roxie glanced at the road, then turned back toward Crystal. "Had to be scary being left alone. I remember when my aunt—forget her name—took me away from everyone I knew. She and her husband were heading to a foreign land—don't remember which one—China or Tibet or Taiwan. One of those Asian places. The idea petrified me." She laughed.

"What's so funny?"

"I was so terrified, I forgot how to enunciate my words. My speech therapist had to start my training from the beginning once my aunt returned me to Mama."

"You'd never know now you had speech problems." Crystal paused. "Except when you're scared. Your r's give away your terror. How old were you when your aunt took you away?"

"Five, I think. Pearl's grandpa moved her to St. Louis. You stayed with Mama and Daddy. After we visited the scary lady in the jail, those people ... I remember their names now, Lisa and Todd. Our aunt and uncle took me to a place I believed to be far, far away. Kentucky, I think." She laughed. "Like we don't hit Kentucky every month."

"I don't remember any of this."

"You were about two. You barely remembered not to pee yourself."

"Hey!" Crystal punched Roxie's arm.

They giggled. Life balanced, and having been ditched in Georgia—for ten minutes, but long enough—lost its sting. Crystal didn't want to break the mood.

"Do you forgive me?" Roxie's voice turned husky.

Crystal knew her sister. Knew Roxie was sorry. Holding onto anger would hurt herself, no one else. "I will. In a year of two."

"Brat." Roxie glanced at Crystal. "Are you tired?"

"Slept enough. You?"

"No." Roxie shook her head. "Driving invigorates me. We should arrive in Jacksboro around nine-thirty. Do you mind if we stop at Walmart and buy supplies, so we don't have to drive back to town tomorrow?"

"Fine."

In the grocery aisles in Walmart, Roxie placed bread in the motorized buggy where her sister sat.

Boone slipped a box of Snowballs into the basket.

"Back on the shelf." Crystal pointed.

"Even though you're the 'cotton candy doll' in our house—all pink and sweet," Roxie said. "I'll never cross you when we shop. You take after Grandma Cora. Healthy." Roxie faked a gag. "You take charge of the boys. Go to the frozen food aisle and grab veggies and french fries. I only need to nab coffee in this aisle. Silly to maneuver the bulky buggy down the row for one item."

"See you in the Tater Tots." Crystal motored off.

The boys ran ahead of her like a ship's prow parting the water.

In the coffee aisle, Roxie reached for a bag of Colombian coffee. The boys would love hot chocolate. She snagged a box then turned to rejoin Crystal. On the main aisle, another motorized buggy paused. Not her sister.

No.

As though the ladies passed in slow motion, Roxie stared. An old lady with an oxygen hose in her nose motored a scooter. A younger one talked. Two familiar people. Scary ladies. Roxie stepped back and grabbed her heart. The pounding in her chest made breathing difficult. A scream crawled up her throat. Her breath choked back her cry. She didn't need to create a scene in Walmart. Why did she need to scream at a stranger in a scooter? Roxie jerked back again, bumping into the shelving. Packages dropped from her hand. The woman in the scooter ... Roxie wheezed. Something familiar and frightening about them. Scary like her night terrors.

Why?

The whirr of the motor faded as the couple moved away.

Roxie stood pressed against the shelves, her groceries on the floor. Like an asthma attack, she gasped for air.

"Is something wrong?" A gentleman paused by Roxie. His voice like a warm fire on a winter's night.

She turned toward him, found peace in his narrowed eyes, his slant toward her.

She shook her head. "I'm fine. Something startled me. Been on the road for hours. I don't know how long-haul truckers manage."

He stooped and picked up her two packages. "Are these yours?"

Roxie took the items. "Thank you. Good thing they weren't packed in glass." With a huge intake of breath, her body relaxed.

The man walked away. Other customers perused the shelves.

Roxie inched away from the hot drink shelving. She licked her lips. *Find Crystal.* Her feet unfroze from the floor, and she wandered the main aisle searching for her family.

In front of the frozen food, Crystal and Boone bickered in hushed whispers. Crystal always had control. Seldom argued.

Roxie dumped her coffee and hot chocolate into the basket. "What's wrong?"

Crystal held up a box of frozen Boo-berrie B'fast Bytes. "They think sugar-frosted sugar constitutes good eating."

"A step below our Pop-Tarts. Mama told us *they* were complete nutrition."

"Grandma Cora always had a fit. Thought we should eat avocados 24/7."

"Avocados gag me still." Roxie took the sugary, fat-laden breakfast food and shoved the box back into the freezer. She turned to Boone. "Go find your brother and meet us by the checkout. No more shopping for you."

Boone ran off, his steps so light, she thought he would fly.

"I think he's happy shopping's done." Roxie took a step down the aisle.

"The boys also insisted we buy these." Crystal pulled out a bag as she motored after Roxie. "Of course, we're keeping the chocolate-coated, marshmallow cookies they found."

"You're making my stomach growl."

"What took you so long?" Crystal asked.

Fear shivered Roxie's spine. *What's gotten into me?*

"Rox?"

She tried for a warm smile, given how her heart still strained against her chest, figured her grin didn't come off. *Why do those ladies still scare me?*

"What's wrong? You look like you do after you wake from your night terrors."

Exactly.

Chapter 5

Roxie lay on her pillows. *Lord, no dreams. Please.* The moon edged through the sky making the shadows shift on her wall like ghouls stalking her.

Why can't I sleep? Roxie closed her eyes and reviewed her photos from the wedding. One had to be submitted to *Bride's* photo contest. The one with Larry's eyes. Pearl's father had the haggard look of a former addict, but her sister adored him. Seemed God valued people no matter how often they fell. *Could I ...?*

Sunlight filtered through her window. Roxie's eyes flitted open. A new day. New potential. No night terrors assaulted her last night, but fragments of her old dreams recurred making her tired and her muscles taut. Today, grades would be posted. She clenched her fists and pulled air into her lungs letting her yoga breathing work off the last of her tension. If all went as planned, she'd have a 4.0. If she messed up Biopolitics—she and the prof argued often, she'd ...

Grades don't matter. She slipped on her soft jeans and orange UT sweatshirt, then ran a quick brush through her hair. She bounded into the kitchen. "Boys, the bus will be here in five. Get moving."

They grumbled something. Thumping from upstairs told Roxie they readied themselves for school.

"Did you sleep okay?" Crystal looked up from her toast.

"I hate you." Roxie slathered peanut butter and jelly on bread.

Crystal stuck out her tongue. "Likewise. What did I do now?"

"Hair uncombed, talking with toast in your mouth, and you still look like a Christmas angel." Roxie nabbed two apples and stashed them into the boys' backpacks.

The twins bounded into the kitchen.

Roxie handed the lunches to her brothers. "I hear the bus coming up the hill. Eat the school breakfast. Now run. We're not driving you to school."

Without coats, the twins dashed outside. They wrestled each other to be the first one up the bus's steps. One would think they liked school.

She stood on the porch as the bus turned in their driveway and headed back to town.

Now. The moment of truth.

Crystal had vanished. Grades haunted her too.

In her room, Roxie lifted the lid to her laptop and logged onto her UT website. Bit her lip as the cursor hovered over the link to her grades. The fine hairs on her arms stood on end. She rubbed her arms as a shiver ran up her back. Would her nervous anticipation ever fade? Her averaged hovered around 3.8. Only once had she gotten a perfect score. Today she'd nab a 4.0 again. She had to.

She clicked. Blinked. The screen began to load— gigabyte by gigabyte. Could she bake a cake before the website loaded?

There.

Her heart pounded as a grin spread across her face. A 4.0 in physiology. Another perfect grade in applied wildlife management—and in senior seminar. Still nothing listed from her boring class. The one area she'd never work in—Biopolitics. Who wanted bureaucracy? Or to listen to Professor Stearns ramble on in his liberal rant on how the government needed policies to make everything good and perfect and lovely? Last she checked, making things perfect was God's domain.

Read Philippians, Dr. Stearns.

Politics. People did nothing but screw things up. Contrary to their assumptions about themselves, humans, not deities, became politicians. So, no wonder society became more complicated. Government officials loved complicating life. Give her the forests and wildlife away from society and officious professors. Although she had to allow Stearns one point. Without governmental controls, the world would lose the animal and plant world she adored. Seemed people never did what they should. Humans acted on what benefited themselves.

She refreshed her screen and searched again. *Come on, Stearns, get your act together. Post my grade.* She stared at her screen. If she concentrated hard, crossed her fingers, and prayed the Apostles' Creed, Stearns would do his job and give her a 4.0. Faith—the substance of things hoped for.

A few minutes passed and still nothing. Straight As were in her grasp. Myriad cups of coffee—venti-triple shot espressos didn't keep her eyes open during Stearns's lectures. The textbook? Reading the tome was like listening to an egomaniac describe his dream. Sleep time.

"Roxie, lookee." Crystal sounded like she did seventeen years ago when one of the goats they used to raise had a kid during the night. Crystal always wanted the baby in her bed to keep the kid warm and not *askeerd* of the dark. Good thing Crystal couldn't wrangle the pooping machine without help, or more chaos than normal would've filled their home. She chuckled at the thought of goat scat skittering like marbles across the floor of the room they had shared. Goats ate and pooped everything out to make room for more food.

Roxie lowered the laptop lid and wandered through the living room, the kitchen, and into the new extension. Even though Daddy added this part of the house sixteen years ago to accommodate Crystal, everyone still called the addition 'the new extension.' She slid onto the bed next to her sister's desk. "What's up."

"I made dean's list this semester. Look." Her finger trailed the print on her computer screen. "Two B+s and the rest A's." She preened.

Roxie leaned over and smiled as she read her sister's grades. "How did you ace a course on Engineering Musical Sounds? Snoozer." She faked a snore.

"My studies will help me when my band makes a recording." Crystal smiled. Light shone from every muscle when Crystal smiled.

Jesse claimed Roxie was prettier than Crystal, but lies from boyfriends were essential sins. Roxie saw how he looked at Crystal when he thought Roxie wasn't looking. He'd never cheat. Every fiber of her soul understood his faithfulness. Maybe not his fidelity. Her sister would rather burn her fiddle than fiddle around with Roxie's man. Still, sometimes jealousy crawled up Roxie's spine.

"How'd you do?" Crystal turned her shining blue eyes—almost too big for her heart-shaped face—to Roxie.

"Straight 4.0 so far. Waiting on Biopolitics. How can anyone want a career in law or government? Minutiae squared."

"You'll get a 4.0. You're smart." Crystal's cell chimed. She glanced at the phone, grinned, then laid it aside. "Besides, you study harder than a Cornell researcher."

Roxie strove to lighten her voice. Crystal thought getting on the waitlist of an ivy league university was a *good deal.* "Remember, Cornell didn't enroll me."

"You got on the waitlist."

Bingo. Always seeing the positive. Roxie rolled her eyes. "I settled for UT. Figured I'd have an easy 4.0. I guess I deceived myself." She stood. "I'm going to take Onyx for a ride. Do you want me to saddle Dover?"

"I'll meet you in fifteen minutes."

In the former goat barn which now housed horses, Roxie hoisted Onyx's saddle. The tang of the leather soothed like the scent of Jesse's aftershave. Pine and leather and the air after a rain. Divine. She closed her eyes and inhaled the calming scent. Fewer than twelve hours separated her from Jesse, and her longing became intense. The memory of their first kiss warmed her. His hands on her nape, soft lips urging deeper kisses. Why did she stop his proposal at Disney? Fireworks and the Magic Kingdom, what a backdrop.

No. Jesse, like Mark before him, was too eager. What was wrong with men? Seemed they wanted a woman, any woman, at any cost. Had to be the sex hormones. Christians didn't—or shouldn't—indulge until marriage. She believed the Scriptures even though some in her church group thought the command had become antiquated.

Again, why did she hesitate? Jesse would make life exquisite. *Why not marry?* They could be married today and consummate her longing.

Jesse was as perfect as any man. Even though he claimed he wanted to stay near the Smoky Mountains, Alaska had more to offer a Phys Ed teacher. Once they married, she could convince him. The Smokies weren't Denali. The Smoky Mountains didn't have tundra or air so cold you couldn't run to the bus without a coat in January.

She wanted those experiences. Where else could he ski and snowmobile and mountain climb? Not in the Smokies.

She cinched Onyx's saddle and turned him out into the paddock. Leaning against the barn, she stared into the distance. Jesse. He was the first man who lasted more than a year. Four years now. Met him freshman year, and from the start, she thought him to be perfect. She glanced toward the house. Within minutes after she brought him home, she discovered Crystal found nothing wrong about him either.

She had to tell Jesse to quit flirting with Crystal. Her sister was getting the wrong idea and her crush kept Crystal from finding her own love. If anyone was going to marry Jesse, she would. Not Crystal. Roxie returned to the barn, saddled Dover, and turned him out. Where was her sister? She gazed toward the house.

A van pulled up to the house. Crystal slipped on her pink sweatshirt and hobbled to the front porch as a woman—looking to be about Mama's age—stepped out of the vehicle and approached.

"Are you one of the Snow girls—used to be a Harrison?"

Crystal hesitated. "Who are you?"

"I'm a relative. My mother's dying." The lady nodded toward the van behind her. "She wanted to meet you. If you're Roxie or Crystal Snow, can we talk?"

Crystal stepped back. *She knows our name? Maybe I shouldn't ... No.* Roxie would be back any minute. No harm in talking.

"I'm Crystal."

The lady smiled. Her shoulders relaxed. "I'll get my mother."

After grabbing the afghan off the porch swing, she sank onto the second step. She zipped up her hoodie and settled the blanket around her seeing as the day proved a mite cold.

The woman returned to the van. She hit controls for a lift and lowered an older woman sitting in a wheelchair.

A van had parked in the driveway next to the twins' basketball hoop.

Roxie skidded to a halt. *Company?*

She strode toward the house. No one sat on the back porch, so the visitors had to be strangers. Anyone who knew her family settled out back where the view was good. As though to confirm the beauty, she paused, looked toward the Cumberlands. The clear day defined each ridge. Even though leafless trees decked the mountains in browns and grays in January, these mountains were most beautiful on clear, cool winter days.

Voices drifted from the front, and Roxie remembered her mission.

Crystal, with the porch afghan wrapped around her shoulders, perched on the front steps talking to two ladies. One sat in a motorized wheelchair. An oxygen cannula hung from her nose. The other, a middle-aged woman stood next to her.

Roxie stepped forward.

Stumbled back.

No. Her heart raced, and breath came hard.

Why did those two ladies follow Crystal and her here?

Chapter 6

The women had barely worked their way back to Crystal when footsteps sounded to her right.

Thank heavens. She didn't want to be alone with strangers. Crystal turned from her visitors toward her sister.

"What …? Who …?" Roxie's shoulders stiffened. She stared at the two ladies in front of her, then slanted her gaze toward Crystal.

"What's wrong?" Crystal asked.

Roxie stood as though the ground anchored her feet. She shook her head.

Leaning forward, Crystal patted the space on the step next to her. "Come. Sit. You're whiter than snow on Mt. LeConte."

Roxie shook her head. "I'm fine here."

I don't think so. Crystal glanced at the women in front of her and back to Roxie. "These ladies say they're related to us. Do you know them?"

Roxie narrowed her eyes. She edged closer to the steps, avoiding the strangers. "No." She tilted her head and seemed to examine their faces. "I saw them last night when we shopped."

"We did make a Walmart run." The younger one smiled and leaned over as though to study Roxie. "We needed supplies. Didn't think we'd be in Jacksboro as long as we have. Came here a few days after Christmas and had a hard time remembering our way. We—"

"Lisa, quit yammerin' and git on with this meeting 'fore I die, which ain't long from now, nohow." The voice of the older woman in the wheelchair sounded harsh like gravel lodged her throat. She sounded as though she'd smoked packs of cigarettes a day for many years.

Lisa straightened but said nothing.

The woman in the wheelchair pointed at herself. "I'm Vernita Barnes, and—"

Roxie's mouth dropped. She grabbed the porch railing.

"Rox! I knew something was wrong." Crystal held out an arm. "Come. Sit by me."

Roxie didn't move. She looked as if she'd topple if she hadn't been grasping the porch rail.

Vernita Barnes continued as though unaware of Roxie's terror. "My daughter here, is—"

"Lisa Simpson," Roxie gasped. Her hand flew to her mouth.

Crystal's gaze held Roxie's as she strained to hear her sister. "The one who—"

"Took me from Mama."

Lisa offered a half smile. "Not our greatest moment. Todd and I meant well."

"Meaning well doesn't always translate into doing well." Roxie still hadn't smiled.

"You're right. We made a mess of things."

"Why are you here?" Roxie demanded. An artery pulsed in her neck.

Crystal patted the stair next to her. "Don't be rude. Come here."

Roxie edged around the railing. She kept as much distance as possible from the two women, like avoiding an attack dog chained to a nearby pole.

The strangers didn't move.

Roxie eased next to Crystal.

Crystal wrapped the end of the afghan over her sister and pulled her close as if she were comforting a frightened child.

Roxie's muscles softened.

Lisa's smile lost its tension, erasing years from her face. "My mother—"

"I kin talk fer myself." Vernita Barnes flung up her hand.

Lisa crimped her mouth.

Vernita Barnes's gaze never wavered from Roxie and Crystal. "Y'all probly don't 'member, y'all were so little all them years ago, but I met you in jail."

"I know."

Crystal struggled to hear Roxie's soft words. "When did we go to a jail?"

"You were wit ..." Roxie swallowed. "Little. Maybe two? Three?" Roxie's trembling settled, and she spoke closer to her normal volume, but traces of her childhood speech impediment filtered into the slow and steady cadence of her speech. "You wouldn't we-recall a thing."

Others wouldn't notice the speech, but Crystal had.

Roxie leaned closer to her sister but looked straight ahead at the two ladies. "Why are you here?"

"My mother—"

"Lisa, I'll speak for myself."

Lisa rolled her eyes and sighed. "Go on, Mom."

"I ain't got long left on this here earth. Month or two. Lung cancer." She fingered her cannula. "That's why I'm sucking air in this hose-thing. Anyway, a year or two—"

"Three years—"

"Lisa, child, shush. I'm atoning. Not you." Coughing racked Vernita.

Lisa pinched her lips shut once more but handed her mother a cloth bandanna.

The coughing continued.

Crystal felt Roxie stiffen as Vernita Barnes tried to breathe.

Finally, Vernita Barnes wiped her mouth. Pink stained the cloth. "Three years ago, I realized what a mess I made of things. I 'membered—if I'm honest, I never forgot—the awful things I said ta you girls in jail. Called you a cripple." She pointed to Crystal. "Told yer sister she was a retard. Walked out on y'all." Vernita Barnes adjusted the cannula as she gasped for air.

Crystal lifted a shoulder. "I was too young to remember."

"I meant them words I said. I ain't got no excuse for being the nasty witch I was, but I was wrong. Dead wrong. Done a lot of bad in the world—bad I can't never fix." Coughing once more interrupted Vernita Barnes. "Somehow those terrible things I said ta two sweet little girls haunted me from that day." She leaned forward. Her cloudy eyes intense. They shifted from Crystal to Roxie and back. "You." She pointed to Roxie.

Roxie inched a few millimeters closer to Crystal, still staring straight ahead. She kneaded her fingers in her lap.

"Still a quiet one." Tenderness laced Vernita Barnes's tone. "Jesus told me—"

"Mom."

Vernita Barnes flung out her hand and smacked Lisa's stomach. "Shush. I'll apologize my way." She looked back at Roxie. "You 'member. Your eyes don't lie."

Roxie's chest rose and fell as though air wouldn't fill her lungs.

Silence weighted the air around Crystal.

"You alwed—already… apowl—apologized, so …"

Crystal gripped Roxie's hand, and the fingers stilled in her grasp. She whispered into Roxie's ear. "Breathe. No one can hurt you."

"Not scared." Fear, though, seeped through her voice. She stood. "You said you were sorry. Thank you. We have work to do. You best be on your way."

"You speak real good now." Vernita continued as though she didn't hear Roxie's dismissal. "Lisa told me how smart you were. How frightening being away from your mama and sister was for you. I was wrong to call you a retard. I was talking smack 'cause I was a loser. My son died 'cause of the rotten mama he had. My daughter hated me. I hated the world 'cause of the choices I made."

Roxie didn't move.

Vernita Barnes turned her attention back to Crystal. "And you. I ain't never seed such a pretty woman. You gotta take after your mama's side of the family. My Daniel … he was a cute one but not pretty like you."

Heat crept into Crystal's face. She tried not to grin at the compliment, seeing how anger still boiled inside her sister. "Thank you."

"Give her the note, Lisa."

Lisa fumbled through her purse and handed a slip of paper to Crystal.

"Here's our number and address." Vernita Barnes nodded toward the paper. "As I said, the good Lord only gived me two or three months more. Would sure love to get to know you."

"Not a chance." Roxie crossed her arms.

"Roxie." Crystal scowled at her sister. She leaned forward and took the paper from Lisa. "Thank you for the contact info." She stuck the note in the front pocket of her sweatshirt.

Vernita Barnes raised her hand and shook her head. "I ain't a fool even though I don't talk purty like y'all. I was a lousy mother, a worthless addict, and I paid the price. I ain't looking ta be yer mamaw. But Jesus ..." For the first time, her face took on a childlike peace. Lines softened. A toothless smile revealed contentment. "I hope you girls know Jesus. If he can take an old son-of-a—"

"Mom."

Vernita Barnes chuckled and gazed up at Lisa. "Was gonna say son-of-a-gun, girl. 'Member? I changed. You better find Jesus too."

"I did."

"Just 'cause you walked the aisle when you was ten don't mean squat." Coughing shook Vernita Barnes again. When the hacking subsided, she turned back toward Crystal. "Find Jesus. He coulda saved Hitler if he wanted ta. I'm proof he'd redeem anyone. Call if you can find forgiveness for me."

Crystal smiled. "I will."

Vernita Barnes raised questioning eyes to Roxie.

"I forgive you, but the damage is done. I have Mama and Daddy. They're my family."

Lisa bit her lip and dipped her head.

"They's a good family by the looks of you two." Vernita Barnes nodded toward the girls. "Don't lose the paper. The wheelchair motor whirled, and she motored back to the van.

Crystal fingered the paper in her pocket.

"Them." Anger laced Roxie's voice.

Roxie sank onto the steps as though she'd lost all muscle control.

"What?"

"They are my nightmare."

Roxie stared at the van as Lisa scooted her mother onto the vehicle's lift and settled her in the back. The two women waved as they drove toward town. Roxie sat several minutes more. Then she shivered as though throwing off her terror and smiled at Crystal, who hadn't moved since the ladies' goodbyes.

Crystal kept her eyes on Roxie.

Roxie slapped her thighs and stood. "Ready for our ride?"

"Why'd those ladies scare you?"

"Didn't. Come on."

"Your posture says other—" The hardened look on her sister's face told Crystal to be quiet.

"The horses will be antsy."

"I'm sorry. I can't." Crystal seemed to blossom like the daffodils who poked their leaves above the ground. In a few weeks, bright yellow blooms would deck the yard. "Remember the text I got when we were checking out grades?"

Roxie nodded.

"Danica Vaughn."

"Your lead singer?"

Crystal nodded. "We have a gig in Nashville next weekend."

Roxie snatched her sister's hands. "For real?"

"At Jack's on the River. We were on the waitlist, and the group scheduled for the weekend bailed. Jack's called us." Crystal grasped Roxie's hands. Glee sparkled in her Disney Princess's eyes. "Agents hang out there all the time."

"Your star's rising."

"Since we'll be in Nashville, we reserved a studio so we can cut a demo."

"You hired a studio so soon?"

"Our drummer's boyfriend has connections. We're leaving Wednesday and will be gone for ten days. Danica's aunt in Franklin will let us stay with her for a while. I can't go riding. I need to practice."

"No, you don't. Your skill rocks without extra rehearsing." Roxie winked. "With an agent and a record deal, you can pay off my tuition when you go platinum."

"Deal."

"Let's ride."

"I need to prep. My fingers are itching."

"Itchy fingers?" Roxie raised her brows. "I can't interfere with tickly digits. You fiddle around. I'll grab my camera, so I can work off nervous energy until Stearns overcomes his indolence and posts my grade."

"I won't see you until nightfall."

"Think Stearns will wait until the end of the day to post grades?"

"No, silly." Crystal looked up at the sky. "The light's wrong for any serious photography now. Won't be good until dusk."

"If I'm not prepared, I'll miss the shot that will land me in *National Geographic*."

An hour's ride brought Roxie to the lake. She gave Onyx his freedom to graze and sat on a log. *Those ladies … No. They're gone. I'll never see them again.*

Nerves unwound as she studied the bright sun shimmering on the green water below the red clay banks. Because of the contrast in light and shadow, the camera lens would never catch the beauty. The camera's exposure would blow out the highlights and no amount of photoshopping would ever get them back. Funny. The eye God made saw what manmade mechanisms never captured. Editing restored much, but Photoshop could only hope to mimic. Never did software duplicate creation's glory.

Onyx munched dried grass clinging to the side of the path. Gentle snuffles and pawing would scare any animals away. Instead of hunting for deer or squirrels as subjects of her shoot, she stared at the lake.

Crystal would become a star in the music world. She sang like a wren. Fiddled better than Charlie Daniels.

Roxie clenched her fists. Her life? No matter how hard she tried, she was always second best.

Second to Pearl.

When Pearl's grandpa took her, Roxie couldn't measure up to Crystal.

Lisa Simpson and Vernita Barnes found her lacking. Lisa and her husband bragged on her being a good girl but never a special one. Never better than their sons. To prove how lacking her aunt had found her, Lisa returned her to Mama like a bad purchase made in Walmart.

Roxie quirked a grin. *At least, she brought me home.*

Home to a house with another foster child and problematic goats occupying Mama.

Jesse. She let out a sigh and her mood turned serious. He loved her. For sure, she was first in his life. Roxie closed her eyes, and her moment of faith drifted away like morning fog. *Does he prefer Crystal over me? Sometimes I wonder.* Tears welled behind her lids. She doubled over and felt like the five-year-old Roxie. If the log she sat on was hollow, she'd crawl in and die.

She had to compete with Crystal. Ivy League colleges accepted others—not her. Ended in a second-rate university. Even in a non-elite university, she couldn't get a 4.0. Always second best no matter how hard she tried.

Lord, help me.

She had one life to live. She had to be like Crystal. See the good.

Even if she didn't graduate summa cum laude, she was smart.

If no magazine ever published her photos, God still found her worthy—after all, he redeemed Vernita Barnes.

Roxie shivered. The woman haunted her. Caused night terrors. How could God love that creature? Redeem her?

"Too much introspection," Roxie muttered. She stood. Her hips and thighs ached from the long ride out. She took Onyx's reins and walked toward the house. Along the trail, she found a spur leading to a pond. When they were little, they used to take the pony cart here and catch frogs.

She turned along the overgrown path.

Within moments, she found the small span of water.

Too cold for algae. Glassy water shimmered and reflected bits of the blue sky. Green pines replicated themselves in the stillness. She inhaled the enchanted scent of pine and crushed leaves. Remembered Mama and Daddy's love.

She sat on a rock and searched the area. Frogs would be hibernating, but indirect light filtered through the pines. On the far side of the pond, a log lay across the water, and an abundance of pine cones flirted with the surface, repeated themselves in their reflection.

What was up? What was down? Where did reflection begin and reality end?

She shot photographs, adjusted her exposure, shot again. After changing her position, a better perspective created a more artistic composition. She shortened her depth of field and obscured background distractions. Laying on her stomach and focusing, she saw what she wanted in her lens, nothing else.

Back home, the smell of fried chicken and oven-fried okra made Roxie's stomach growl.

The twins sat at the table scribbling on the lines of their notebooks.

"Hey, Rox," Grant glanced her way.

"Hmph," Boone grunted.

Roxie peered over their shoulders. Deciphering their scrawl took talent. "Going to be authors?"

Grant scowled. "How I spent my Christmas vacation." He scrunched his nose like he smelled decay. "Watching old people get married. Boring."

Boone kept his focus on his scratching.

"When's dinner?" Grant asked.

"Ten minutes," Crystal said.

"I'm going to check my Biopolitics' grade." Hope pounded Roxie's chest. She didn't believe she'd make an A, but she would earn no lower than a B+. She slipped onto her bed and tapped in her information onto the website, clicked on Stearns's class.

No! Her jaw dropped. Never, ever had she gotten a *minus*.

"Dinner," Crystal called from the kitchen.

The hunger roiling her stomach five minutes ago turned to nausea. *A B-minus?* No. Clatter of dinnerware sounded, still she stared at her screen unable to move.

"Hey, Rox?"

Roxie looked up.

Crystal stood in her bedroom doorway. Her eyes turned dark, and she stepped forward. "What's wrong?"

Roxie didn't move on her bed. The laptop balanced on crossed legs.

Crystal peered over her shoulder. "What? No way."

"Apparently."

"Oh well. Come. Eat. You'll feel better."

Roxie shook her head and lowered the lid of her computer.

Dinner didn't help.

Roxie couldn't scream. She fell into the pond and every time she opened her mouth to yell for help, water filled her lungs. Someone had to help her. She thrashed. Fought. Struggled to break the surface. Each time she did, pine cones whacked her head.

Again.

And again.

The water burned her lungs, seeped into her eyes. She rubbed her mouth and tasted the iron or copper.

She bolted upright. Grabbed her hair. Wet. Wet and dripping into her eyes. Pain seared. "Help! Help me."

"Boone, Grant, your sister needs us. Now!" Crystal fumbled for her wheelchair. "Go help her but don't touch her."

Her brothers yelled from upstairs. "How can we help and not touch?" They thumped out of bed.

Crystal wheeled into the room as Grant shook Roxie.

"Gun! There's a gun." Roxie, with unseeing eyes wide, screamed. Blood streamed from a gash in her head. She snatched Grant's hair and yanked.

"Stop! Stop, Rox." Tears filled Grant's eyes as he grabbed his sister's hands to stop the pulling. "You're hurting me."

Crystal wheeled close and seized her sister's hand. She unfurled her fingers from her brother's hair and whispered. "Wake up, Roxie. Night terrors."

Something in her voice penetrated Roxie's consciousness. Her open eyes focused. Her hand swiped her forehead. She stared at her hand. "Blood? I thought the pond's water sucked me down. I kept fighting, but the pine cones whacked my head. Must've hit the headboard." She threw herself flat on the bed and tears welled. "I'm crazy. Crazy."

"I want Mama and Daddy." The tears slipping down Boone's face defined his terror. They spoke of the little boy he was.

Crystal stripped a case from a pillow and shifted onto the bed next to Roxie. She wadded the cloth against Roxie's head. "Boone, go call Ma Jaynes. Have her come over." Ma Jaynes, the mother of Mama's late husband, lived closest to them. As much a grandma to Crystal and Roxie and the twins as Grandma Cora or Grandma Snow. Ma Jaynes always came in emergencies.

Boone ran from the room as though chased by Count Dracula.

"I'm sorry." Grant sobbed. "Why'd she hurt me?"

"She has no control. No one can touch her when she has night terrors."

"But she was awake. I seed her eyes open." He sniffed.

"Open, but not awake. You have nothing to be sorry about. Go fetch my braces and a dish towel."

Grant didn't move.

Within minutes, Boone returned. "Ma Jaynes is coming."

The boys stood flanking Roxie's bed, their focus on their bleeding, terrified sister. Something other than intrigue in their sister's gore held them. "What's wrong with Roxie?" Grant asked.

"Night terrors. Go do what I ask."

Grant grabbed Boone's hand, but the boys didn't bound out of the room like normal. By the door, Boone turned. Stared in the sisters' direction.

"Go." Crystal waved the twins out of the way.

Roxie eased into a sitting position.

"You're going to need stitches. Get dressed. We're heading to the ER."

"Not necessary."

The boys trotted back into the room. "Is she gonna live?" Grant handed Crystal a towel and dumped her braces on the bed.

"I'm going to live. For now. Someday, though, these dreams will kill me—"

"No." Tears clogged Grant's voice.

"She's exaggerating. Go on up to bed." Crystal pointed.

Boone stomped his foot, and tears clouded his eyes. "But—"

"School in the morning. Go."

The twins stomped out of the room. They pounded up the stairs, the noise underscoring their lack of enthusiasm for bed. Or school.

Crystal lifted the wadded pillowcase from Roxie's head. "The bleeding's slowed down." Crystal tossed the linen away. "Hold this towel against your head. Go dress."

While Crystal strapped on her braces, Roxie took the towel.

She yanked on a dresser drawer with her free hand and pulled out a T-shirt. Tossing the towel on the bed, she slipped the shirt over her head. "Ouch. Should've used a button shirt."

"You've got blood on your shirt. Hope this one wasn't a favorite." Crystal tossed the towel back to her sister. "Keep pressure on your gash."

"What time is it?" Roxie asked.

"One. When you finish dressing, head to my car." Crystal, using the handles of her wheelchair for balance, returned to her room to dress. Before she finished pulling up her wide-legged jeans, a vehicle rattled up to the house.

Ma Jaynes hurried into the kitchen. "Hello."

"Be there in a minute." Crystal zipped her pants and made her way into the kitchen. She threw Ma a smile. "Roxie had a bad go of night terrors."

"I thought she outgrew them."

Crystal quirked her lips. "Something triggered them again. The boys are probably not asleep. You know the morning drill if we're not back."

After a CT exam, Roxie lay on the exam cot. Every muscle in her body tensed while the plastic surgeon stitched her head. "The CT scan indicates a mild concussion. You will have a headache for a few days. Take acetaminophen and ..." He jabbered on about something else.

Eventually, he shut up.

Roxie's stomach soured. "Going to be sick."

The doctor lurched back, grabbed a kidney-shaped bowl, and handed the container to Roxie.

She hoisted herself half up. Her stomach settled, and she didn't upchuck.

"Nausea's another side effect of concussions. Eat light." The surgeon removed the bowl and resumed stitching.

Roxie tried to shift up.

"Hold steady." The physician pressed down on Roxie's shoulder. "Three more stitches."

"I'm looking for a padded headboard tomorrow." Roxie glanced at the large, industrial clock. "My mistake. Seeing as it's almost five a.m., I'll buy a padded headboard today."

The doctor finally dropped scissors on the tray. They clattered in the quiet ER. He stepped back. "Remember what I told you about the scar care. More important, look into therapy. Your primary care can recommend a good psychologist."

Blood pounded against the stitches, and Roxie's head whirled. "I don't need a shrink."

"Your dreams indicate something unresolved. Most people's nightmares don't give them concussions and fifteen stitches. You need professional help, Roxie."

This time, she vomited all over herself.

Chapter 7

Jesse, warmed by his hike with best bud, Geoff Upshaw, sat on his jacket and watched as water cascaded over the rocks of Indian Flat Falls. He and Geoff ate their late lunch under the rhododendron bushes anchored to the rocks. "Have your feet thawed from crossing Panther Creek?"

"Fresh socks and a few hours hiking? Feeling good." Geoff stuffed his sandwich wrapper into his knapsack. He stood and studied a patch of ground where icy water flowed around scrub sourwood. The high water created an island six feet away.

"Don't tell me—"

Jesse didn't finish his sentence because Geoff leaped. He skidded on ice and plopped on his rump on the one dry bit of ground.

Sort-of-dry. His body skidded inches, and his foot hit the water.

"Icicles on the falls, frost on the rocks. We skidded all the way down here, and you think leap-frogging the falls is a good idea? What an idiot." Jesse's laughter would tell his buddy that he amused him.

Geoff stood and leaned across the flowing water. "Give me a hand off this island."

"And pull me over the edge?" Jesse leaned toward his buddy, and Geoff grasped his hand. When he leaped, he stayed dry.

"I don't have dry socks anymore. You have some?"

Jesse rummaged through his pack and handed Geoff a pair. He hoisted his backpack. "Good thing I had good balance on the log we used to ford Panther Creek. The water this time of year has to be colder than the Arctic Ocean."

"The water was. Believe me." Geoff tightened his laces. While still sitting, he grabbed a few loose stones and skipped one into the high pool of the falls. "Crossing Panther Creek with the water high at six in the morning 'bout gave me hypothermia."

"Because you can't balance on a log and went swimming."

Geoff tossed a stone at Jesse.

Jesse stared at the late afternoon clouds scudding above the rhododendron leaves. "Roxie would love the lighting right now. She'd sit here until sunset to get the right exposure. We'd wait until the dark made photos impossible."

"Glad she gave you time off."

"After the five days at the wedding, we needed a break." *And after Dad's binge last night, ain't staying home.*

"Feeling colder." Geoff stood, hoisted his pack, and cinched the straps. "So have you popped the question?"

Jesse's mouth dried.

"I don't see why you want to tie the knot and tie yourself down." Geoff took a step up the rock incline. "Enjoy the benefits of love and be free of the 'until death do us part stuff.'"

"No benefits." Even to himself, Jesse sounded forlorn.

"Oh, yeah. Christians aren't allowed to have fun. Why?" Geoff called over his shoulder. "I know guys in the church you go to who play the field. If she won't marry you, she's being a ..." Judging from the breathlessness of Geoff's words, exertion cut off his words. He stopped, gulped air, and faced Jesse. "Why don't you find someone who likes to ... get physical?"

"Going to be dark before we hit the trailhead. Seven miles done. Four to go. No more river crossings, which is a good thing for you."

"Speaking of rivers—"

"Since when?" Jesse spoke to his back.

Geoff turned. "This spring, we kayak the Sinks."

Jesse froze, and not from the cold. They'd chatted about skydiving. They'd kayaked class III rapids and even bungee jumped. Once. Class IV rapids around the narrow curve of the Sinks? If he kept his mouth shut, maybe Geoff would forget.

Thirty feet ahead of Jesse, Geoff turned. "You coming or going to daydream until it's time for night dreams?" He turned and set a fast clip. The pace Jesse loved most. Some days, he came to Middle Prong to trail run. Fast and furious. That was living. Today, the speed would chase the fear of shooting class four rapids.

The men climbed the slope to the main trail. Jesse's lungs pumped as he followed Geoff up the rocks. Each bobble of Geoff's orange pack brought back his buddy's query. Before he knew Christ, Jesse knew women. He should find someone "fast and furious." If he had a girl on the side, his love for Roxie wouldn't hurt. He smiled at his dumb idea. *I wish I'd never indulged. If I didn't know what I was missing by being celibate, I wouldn't feel so ... desperate.* His love for Roxie had to be more than a pursuit of the physical. She deserved better.

Maybe better isn't me.

Crystal was right. Roxie would find a reason to break off their relationship. She ran so hot and cold. *I know why dudes married by twelve in biblical times. Sex.* He imagined Roxie in his arms, relived the liberties he shouldn't have taken. His heart pounded as he climbed over boulders on the narrow path. The pounding wasn't from physical exertion.

Think something else, Maxwell.

Roxie sat cross-legged on her bed. Her head still throbbed, but the pain from the stitches lessened. She amended her course registration on the UT website and snapped her laptop closed. *Done. I'll show you, Stearns.*

She stared at the wall. All morning, she debated her decision. Then the solution came for certain. Nothing would keep her down.

Now? Her momentary triumph faded, and she lifted her phone. Clicked on texts. Found what she knew she would. Ten from her to Jesse. None from him. She gave herself a concussion, and a surgeon stitched fifteen teeny sutures into her head, but none of this mattered to him.

Crystal's fiddle had replayed the same melody all morning. The music had grated like the blood thumping against Roxie's sutures. Now? Nothing.

She climbed off her bed and tucked her hair behind her ears. She pulled the strands back over the bandage covering her wound. Of course, Jesse cares. She tapped out one last note to him.

ROXIE: Where are you? I've texted and called and need you.

She tapped her thumbs on the phone's face and stared. Willed Jesse to answer.

Nothing.

tangled lives

Was she sad? Angry? Roxie couldn't define what roiled her heart. She jiggled her leg and tried to quell her nerves. Something kept Jesse away. Maybe her jealous argument on the way back from Pearl's wedding?

No.

Did his father need him in his welding shop because he was hungover? Perhaps his mom wanted him to … No. All those activities would keep him close to his phone. She tossed aside her cell. *Too beautiful an afternoon.* On the front porch, she joined her sister. "This weather's divine. Has to be around sixty degrees."

"Sixty-four last I checked. Look at the sky. Beautiful clouds, bright blue sky. Too nice to practice a moment more."

Roxie plunked down on the porch swing next to Crystal. "Thank heavens. All day you plied your screeching strings. Think your squealing gave me the headache, not the concussion."

"Brat." Crystal slapped her sister's arm. "You've turned into a head-banger."

"Shouldn't the boys be home from school?"

"Aunt Sunny picked them up. Cousin Owen's teaching the twins to shoot hoops." She pointed to the hoop on the side of the driveway. "Maybe they'll make some baskets."

"If we lower the hoop." Roxie's chuckled warmed the cool air.

Crystal swiped the lock of hair away from Roxie's bandage. "Aside from my migraine-inducing fiddling, how's your head?"

"The throbbing quit. The pain's turned into a dull ache."

"Have you gotten hold of Jesse?"

Roxie shook her head.

"Must be off on a run—"

"For ten hours?"

"Give him—and me—a break." Crystal stood. "I'm going to practice. If my bowing annoys you, your whining is enough to send me back to my strings."

Roxie swallowed hard and reached for her sister. "Sit. Keep me company."

Crystal settled back into the swing.

"Two bits of good news."

Crystal arched a brow. "Good news?"

"Don't snark at me." Roxie pushed against the porch floor and set the swing in motion. "I've reregistered for Stearns's course."

"What?" Crystal twisted to face Roxie. "Why on earth?"

"I'm not ruining my GPA because of Biopolitics. I've never done so poorly."

Crystal grasped her arm. "Roxie, retaking Biopolitics is *not* good news. You're an idiot."

"I don't want a B-minus." Roxie crossed her arms.

"Your grades don't mean anything. You're not going into government. Take something you love, like a photography course."

"Photography won't pay my bills." A grin struggled on Roxie's lips. She bit back her smile. If she didn't, she'd prove her baby sister right—again. "I semifinaled in the *Wild World* Photo contest. I'll hear on April first if I'm one of the three winners."

"What will a win do for you—besides make you impossible to live with?"

Roxie smirked at Crystal. Teasing said her sister loved her. "Along with ten grand, first place wins a photo tour free and clear. Guess where?"

"By your smile, Alaska?" Crystal's smile and happy eyes told Roxie Crystal's anger stalled.

"Long shot to win. Second place wins a thousand bucks. Third, five hundred. Plus, we can join the tour—for a cost. Honorable mentions only earn bragging rights."

"Start bragging, Rox. You're guaranteed to be honorably mentioned. I'm going to start dinner." Crystal grabbed her crutches and stood. "You go pick up the boys."

"Want me to buy dinner in town?"

"Perfect. I can practice instead of cook."

"Haven't you plied the screech machine enough?"

Crystal scowled at Roxie.

She held up her hands in surrender. Crystal had an even temper, but if Roxie insulted her violin, she'd be sure to lash out.

"I need to perfect my performance."

"You play for twenty-three hours a day, and you have the nerve to say I overstudy? I'm not as obsessive as you."

The sisters laughed, and the action eliminated Roxie's sorrow about Jesse's indifference.

On her way to town, she hit the call button on the steering wheel. The mechanical voice intoned, "No phone is connected. Would you like me to connect one now?"

No phone? Roxie dumped her purse on the passenger seat. Grinned. Yep. No phone. Tossed the dumb cell on my bed. Didn't matter. She'd enjoy being untethered to the world for an hour or so.

Two hours later, after chatting with Aunt Sunny, watching her brothers show off their basketball skills honed by their older cousin Owen, and picking up pizza, Roxie drove two sweaty boys up the darkened Hen Waddle Hollow. The aroma of hot pizza made her stomach growl despite the garlic knots the three of them had devoured as soon as they left Pizza Hut. She topped the hill, and her world turned right.

"Jesse's here." The twins whooped in unison.

Jesse.

The boys tumbled out of her car, each clutching a box of pizza.

Roxie inhaled to slow her heart. She turned off the ignition and tried not to run from the vehicle.

Jesse bounded around the front.

She stepped out of her car. "Why are you here?"

Jesse caught her into a bear hug. "This is the only way I can check on you if you don't answer my calls. What if you were seizing with a concussion?" He inched away and brushed the hair from her wound. "Looks awful."

"You didn't answer my texts or calls."

"Hiking with Geoff." Jesse pulled her closer and nuzzled her ear and whispered. "You gave me orders to stay in Townsend. My choice then was to work with Dad and Bradley or hike, so we hit Middle Prong."

"Hmm." She didn't want to speak. The warmth of his body nudged into hers. His scent of pines. Roxie ran her hands along the nape of his neck, fingered strands of hair. Breathed in. Inhaled his peace.

The two leaned against the car.

"I like your hair down." Jesse's breath tickled her ear.

"Right now, I want to shave off every strand, but then I'd have no way to hide the stitches."

"No need to hide them." Jesse stepped away, but still their shoulders touched. "They testify to your wild, untamed nature."

"I'd rather be tame like my sister."

"You told me about your childhood night terrors. I never realized how awful ..."

Roxie gazed at him, waiting for him to finish.

"What brought them on again?" Jesse asked.

"Supper's going to be devoured. Let's eat."

"Why aren't you answering my question?"

Why? Right now, she'd say the visit from Vernita Barnes and Lisa, but she'd had no reason for them to resurrect at the wedding in Kissimmee.

"Roxie?"

"Who knows what brings them on?" She edged away from the car. "Tell me about your hike while we eat."

After dinner, Jesse gripped Roxie's hand as they walked up the road. Only the flashlights on their phones illuminated their way. No car ventured so far down Hen Waddle Hollow unless someone visited Ma and Pa Jaynes, who owned the last farm on the road, or they were lost.

Silence was palpable. The air nipped their noses.

Jesse looped his arm around Roxie.

Roxie pulled close to him as they reached the road's end. They turned around. "You should be tired of trekking in the countryside.

He shook his head. She wouldn't see his response in the dark. "Movement energizes me."

"Like Crystal." Her voice sounded wistful. "If not for the spina bifida, Crystal would be running marathons instead of racing on her fiddle."

"Do we thank God for her disability? Your sister rivals Vassar Carlton."

"You know about the Father of Hillbilly Jazz?"

"Anyone who talks to Crystal for a moment learns about the fiddling greats—Carlton, Tennessee McMaster, Charlie Daniels."

"You'll come to Jack's on the River in Nashville on Saturday, won't you?"

"I wouldn't miss the day Crystal signs a recording contract."

"Funny. If I had her opportunity, I'd assume I'd fail."

Jesse stopped and turned her in his arms. "I don't know why. You're a brilliant photographer."

"Almost a contest winner." Roxie straightened in his arms.

"You'll nab first place. Guaranteed."

She winced. "Mediocre student, though."

"A 3.8 is not second-rate. I've attended one of Stearns's lectures—I'll never let you drag me to another. His doctorate is in boring students. I can't believe you enrolled in his course again."

"You know me."

He did.

Silence swallowed them once more. In the distance, an owl hooted. A lonesome train rumbled down in town. Sorrowful sounds.

The quivering of a fiddle wafted in the night breezes. The musical strains were also mournful and slow.

The Snow girls had an intriguing depth. Roxie, willing to serve her family and friends, loving and kind. Determined. Insecure. And a temper. Like a tornado, her anger passed quickly, but sometimes caused mayhem. He peered in her direction. A breeze blew her loose hair which tickled his nose. He leaned toward Roxie and kissed her head. Her determination was bullheaded like her temper.

The music grew louder as they approached the house but not more cheerful.

Funny. Crystal's always happy, even when I ditched her in Georgia. Good thing she didn't hear the subject of Roxie's and my fight. Would she remain cheerful?

The sounds from the fiddle echoed the lonesome train or a sound of an owl. Made Jesse feel what? The plaintive tunes drew him in. Pulled his heart. Made him want to protect Roxie and her sweet little sister. "Do you think Crystal will stay in Nashville?"

"No. She has two more years left in UT. I won't support a starving artist, so she needs a degree."

Minutes ticked away. Jesse *had* to understand what issue plagued his future wife. "Are you ever going to tell me what brought on your night terrors?"

Silence surrounded them.

No answer? Again?

They stepped into the yard. Soft light from the porch lit the night.

"What brings on any dream?" Roxie sounded almost clinical. "I'd guess I'm worried about Stearns."

Roxie stared at the ceiling. She should be exhausted. Long ride back from Pearl's wedding. Longer night in the ER last night. Sluggish all day today. Sleep should come easy. Every time she drifted off, she lurched. Minutes would tick by before sleep would tease her, make her believe she'd sleep. If she slept, would she dream?

Blessings. Count your blessings. Mama made up counting songs about their blessings when Roxie was little and bad dreams assaulted her. After her songs, Roxie had always felt loved and whole. *Okay. I'll count.*

Mama and Daddy love me.

Crystal and Pearl love me.

Jesse loves me ...

She bolted upright. She slept—for what—a minute? An hour? She lay back down. Sleep erased fear, then terror resurrected and ruined everything.

She knew the sole way to conquer dread. Face the terror. Her biggest fear? She lay down and propped an arm behind her head and let her heart settle. Her biggest nightmare would be vanquished.

I can't wait for Saturday night. Jesse will be shocked. She hugged herself and slept.

Chapter 8

Friday noon. Done. The Girls from the Hollow finished their demo. For twelve hours a day over the last three, they fine-tuned their music. Now came the moment of truth. Crystal and her bandmates sat in the studio. They focused on the sounds coming through their headphones. Crystal bobbed her head to the final cut.

Leanne's long braid danced with the rhythm. Her fingers tapped against her jeans, and her foot kept the beat. Energy in action. A natural born drummer. Her snub nose seemed to express her character as much as her drumming.

With closed eyes, Crystal felt herself clog in a field of columbines. She cried in the wind and laughed in the rain.

Too soon, the music ended.

She removed her headphones. "I'd say we nailed this tune."

For the first time Crystal could remember, Danica said nothing. Her face told the story of her heart. She—and the others—agreed with Crystal's assessment.

Minutes ticked away, and no one moved until Danica whipped out her phone and spoke as she thumbed a text. "Did I, or did I not, score when I organized my group?"

"We work well together." Leanne beat a drum roll.

"Mike and I are going out to celebrate." Danica shoved the cell into the back pocket of her jeans. "Will you ladies join us?"

Leanne twirled her drumsticks like a baton before stashing them in the holder. "I will. Richie has no choice. He's in too."

Abilene, the string bassist, had already slipped on her hoodie over her spiked, dark hair "Count on Conner and me. Loverboy never misses a chance to party." She fingered her lip piercing and winked.

Danica turned to Crystal. "How about you?"

All of them were paired up. Since Wednesday, Crystal tagged along with the couples. She alone remained single. After two days of being the spare tire, she'd had enough. "I'll catch up tonight. I'm heading back to your aunt's."

"Don't be a party-pooper." Danica pouted. "Your presence makes us happy."

Crystal tossed Danica her sweetest smile. No way would she let her friend know how she envied them. To be loved by a man would be divine. She glanced toward the braces hidden beneath her wide-legged linen pants. "I need to call Roxie. See what's going on." *If Jesse's not hogging all her time.*

Roxie studied the jewelry case in Walmart. The occasion called for a nice ring, not a joke, something promising her love. A band Jesse would wear. She slipped a silicone band onto her thumb. The ring, a size ten, seemed to have the same wiggle room as Jesse's other ones. For ten bucks, she'd take a chance it would fit. She picked up a pretty, cubic zirconium for herself and slipped the ring on her finger. The stone danced in the light. Simple and cheap, perfect for her. Didn't matter if she lost the band in a stream or left the thing in an outhouse in the backwoods.

Tomorrow night, she'd shock Jesse.

The salesclerk rang her up and slipped both pieces of jewelry into a bag. As the lady handed her the purchase, a motorized buggy whirled behind Roxie. She jumped.

"Are you okay?" the clerk asked.

Roxie nodded toward the customer motoring past. "Didn't hear the lady."

"Some of the scooter drivers don't watch where they're going." The salesclerk turned away. "You have to watch out for the old coots. They're crazy reckless—like teens learning to drive."

Roxie studied the older lady as she wended her way down the aisles. She wore her gray hair in a ponytail like Vernita Barnes. Those three things—hair, age, and buggy—were all the similarities the customer had to her supposed grandmother. Still Roxie stared. Looked closer. Made sure.

Roxie clutched her package, and her purchase made her feel alive like Jesse must feel at the start of a race. *Tomorrow night ... look out, Jesse.* Humming, she swung her arms as she strolled out of the store. The urge to skip to her car overwhelmed her. She glanced around. Nobody watched. *Why not?* She skipped.

On the way home, she phoned Jesse. She couldn't tell him about her plans, but still, she needed to celebrate.

The cell rang. Rang some more. Voice mail picked up, and she disconnected. Right. He worked in his father's welding shop today.

Seeing as she'd be gone most of tomorrow, her brothers were visiting Aunt Sunny for the weekend. Her folks' cruise would dock in Cozumel today. Not home until Monday. Well, not in the States until Monday. Home when they decided their love tryst vacation ended. She puckered her lips. Yuck. Her parents were in their fifties. They didn't still ...?

As Roxie pulled into an empty driveway, a cloudburst blanketed the hills. She dashed into the house. The rain soaked through her clothes in her thirty-second dash.

What to do now? She stared out the kitchen window.

Couldn't take pictures in the downpour. Although? The raindrops splattering on the pane often looked nice in a macro shot.

Nah.

Riding in a cold rain didn't thrill her. Onyx hated the wet, anyway.

She dialed Jesse again.

Nothing.

She found her Biopolitics book on the end table where she'd left the text and read a few pages. Her head nodded, then jerked upright. She tossed the tome away.

The house, the emptiness, the weather jailed her. She had to escape.

If Roxie drove to Nashville a day early, she'd have company. Perhaps crashing at Jesse's for the night was a better idea. Together, they could drive to Crystal's gig.

No. She had the horses to tend. After gashing her head, she couldn't bother Ma and Pa Jaynes again to care for the horses. They had their jobs and steers and ... lives. She fingered the bandage.

Why do I feel so trapped? She thrived in remote settings alone with a camera or a notebook, studying God's beautiful world. Nature rained down outside her home— literally. Why not relish the beauty of the downpour, the heavy clouds over the hills, or the raindrops in the big pond out back?

She threw on her yellow slicker and shoved her feet into her red barn boots. Swaddling her camera in plastic, she headed for the stalls. She'd lose herself in the horses, take pictures from the barn, and quit obsessing over whatever. She wasn't in jail.

Never would be.

Even if today felt that way.

On Saturday night, crowds thronged Jack's. The clatter drifted into the backroom where Crystal and her bandmates sat. She closed her eyes. The murmurs from the patrons drifted through the doors and pounded Crystal's heart until the two discordant noises harmonized like one of Mama's jazz numbers. How her Mama loved to sing—a capella, improvised, and lots of scat singing. Mama filled her childhood with music which now filled her heart. Crystal placed a palm over her heart and felt the sounds around her. Which was louder? The audience or her heartbeat? Her fingers twitched, remembering the rhythms and melodies they memorized over the last three days. A half hour to go. Nerves heightened her senses. Was her sister here yet?

Crowds and performances and speeches terrified Roxie.

They energized Crystal. She picked up her fiddle. Keeping the volume soft, she harmonized to the dissonance from the crowd in the club.

"Crystal? What on earth are you doing?" Danica stared. Her eyebrows squished together. "You better not sound so discordant tonight."

"Do you hear?" Crystal nodded toward the closed doors. "There's music in the crowd's clamor. My harmony complements what I hear out there."

"You're crazy. That's why we love you." Danica turned toward the other group members. "Ladies, remember our sequence. Our encore will be "Barefoot in the Hollow.""

"What if we don't get an encore?" Abilene asked.

Crystal chuckled. "Danica will make them sit down, and we'll play the song anyway."

Jack stepped into the room. "Fifteen minutes. Anyone want a drink?"

"A beer." Leanne raised her hand.

"Me, too," Abilene said.

"Danica?" Jack looked to their lead singer. "How about you, Crystal?"

"They're prudes." Abilene winked. "Seltzer with a twist of lime and a swizzle stick for Danica so she looks like she's drinking. Sweet tea for the pretty one who isn't old enough to drink, anyway."

Leanne whooped and pointed at Crystal. "We're going to rock our set, Abi. Crys is blushing."

Indeed, Crystal's face heated. The standard joke was they'd floor the audience if they made Crystal blush. Whether their prophecy worked or not, she couldn't tell. Someone had only had to tease, and her fair skin ripened like a cranberry.

Jack returned with their drinks.

The other three chatted.

Crystal bowed her head. *Lord, good or bad, thank you.* Maybe they'd bomb. Signing with an agent was a long shot. She also understood the meek were blessed in the present. God executed the promise in the future according to his will. Sometimes her desires coordinated with God's, but not always.

At ten minutes to nine, Roxie made her way to the table reserved for guests of the band. All men she'd hung out with before, all but one.

"Roxie." Mike, Danica's fiancé, stood and pulled out a chair to his right. "Saved you a seat."

"Where does Jesse sit?"

"Out on the curb." Mike's hearty laugh made her smile.

"You know everyone, right?" Mike pointed to his left. "Richie belongs to—"

"Leanne." Roxie nodded. "Richie's stage production is going to dazzle the audience when Girls from the Hollow get the big gigs."

"At the least, my company will nab them recording studios." Richie lifted his beer.

Roxie's gaze moved around the table. "Hey, Conner, heard you found a PT job. Where?"

"Vanderbilt. I love this town. Nashville knows how to party."

"I hear you." Roxie plugged her ears. "Can't come within a mile of Broadway without going deaf from the party-goers."

"Not sure how I'll manage my work at Vanderbilt when my girl's on the road winning Grammys."

Roxie laughed. These guys adored their ladies. She turned to the good-looking guy sitting next to her. "I don't know you."

"Kenji. I belong to no one." He winked.

He was a cutie. Dark, full-bodied hair. Straight nose. A full bottom lip, well-defined top one. She wished Kenji would stand so she could check his height.

Her phone chimed with a text. Jesse.

JESSE: Sorry I'll be late. An accident has me stuck between exits. About twenty minutes away from the club once this mess clears.

Another text materialized before Roxie replied.

JESSE: If the traffic jam ever unclogs. Haven't moved for ten minutes.

ROXIE: Jack's is packed. Text when you arrive.

She placed her phone face down on the table.

"Boyfriend?" Kenji asked.

For a minute, Roxie wanted to deny her relationship. Guilt swept over her. "No." *Not a boyfriend after tonight.* She opened her mouth to explain, but Kenji turned toward Connor and spoke to Abilene's man.

Roxie looked toward Mike who seemed immersed in conversation with Richie—or what would pass for talk in the noisy club.

"So, you're Crystal's sister?"

Roxie jumped.

"Sorry. Didn't mean to startle you." Kenji raised his voice and cupped his hand over his mouth as though he'd yell. "If you don't yodel or bellow, no one hears anything. You look like Crystal."

Roxie tilted her head and smiled at Kenji's observation. How often had people compared them? She ducked her head and lowered her lashes. "I'm the pretty sister." She shuddered and stiffened. *Why am I flirting?*

"Do you work? Go to school?"

"I go to UT. Studying wildlife research. You?"

"I'm a zoologist at Zoo Knoxville."

A zoologist? Her heart sped, and she couldn't stop the grin which probably stretched to her ears.

"Seems you like my profession." Kenji sipped his red, icy concoction. "As they say, it's all happening—"

"At the zoo. I like Simon and Garfunkel."

"Me too." Kenji winked.

"I guess fate put us together." Roxie clamped her lips. She opened her mouth to correct her impetuous remark.

"What happened to your head?" Kenji brushed a lock of hair away from Roxie's forehead.

His fingers grazed her skin, and she trembled. "Hmm." Roxie glanced away. *Do I tell him I beaned myself on my bed? How embarrassing.*

tangled lives

Jack, the club's owner, spoke before she answered. "Ladies and gentlemen, tonight's guests are going to amaze you. Give a warm, no, not warm, give a Jack's on the River welcome to Girls from the Hollow."

Applause, especially the hoots and hollers from her table, made speech impossible.

Thank heavens.

Crystal took the stage. Her stool sat stage left, closest to their entrance. She laid her crutches on a table behind her chair and with the agility of a gymnast, hoisted herself onto her stool.

Dead center front, in a packed club, sat Roxie along with all her bandmates' beaux. Her sister waved. Her smile as warm as any Crystal had seen.

She readied her fiddle.

Where was Jesse, though? She scanned the crowd of eager patrons—drinking, laughing, loving. For a moment, Crystal's heart sank like popping bubbles in a soft drink. He didn't come. She should be happy Roxie showed up. Enjoy the company of her friends' lovers. Celebrate the fact an agent watched and listened somewhere in this club.

But she was close to twenty years old. No man had ever loved her. Tons of men-friends. Never a boyfriend.

Danica took the microphone. "What a pleasure to ..."

A couple walked into the nightclub.

Malachi and Pearl?

Crystal's heart leaped. They made a ten-and-a-half-hour trip from Florida to celebrate her big gig. This road trip came at the end of their honeymoon. They came for *her*. She threw them her brightest smile.

Who needed a boyfriend?

91

Roxie saw her sister smiling at someone in the distance. The brightness of the grin said she loved whoever she acknowledged. Was Jesse here?

She twisted around. No Jesse. Wait. Pearl and Malachi? How wonderful! Roxie yearned to leap from her seat and hug her sister and brother-in-law, but she couldn't disturb Crystal's performance—if Danica ever stopped yapping. Roxie pasted on a smile and listened to Danica's spiel. The girl had an ego. *Play, already.*

As though the lead singer heard her, Danica strummed a few, slow chords on her guitar.

Roxie shifted to face the band. Her shoulder brushed Kenji's sending a thrill rippling down her spine. She stole a peek. Jerked away. *Had he smiled at her?*

Abilene's bass thrummed on the same register as Roxie's heart. Each note resonated inside her chest.

The fiddle—low and plaintive. Slow. Each note held, in tune at the same volume, for eight beats.

Roxie held her breath.

She forgot to think. Feelings overtook her. The music brought her into the Appalachians and led her through rippling streams and violent storms. The sweet scent of magnolias wafted around her as though she sat under a tree in bloom. Every note flowed through her like blood giving her life.

After a span of time—an hour? A day? Her lifetime? Danica chatted again.

Never had the Girls from the Hollow sounded so good. All her sister's practicing had paid off.

If she studied her Biopolitics harder, she'd see similar success.

tangled lives

Danica interrupted Roxie's musing and introduced the band members. Roxie straightened and listened for her sister's name.

"On fiddle, our alto, Crystal Snow."

Roxie leaped to her feet and whooped.

Crystal's face reddened, but her sweet smile told Roxie how she'd blessed her sister.

The a cappella for the opening for "Life in Tennessee" forced Roxie back into her seat. The first, slow strains of the fiddle began. The tempo kicked up. Before long, Roxie couldn't understand how her sister's fingers moved so fast.

A clumping to the side of their table behind Kenji drew Roxie's attention from the stage. She leaned forward. Her arm pressed against Kenji's. *What?* A couple of ladies clogged to Crystal's music. Usurped her sister. *Rude.* She glanced at the band.

"Way to go, girls." Danica gave a thumbs up. "Anyone else want to join in? Now's the time." She turned to Crystal. "You go, Crystal Snow."

Crystal's face looked like someone in a dream. Not Roxie's nightmare, but a dream where you didn't want to wake. One keeping you curled under down covers, savoring the morning light. Or maybe a dream where you jigged with elves chasing rainbows.

Girls from the Hollow loved the cloggers.

Roxie sat as though glued to her chair.

Kenji leaned in to her as the fiddle intensified.

The smell of the man whose arm pressed against Roxie mingled with the sounds of the band. Intensified her mood. What scent? A sweet-smelling aroma like the firs in the Smokies. The hay fed to goats. The zoo. The outdoors.

She jerked away.

She had two rings. Tonight, she was going to propose to Jesse.

If he ever got here.

Three encores.

The band looked at one another—spent and euphoric. Had to be beyond overjoyed if Crystal's friends felt like she did.

Crystal's bandmates scurried off stage and into their lovers' arms. Crystal twisted to nab her crutches. She found herself airborne, swooped off the chair, feet off the floor. Strong arms held her like a bride heading over the threshold.

As Malachi whisked her away, his breath brushed her ear. "You. Were. Amazing."

How could this bear of a man move so fast? How does he have such finesse?

Malachi settled Crystal next to Pearl, like a mama settling her baby—soft and tender.

Pearl and Malachi talked over one another, the speech fast, their gestures animated.

"You were divine."

"Got soul, girl."

"I couldn't believe ..."

Another voice, a tenor both warm and melodic, joined the duo.

Jesse.

Crystal's breath settled enough to speak. "I didn't see you come in."

"Traffic accident. I arrived in time for your last number and the encores. Judging by crowd reaction, I'd be surprised if you don't have an agent and a contract by the end of the evening."

"Being discovered happens in novels. Not in real life," Pearl said.

"As if you know what happens in books," Crystal teased.

Pearl playfully slapped her. "I read what I need to. Recipes. Gossip magazines. TV guides."

"Anyway, happy endings don't come in all books." Crystal wagged her finger. "Remember, I favor Koontz and Rice and Lovecraft."

"Give me a Hallmark movie." Pearl gazed at Malachi. Her cheeks glowed, and she didn't look away from her man. "Get this girl a drink, Malachi."

Malachi stood. "Name your poison, Crys."

"Sweet tea."

"You don't need any more sugar." Jesse's hand touched hers. "You are the most amazing and sweetest Snow I've ever known."

Crystal's heart stopped.

Jesse's here? Why isn't he ...? Roxie's thoughts sputtered. She studied him across the room. He leaned in toward her sister.

Malachi stood.

His movement gave Roxie a clear view of her sister and Jesse.

Jesse had gripped Crystal's hand from across the table. He didn't let go.

Kenji's hand on her shoulder made Roxie shake away her emotions. "Can I get you something from the bar?"

She looked up. His sweet face and those large brown eyes—soulful and deerlike—almost hypnotized her.

If Jesse can flirt, so can I.

She closed her eyes and inhaled to steady her thoughts.

"Roxie?" Kenji peered down at her.

Roxie fingered her purse with the rings.

95

Chapter 9

Crystal looked up from her conversation with Jesse while Pearl and Malachi canoodled across from her. She waved to her sister. "Come. Join us."

Roxie's smile said she either loved the show, or she loved Jesse. Of course, the two didn't exclude each other. Roxie bent over Crystal and kissed her cheek. "You were phenomenal."

Words stuck in Crystal's throat.

Roxie's hand reached for Jesse. She moved close and kissed his ear.

No. Didn't kiss.

Roxie whispered something, and Jesse's face flushed. His eyes glistened, and he nodded—one quick jerk. Jesse pulled out a seat for Roxie. She squeezed herself into their table. "Pearl, I didn't expect you to cut your honeymoon short. I'm so happy you're celebrating our sweet pixie's triumph."

"How could I miss our baby sister's big break?" Pearl leaned across the table and squeezed Crystal's hand. "When I lived with you, I'd never dreamed your scratchy, pitchy violin could sound so good. You can play, sister."

"I had picked up the violin a year or two before you left. I was what? Twelvish?"

"I think so. I forget because I tried uber hard to block out the awful noise you made nonstop. Had I known your talent, I'd have hired you to play at our wedding. I'm sorry."

"We barely know each other, and I wouldn't have taken a cent from you," Crystal said. "I'm thrilled you came up to see our show."

"I was your mama for two years. A mother never forgets her child—"

"Even if the child forgets her?" Crystal laughed.

"You were two when Grandpa adopted me." Regret tinged Pearl's lowered voice. "Two-year-olds don't know who they are. After I left, jealousy ruined ..." She spoke with a long exhale. "Malachi tells me I was a child back then too, and children do foolish things. I missed my sisters even if I ditched them."

Malachi returned with drinks and a frown. "Here we go."

Pearl looked up at her husband. "What took you so long?"

Malachi hiked a shoulder. "A pitcher of sweet tea for sweet southern belles."

Pearl ground her teeth.

"What's wrong?" Crystal asked.

Pearl quirked her lips. Her voice held an edge. "Sometimes, boors treat Malachi as though he's not important."

"Why on earth?" Roxie asked.

Pearl ran a finger along her skin.

"We have no proof." Malachi's grin looked genuine. "We can't assume bias because customers overwhelmed the barkeepers."

"Color? Here in Nashville?" Crystal frowned. "Didn't bias go out in the sixties?"

Silence answered her.

"I sympathize. Sometimes, I get shunned because I can't walk. No one sees the fiddler who will win a Grammy—"

"Invite me to the award ceremony."

"Sign my napkin. Need an autograph."

"You go."

Everyone spoke over one another.

Crystal held up her hand to stop the chatter. "Boors don't understand that beneath crutches or skin or mental status, we're all the same. All important to God."

"Let's not get melancholy or philosophical" Malachi raised the pitcher. "Pour a glass and drink a toast."

They each filled their glass.

Malachi lifted his. "Here's to an agent, a contract, and continual platinum albums, so Crystal can support us in a manner to which none of us is accustomed."

As they laughed, the crew clicked glasses, and sipped.

Crystal's cheeks hurt from smiling. "The way everyone's taking a cut from the millions we haven't made, y'all will have to support me and keep me off welfare after my success." She looked from face to face, and love wanted to burst her heart.

Roxie's shoulder nudged Jesse, and the two of them stood. "We'll catch you in a few."

Crystal frowned as she watched them leave.

Roxie's heart thrummed, and she stiffened to keep every limb from shaking.

They stood on the rooftop patio overlooking the Cumberland River flowing northwest toward Kentucky. Music from downtown twanged and rocked. Lights twinkled around them from the clubs in full bloom, not to mention the lights strung along the deck or on First Avenue, three stories below the dark brick building. Across the river, Nissan Stadium stood dark.

The rest of the riverfront danced in light. To her right, the Ghost Ballet—a sculpture looking like a broken roller coaster, glowed in red light. The reflection repeated in the quiet water below. Life danced beyond the sculpture in lights and traffic. An icy wind blew off the river. She shivered.

Jesse took her in his arms and drew her close. "Are you cold?"

The wisp of his words warmed her ear, and she wriggled closer. "Yes, but I love the cold. You know that." She buried her head into his chest.

He kissed the top of her head. Each lean muscle pulled her closer. "Let me keep you warm."

Oh, they had to marry soon. She trembled—and not from cold. If she didn't pull away, they'd ... How she wanted to make love with him. She stepped back, her hands against his chest. The cold air urged her to rush into his arms once more. If she didn't propose now, her nerve would fail. She'd lose Jesse like every man—well, every boyfriend—before him. He *was* good, and she didn't imply good *enough*. Enough meant settling for something less. Jesse was as perfect as any. A 4.0 of a man.

He peered down at her. His wide eyes looked like he feared she'd run from him. "You're going to get cold. We should go in."

"In a minute." She shuffled through her purse and grasped the ring. *Do I go down on a knee? Or do only men kneel? Mama didn't get on her knees when she proposed to Daddy.* Her mind drifted to the family tale of how Mama asked Daddy to marry him the day Lisa Simpson stole her away from everyone she loved. Daddy refused her. Mama never let him live down his mistake.

"Roxie, are you okay?"

She looked into his eyes. Light sparkled in their deep brown. "More than all right." She held up the silicone band. "Here."

What an idiot. You don't say 'here' when you propose.

"What's this?" Jesse's eyes narrowed.

She licked her lips. Plopped down on both knees. "Jesse Maxwell. Be my husband." *Ooof. Klutz.*

"What?"

Still on her knees, she faltered but grabbed his hands. "I practiced my proposal over and over and over. Nothing I've done tonight matches what I rehearsed. And the wood I'm kneeling on is biting into my knees. I think they're frostbitten."

"Then stand." Jesse laughed as he pulled her to her feet.

"I love you. I never want to be separated from you. Will you marry me?"

This moment was all Jesse had ever dreamed of. He peered into the pretty eyes of his girl. No. Of his fiancée. Crystal was wrong about her sister and him. He should've proposed in Florida. His gaze danced over Roxie's face, down her neck. Lower.

"Jesse?" Roxie sounded like she held back tears.

He smiled. Pulled her close. Kissed her, let his lips travel to her neck, caressed the hollow in the nape. "You are my dream. Of course, we'll marry."

"Put the stupid thing on." Roxie grasped Jesse's hand and slipped the ring onto his finger. "Your band fits like it was made for you. Like us." She curled into him.

Jesse ran his hands up and down Roxie's arms. "Aren't you cold?"

"Nope. Love winter."

"I am. Heat and humidity are why I'm a Southern country boy." He pulled away and stared at his ring.

"We'll get a real one, of course." She gazed at his hand as her heart pounded like Leanne's drums. *I did it!* She stiffened and grinned. "I almost forgot. I bought one for me, too." Roxie pawed through her purse. She waved the zirconium in front of him. "The one you buy for me doesn't have to have as big a diamond as this, but you get the idea."

"If I bought a two-carat diamond, you'd submerge the ring in moose-muck." Jesse took the ring from her and grasped her left hand. "Roxie Snow, I love you. The sooner you're my wife, the happier I'll be." He slipped the band on her finger. "Let's go tell the world."

"Danica, you look like you lost a war." Crystal's heart sunk a mite as the band's lead trudged toward the table. If Danica was sad …

"We did lose." She slumped into a vacant chair. "The agent didn't show. After all my conniving and calling. I don't know what I did wrong."

"You did nothing. Our performance is a group effort. Not your solo. We share victory." Crystal grew silent.

"And defeat."

Crystal closed her eyes. Another smidge of joy drained. She dredged her spirit to find the positive to this news. "Everything's good. We lost one battle, not the whole shebang."

"At least, we have a good demo." Danica fingered an empty glass sitting on the table in front of her.

"All's not lost. First," Crystal held up a finger, "we'll email links to the demo to every agency in town." She held up a second. "We'll cold-contact every agent we can find in—and out of—Nashville." She raised her third finger. "Better, yet, Mike's on his way over."

Danica craned her neck and looked back.

Mike leaned over Danica and kissed her head. "Ready to celebrate?"

Danica stood. She gazed down at Crystal. "Sure you all don't want to come? Pearl and Malachi are more than welcome to join us."

"No. We're going to head to their hotel room and catch up on the honeymoon details."

"Excuse me?" Pearl jabbed Crystal with her elbow.

"We'll talk about the ones they're able to share." Crystal winked at Pearl.

"You can go with your friends," Pearl said. "We're good."

"Do you need more honeymoon time?"

Pearl flushed the Snow sisters' trademark blush. "No. We've got a lifetime of loving. We're here to help you rejoice, not to hamper your celebration."

"You're not intruding." Crystal didn't want to hang out with couples any longer—although Pearl and Malachi technically were a couple. "We need to catch up."

"Danica!" Roxie called as she strode across the crowded club. Her hand, clasped in Jesse's, dragged him along. "Wait."

Danica turned toward Roxie. "Are you coming or hanging out with your party-pooper sister?"

Crystal grinned then stuck out her tongue at Danica. "Your joke's stale. But I love you, anyway."

"Jesse and I will join you." Mischief glinted in Roxie's eyes, one of those cat-eats-mouse expressions. "Look." She grabbed Jesse's hand and thrust out his and hers. "Guess who's getting married?"

Danica whooped.

Pearl bolted out of her chair and hugged Roxie. "When?"

"A few minutes ago." Roxie beamed.

"You married a few minutes ago?" Pearl laughed, her grin showing her perfect teeth. "You're fast."

Roxie swatted her. She gazed at Jesse, her eyes turning dreamy. "When?"

"After graduation?" Jesse's eyes sparkled.

Roxie turned back to her sister. "You heard the man. Are you coming along with us tonight?"

Pearl said something.

Crystal's mind wandered as the last of her joy seeped away. Her shoulders sagged. Breathing weighted her down as though the air thickened in her lungs. *No agent. Jesse engaged. Danica taking all credit. All I'll have is a degree in music business and a house full of cats.* She bit back a grin. Roxie was more apt to be the crazy old maid adopting hundreds of felines. Every time they went to Grandma Cora's, Roxie had to dose herself with bottles of Claritin, but she always cuddled the kitties. Crystal didn't much care for them. She'd be an old maid collecting violins. She suppressed the chuckle over her internal joke.

"Crystal, you get bad news about the agent and still you grin." Roxie's statement brought Crystal back to the moment. "I never understood your good humor."

"Not all of us are grumps like you."

Roxie stuck her tongue out at Crystal. "Brat. Now, answer me."

"I didn't hear what you asked."

"Are you coming with us?" Roxie waved her hand around to indicate Danica, Mike, Jesse, and her.

Crystal looked from her sister to Jesse. His eyes gazing into hers seemed to beg her to come along. She straightened, willing her normal good nature to chase the ache of being the odd-one out away. "No. If Pearl and Malachi are still hanging out, I want to visit with them."

"See you at home." Roxie bent and kissed Crystal's cheek. "When are you heading back to the homestead?"

"Sometime mid-week. School starts and won't wait on my career."

Roxie scoffed. "Not talking school tonight. This evening calls for celebrations—you, me, life, love."

Crystal watched the crew bounce their way across the crowded club. All her friends chased their dreams. She played life safe by staying in school studying business. Had to prepare for her future alone. Chances were good she'd live a solitary life with no Grammy award for comfort.

No. *Not going to happen that way.* Girls from the Hollow had four more days in Nashville to nab an agent and another gig at Jack's. Her world hadn't ended.

Three hours later, Crystal climbed onto Leanne's bed in Leanne and Abilene's bedroom. Three a.m.—the duo would stay with their lovers. Seeing as Danica slept in the queen-sized bed they shared, Crystal would camp out here until sleep claimed her.

Crystal sipped hot, herbal tea. The scent of mint didn't soothe her as usual. The last hour dragged along as though a full day had passed.

Listening to Pearl and Malachi's joy had sapped hers. Pearl and Malachi were so welcoming. Their conversation never flagged, but their touching and kisses and endearments showed they wanted to continue their honeymoon.

Sometimes optimism devastated you. When she believed in faith, she'd fail. Hope would resurrect only to dash her back on the rocks. Being optimistic often dished out disappointment after disappointment. More often than not, faith sucked you into the muck of misery.

She sipped her mint tea and inhaled the fragrance. Like weeding Mama's garden, the scent reminded her how this herb refused to die. Pull out every root, and somehow, the mint grew back as fragrant and delicious as ever. She was barely out of her teens. The world waited for her. *Why am I sulking? I need to be a mint root and pop back up.*

God knew the plans he had for her and Girls from the Hollow. Plans for hope and a future. A song bubbled up. She had to believe the melody confirmed the Lord's plans. She had a plan on how to fix her musical dreams.

Roxie drove through Dutch Valley. Her head bobbed as sleep tried to claim her. She jerked up and pulled off the road. *I'm not going to make it home. I should've taken a room for the night.* She climbed out of her car and studied the houses shadowed in night, all swaddled in pitch as families slept.

Families.

Roxie's stomach turned to rock as the vestiges of fatigue fled.

Jesse started talking about a family and babies and settling down after being engaged an hour. He also talked about living in Townsend or Tuckaleechee, so she could work in the mountains or close enough to UT to teach. She didn't want to be a professor. Didn't want the Smokies. She told him on their first date she didn't want to live in Tennessee. Moose only lived in the north. Snow came less and less in Tennessee. She couldn't change the environment, but Jesse could find a teaching job anywhere. Even Alaskans needed teachers.

Since her teenage years, moose and Alaska and caribou intrigued her. Frozen expanses. Snowcapped mountains in July. To experience the tundra cold instead of the muscle melting humidity of the South.

The cool night wrapped around her. Invigorated her. She looked up at the starry sky. "I want the fresh, cold air. I need the Northern Lights. Twenty-four hours of sunlight."

She listened.

No creature answered her.

Lord?

Nothing.

If not Alaska and the moose and caribou, she wanted to see yak. Tibet became cold. The panda of China, although not in the deer family, would be cool to study or photograph. Cold there too.

The world was bigger than Tennessee.

Oh, Lord, what did I do? She paced away from her running car, pivoted, and strode back. Wide awake now, she climbed in, shifted to drive. Clutching the steering wheel, she made up her mind.

No way would she ruin her life.

Chapter 10

On Wednesday morning, after three hours of interviewing at Knoxville Academy, Jesse stood and shook the principal's hand. "Mrs. Sanford, Knoxville Academy is my dream school."

"Since your student teaching days, we wanted to hire you." Mrs. Sanford stepped to the door. "We hate to lose Stanley Wilfred, but retirement comes to us all."

Jesse bit back a chuckle. "In one form or another."

"I'd rather retirement come from work and not in meeting my Maker."

The two laughed.

Mrs. Sanford opened the office door. "Sometimes bureaucracy stinks. We have to go through the hiring committee. Bureaucracy ties my hand as much as it ties up time. You have my vote."

Jesse soared as he left Knoxville Academy. He called Roxie. After two rings, though, he hung up. He had a better idea.

Crystal's plan wasn't going to sit well with Roxie. Mama and Daddy would come around quicker than her sister. As she pulled into her driveway, her hands turned clammy.

The motor still rumbled as Mama came running down the walkway.

Daddy followed close behind.

"Roxie told me Saturday night rocked the joint," Mama said.

Crystal scrunched her eyes. Old people shouldn't use slang. "We did." She edged out of the car, gripping the door for balance.

Mama's arm clutched Crystal in a tight embrace, then passed her on to Daddy.

"How was your cruise?" Crystal asked.

"We have time to talk." Daddy hung onto her as Mama handed Crystal her crutches. "I'll grab your bags."

"No bags." Crystal edged to the front of the vehicle hoping to avoid the confrontation sure to follow.

Daddy held her arm. "Why not?"

"I've got to run to the ladies' room." *Lord, forgive my lie. I need your courage.*

Jesse climbed out of his car as the school bus pulled in front of the house.

"Jesse!" Boone bounded off the bus followed by his twin and grabbed Jesse in a bear hug. "Come, shoot hoops. Roxie stinks. Girls can't play."

Boone and Grant tossed their packs onto the lawn.

"Don't let your sister hear you. She'll wear you out playing until she proves you wrong. Go get the ball. You know Rox's competitive streak."

"My what?" Roxie strode toward Jesse.

"Nothing, my love." Jesse turned to his fiancée—he loved the word almost as much as the noun wife. He pulled her to him. Her kiss made him want to forget basketball. Wanted his wedding night. She tasted salty and smelled like she'd been in the barn. Not a nasty scent—all leather and oil and horse. He inhaled. He'd never breathe in the scent of leather and not have to fight ... his urges.

"Gross." Grant dribbled the ball in the road. "Quit passing germs and shoot the basket. That's what we're here for."

Jesse chuckled. *Kids have no clue.*

"Why *are* you here?" Roxie inched away.

"I have news."

"Come on, Jesse." Grant tossed the ball into the hoop. "We have the first points."

"Go." Roxie ran her fingers along Jesse's jaw. "News can wait. My brothers can't."

"I'll be in after they cream me." Jesse threw Roxie a smile and dashed to road to prove the twins wrong in their challenge.

Roxie crossed her arms and watched the scrimmage for a few seconds. Her mind drifted from the pickup game. *We'll be back at UT on Saturday, so why'd Jesse come all the way to Jacksboro?*

Love brought him up here. She smiled, and her crossed arms turned into a hug. *Love will make him see my needs.* She watched Jesse's lithe movements, like a ballet dancer, though they'd argue over her analogy. Jesse called ballet and figure skating and gymnastics girl things. Still, his leaps and pirouettes along the road proved manly men could dance.

Roxie fingered her ring finger. The zirconium lay on her dresser. It caught on the horses' leather and dirt clogged the setting. No ring. Needed to wear it, but she hadn't told her folks. Wait until Mama and Daddy learned her news. They loved Jesse almost as much as Crystal did.

They'd rejoice for real. Had her sister come around to the fact she, Roxie Star Snow, would soon become Mrs. Jesse Maxwell?

No.

Never.

She was going to be Dr. Roxie Star Snow, PhD, star researcher. Never would she take a husband's name.

"Score!" Grant danced along the road in victory.

The dunk shook her out of her daze. Basketball bored her. "I'm heading in to help with dinner, so Crystal and I can catch up."

The males battled for baskets in the road.

Men. Didn't know I was here. She shook her head. Jesse lost himself in action, much like Crystal. *Me? Give me stillness and God's glorious creations.* Back in the house, she slipped on her fake engagement ring.

A half hour later, the family crowded the table.

Jesse, his face damp from washing after his workout, squeezed in next to Roxie. The dampness made him look dewy. Given her earlier thoughts about his ballet skills, she smiled.

"Why are you giggling?" Jesse's whisper tickled her cheek.

She couldn't tell Jesse he reminded her of a prima ballerina. Or would he be called a ballerino? What's the noun for a male ballet dancer? She shook her head.

Crystal settled next to the twins across the table.

Mama and Daddy reigned in their usual spots at both ends of the table.

The twins reached for rolls, and Mama gave them her evil eye. When she used her piercing stare with her lips pinched, no one crossed her.

The boys dropped their hands into their laps and bowed their heads while Daddy asked the blessing.

tangled lives

With the final amen, Roxie twisted her zirconium engagement ring. She turned the stone downward. When she closed her fingers, the ring looked like a simple, silver band. *Do I tell them now?*

Mama settled her question as she passed the salad. "Our cruise ..." Mama's eyes glowed. She peered at Daddy like what? Like a newfound lover.

Ew. Old people sex. Gross.

"In Bonaire, your father convinced me to scuba dive." Mama leaned forward as enthusiasm laced her voice. "At first, thinking about breathing underwater—"

"You snorkeled plenty." Daddy gazed at Mama like a teen in love. "You know—"

"My story. My style of telling the tale." She blew him a kiss.

"As your mother sat on the edge of the boat ready to dive, she trembled like—"

Mama wagged a finger at Daddy. "My story." She looked around the table. "Your father forced me to be brave."

"I didn't *force*—"

"Encouraged me."

Mama and Daddy gushed, each finishing the other's sentences as the adventure of their cruise unfurled.

Roxie'd have to wait until the boys went to bed and Mama and Daddy finished regaling them with the details of what sounded like a honeymoon of new lovers before she mentioned her engagement.

Daddy gazed across the table at Mama. His voice became husky. His eyes misted. "We never had a real honeymoon after we married. So, this one ..."

Roxie wasn't wrong in her assessment. The cruise had been a honeymoon. Seventeen years late, but real. She looked at Jesse. Would she feel the same way about him in ten years? Fifteen? Her heart quivered. She loved his youth. What would she think when his jowls sagged, and he lost his hair?

Mama and Daddy continued to gab about beaches and coral and the food on the cruise ship. Love glistened in their glances, like Malachi and Pearl.

Roxie looked at Jesse whose focus shifted from speaker to speaker. Did he see her like Mama and Daddy saw each other?

"Enough about us." Daddy passed around the pasta. "You all have news for us." He looked toward Crystal. "Tell us about your gig at Jack's."

"The show went well. We have an appointment with an agent on Monday." Crystal shoved pasta into her mouth.

"How will you fit in a Nashville trip? Doesn't school start?" Mama asked.

Crystal chewed slowly and studied the table.

Roxie knew her sister. She had secrets too.

Crystal swallowed and licked her lips. "I'll manage."

Daddy picked up Mama's inquisition "How—?"

"Hey, this dummy," Grant interrupted Daddy as he pointed to Roxie, "is taking her boring course again with Dr. Stupid Stearns. Good thing you wasn't here—"

"Don't call people stupid, and you say weren't here, not wasn't." Mama frowned.

Grant rolled his eyes. "Whatever."

Mama's flinty eyes speared Roxie.

The look meant one thing, and not something good.

"Why on earth?" Daddy laid down his fork. His eyes pierced her. "Didn't you hate the course?"

"Stearns gave me a B-minus."

"You passed. When I had to study about social work agencies dealing with adults—"

"And my course on sheep's bowel issues—"

Daddy continued as though Mama hadn't spoken. "I about fell asleep." He looked up at Mama. "And she put me to sleep regaling me with the details of intestinal issues in large animals."

Daddy did hear me.

"Was this before or after you clunked your head?" Daddy's scowl said his joke wasn't meant to be funny.

No way would Roxie tell them tonight about Vernita Barnes's visit. Stearns and stitches were enough to handle.

"B-minuses were my," he looked at Mama. "Our— success stories."

Crystal stopped forking pasta into her mouth. "She thinks a grade so low makes her stupid, so she—"

Daddy raised his hand to stop Crystal's explanation. "You're not—"

Roxie ground her teeth. Daddy. He didn't understand.

Jesse grabbed Roxie's hand under the table. His warmth calmed her nerves. "A high grade-point makes her happy. Isn't that what matters?"

"Happiness, yes. Grades? No." Mama pushed her plate away and leaned back. "You're smart. More than smart. You threw your soul into your studies. Doing your best is the thing that matters."

"Mama." Roxie half rose. "I'm not going to be second-rate."

"Sit down." Mama pointed to Roxie's chair.

Roxie sat.

"You'll never be second-rate, even if you earn a D in a college course. You are more than your intellect. You—"

"Mama—"

"Remember Grayson, Roxie?" Mama acted as though she hadn't heard Roxie's protests. Typical of Mama. Why didn't Daddy interfere now? He always defended her against Mama.

Daddy cleared his throat. "Listen to your mother."

So much for Daddy defending me. "Which of our fosters was Grayson?"

Mama continued as though she didn't hear Roxie's question. "You didn't like Grayson and called him stupid."

"How do you remember those little details from fifteen-sixteen years ago?" Roxie's stomach clenched. Every time life became good when she was young, Mama took in another kid.

"Because of circumstances, some things stick out." Mama's voice turned sad. "Grayson was our foster with Down syndrome."

Roxie raised her eyebrows. "The one who didn't speak? Only grunted?" Roxie hated that foster. Grayson took up all Mama's time and didn't add anything to the house. "Right after you lost the baby."

Mama nodded. "He lived here for one week."

"What does he have to do with me retaking Biopolitics."

"Grayson couldn't speak. He needed help getting shoes and socks on and loved animal documentaries." Mama's eyes turned dreamy as though she described one of her own kids. "His father loved him. His sister gave up her way of life in Duluth to make room for him and her dad who suffered from Alzheimer's. Grayson, and his father, mattered. Not because of their talents, but because God created them. Loved them."

"Grayson has nothing to do with me. I can do better than a B-minus."

"Yes," Daddy said. "If grades are important to you, then bore yourself to tears. Your mother's right, though."

Her folks dropped the subject and resumed their meal. Still, their disapproval tore a hole in Roxie's soul.

I never choose right. Lord, help me. Please.

Daddy pushed his plate away as though he lost his appetite.

If they hate all my decisions, what will they do when I tell them I'm getting married? She turned to Jesse. "Let's go for ice cream. Don't you have news for me?"

"We've got ice—"

Roxie cut off her mother and strode out the back door.

Crystal worked her way to the sink and washed pots. Leaning against the countertop, she could handle this chore without help. Wash dishes. At the moment, she loved Roxie. Her sister's schooling took the focus off her. Maybe she could move to Nashville and not tell her folks.

Of course, tuition payments would be a problem.

At any cost, she wanted to avoid the conversation about Nashville and record contracts. Now wasn't the time to tell her folks her plans. If Roxie's excellence in school upset them, what would her issues do?

"Let me get the dishes." Mama held Crystal's shoulder and turned to Boone and Grant. "Boys, you're on clean-up tonight."

"Maaaa." Both whined, almost in harmony.

"You said you'd wash the dishes," Grant grumbled.

After giving the twins her *don't argue with me* stare, Mama turned back to Crystal. "I'll bring out coffee and cake, and we can catch up in the living room."

"I can manage here." Crystal gritted her teeth and prayed Mama would let her clean the kitchen. "Let the boys—"

Mama gave her *the* stare.

No use arguing.

In the living room, Crystal sat on the edge of the recliner. Her heart resonated like Abilene on her bass, and she tapped her fingers against her pants' leg. Her folks took forever. Crystal wanted to tell them her news, listen to the fireworks, then get on with life.

"Here we go." Mama handed Crystal a cup of decaf.

Daddy carried sweet treats from Flour Child's bakery. He set the plate on the coffee table and pushed the plate toward Crystal.

She eyed the sugary petit fours, Napoleons, and cream puffs, and her stomach soured.

"What's got you so keyed up?" Mama reached across the coffee table and grasped Crystal's hand.

Crystal shoved an entire petit four into her mouth and stared at the ceiling while she chewed. *Why weren't these things bigger? Take longer to swallow?*

"Crystal," Daddy said, "answer your mother."

Spew out your plans like ripping off a bandage. Crystal's throat constricted. "I'm not going back to college."

"What?" Daddy stiffened like someone rammed a board down his back.

"The band and I are going to make our way in music."

"Can't you pursue this once you earn your music business degree?" Daddy used his rational tone. "Or record while you study?"

If he had yelled, Crystal would've found things easier to argue. "Timing."

"Timing? What do you mean?"

She was in trouble because he crossed his arms and leaned back on the sofa. *Case closed. No argument.* Daddy may think so, but he had another think coming. She licked her lips. "Momentum is on our side."

"Getting your degree so you can support yourself is what's *on your side*." Daddy looked at her mother whose face looked what? Stoic? Disapproving? "Mama regretted not getting her degree. Ended up settling as a vet tech."

"She likes the job." Crystal relaxed. Turning the focus to Mama took the pressure off her.

Crystal studied her silent mother whose eyes flickered as though searching for a response. "I do love my job.

However, I could've been a vet." Mama leaned forward. "You cannot make the same mistake I made."

"Given the lives you two shared, you should know one thing." Crystal couldn't hide the edge in her voice. Upsetting anyone always bothered her. She wanted the world happy, but the time had come for her to live the life she craved. "Timing is never convenient but is always perfect. I've withdrawn from UT already. Done deal."

"Not if you're under our roof," Daddy said.

"No problem." Crystal rose. "Tomorrow, I'll be in Nashville. Danica's looking for an apartment for us." She worked her way toward her room. At the kitchen doorway, Crystal turned back to her folks. "Unless you want me gone tonight. The choice is yours." Crystal hurried out of the room as her soul bled. Why did her dreams conflict with everyone else's?

Jesse pulled into the Dreamery Creamery, Jacksboro's premier ice cream parlor. "Ready?" He grinned at Roxie as he stepped out of the car.

"Going to leave the vehicle running?" Roxie turned off the ignition and climbed out.

"Oops." Jesse held out his hand.

"Nope. You'll lose them." She slipped the key into her pocket and skipped toward the Dreamery.

Jesse caught her by the door and pulled her into his arms. Her kiss curled his toes and urged him to linger.

Roxie broke away. "I came for another kind of sweet." She flung open the door. "I'll take the usual."

Five minutes later, Jesse slid the cup of black cherry ice cream in front of Roxie and slipped into the booth across from her.

"Treats to eat. Family gone. No interruptions." Roxie leaned her elbows on the table and pointed her spoon at Jesse. "Time to tell me what brought you up to Jacksboro."

"You." Jesse winked and dug into his hot fudge sundae.

Roxie grinned.

Jesse put down his spoon. *Why the nerves?* He inhaled to steady himself. "I'm guaranteed a job at Knoxville Academy."

Roxie frowned.

His plan wouldn't go well.

"You're not going to take the position, are you?"

"The academy is my dream job."

"But the Academy's in Knoxville."

He nodded as his ice cream melted under the heat of the fudge.

"I'm going to Maine for grad school."

"Why not finish at UT?"

Roxie shoved her black cherry scoop away. "You know I've been accepted in Maine."

"We could marry when your grad school finishes." He grabbed her hand.

Roxie said nothing. Her face, though? The scowl, the hard, blue eyes hinted of more.

Roxie stared at her hand. Wiggled her fingers. "Is working in Tennessee what you really want?"

He nodded. She understood. Roxie would compromise. His heart rate settled for the first time since they started their drive to town. "With all my heart."

Roxie stood. "You've never listened to me since we started dating. I don't think you want me." She strode out of the Dreamery.

Chapter 11

With elbows on the table, Jesse propped his head on his clasped fists. Roxie had to listen to reason. *Lord, wisdom here. Please?*

After several minutes, he leaned against the booth. She would come back into the shop. He drove. Had the keys.

Keys.

He patted his pockets. No. He'd left the car running, and Roxie had grabbed them when she turned off the ignition. *She wouldn't, would she?* He knew Roxie, though. After easing out of the booth, Jesse stepped into the parking lot. He growled into wind biting into him. *That woman will stroke me out one day.* No car. He looked up and down the main road. Cars whizzed by filled with men connected to reasonable women—not one who would strand them. He sighed, reached for his phone and called her. Each ring vised his chest until voice mail picked up. Steadying his voice to hide his anger, he spoke. "Roxie, come back. Let's be reasonable." He scrunched his eyes. He heard her reaction to his message.

I am reasonable. You, though?

Why didn't voice mail have an edit button? Since he couldn't change what he already said, he apologized. "I'm sorry. We need to talk. I love you." He hung up.

Why couldn't she be like Crystal? Never an issue. Never an argument. Happy. Content. Talented. Beautiful—far prettier than Roxie. He grinned. He'd never tell his girl her sister was prettier. Truth, though, Roxie intrigued him. Kept him on his toes. Made him be the best version of himself. Crystal worried too much about offending anyone. So sweet, but too much sugar wasn't good for you. Besides, Crystal would never be spontaneous like Roxie.

He found an empty table on the outside patio and waited.

Fifteen minutes later, Roxie pulled up in front of his table. She lowered her window. "Ready to head home?"

He didn't move. "Why'd you run off?"

"I had errands."

"Couldn't you have told me?"

She smiled her beautiful grin. White, even teeth, full lips.

His heart pounded even as he understood her words were going to pound him once he sat in the car.

"I didn't think we needed to discuss our day-to-day decisions. Errands or where we'd live, study, the number of children we'd have."

Jesse glanced around. A few customers hunkered around their food stared. Heads cocked. Seemed they relished the budding argument as much as their frozen treats. Their argument didn't need to be a public display. He stepped toward her window. "What do you mean?" He grabbed the door handle. Locked. "Open up."

"You take a job at Knoxville—"

"I didn't take one. They're working through committee."

"When they offer you the placement, what are you going to do?"

He yanked the door handle. "Unlock the door."

"Answer me."

"Be reasonable." He reached inside the open window of the door and reached for the lock.

Roxie shifted the gearstick. The car lurched back, and she curved out of the spot.

As the car paused, Jesse held up his hands. "Roxie. Be ..." He wanted to say reasonable. Again. As if the first two times he told her to be reasonable didn't anger her enough. In her current state of mind, rational thought escaped Rox. "Let's talk somewhere private."

"Get in."

He headed for the driver's side.

Roxie jerked her head toward the passenger seat.

Jesse bolted around the car and dove inside. They drove in a silence so sharp he thought he'd bleed.

Roxie turned in toward Cove Lake State Park.

"Where are you going?"

She pulled into an empty spot near a gazebo. "Time to talk." She climbed out of the car and took a seat under the shelter.

After the heat of the car and Roxie's anger, the frosty night soothed Jesse. At the picnic bench, he slid into the seat across from her and reached for her hand resting on the table. He expected her to jerk away. She didn't. Her hand, warm in his, settled the last of his anger. "Talk to me."

"If you take this job, how can we get married? I'll be in Maine."

"You can take grad courses at UT. The university has a great wildlife program."

"They don't offer moose research."

"You've seen a moose once when your folks brought you on your undergrad college tours. Why not study deer or bear or—"

"I want to move north. You've known my goal since we first met."

"I want to stay here. My family lives here. Mom and Dad are aging—"

"Mine aren't?"

"Meredith and Parker are ten years younger. The North doesn't have the Smokies. Knoxville Academy has stellar track and field and cross-country teams. One of the best in the nation."

"Maine has *stellar* studies in moose biology. I want the wilds of central Maine. I want to explore Alaska and Canada and the Hudson Bay and the Adirondacks. The world is wider than East Tennessee."

"Then go to the University of Maine."

"Really? What about Knoxville Academy?"

"I'll work until you graduate. When we marry, we can readjust our plans." *I'll convince you East Tennessee and our families matter more than subzero temps and gangling moose.*

"You'd move north?"

"I won't rule out relocating if you don't." Jesse studied their clasped hands. Compromise hung in the air. "We've always found agreeable compromises."

A breeze blew through the shelter, and a shiver coursed through him. Her hand, though, had softened beneath his. Roxie peered up at him. "I love you. I want our relationship to work. Promise me you'll talk to me before you make any decision."

"You didn't talk when you applied to Maine."

Roxie threw the car keys at him. They glanced off his nose. "So much for compromise." She swiveled away from the picnic bench, stood, ready to run.

Darting from the table, he grabbed her before she stormed into the night. He ground his teeth as he pulled her to him. *Why can't she be like Crystal?* He held her stiff body.

Her icy eyes stared into his. "We weren't engaged when I applied to U Maine. You didn't stop me, and we hadn't decided to marry."

"Do you want to marry me?"

Silence met his words.

Crystal picked up Lovecraft's book. Murdering fictional characters worked off her anger. Soon she lost herself in the shadows of evil kidnappers and hapless victims. Somehow the hero would work out the mystery. He'd conquer the existential evil haunting the protagonist. Somehow life would return to balance. If not for her parents' anger about her quitting school, at least for these characters.

"Want company?" Roxie startled her as she hopped onto the bed. She grabbed Crystal's book.

"Hey." Crystal reached for her novel. "You'll lose my place."

Roxie dogeared the page and studied the book. "Lovecraft's cover with the knives and blood and entrails ..." She shuddered at the picture. The cover will induce my night terrors." She tossed the book aside.

"Your nightmares and screaming don't scare me. You sleep on the other side of the house. No sweat." Crystal reached for her novel.

Roxie shouldered her away. "No. Talk to me." Roxie nestled next to her, their arms touching.

"How'd your ice cream date go?"

Roxie hiked a shoulder.

"What did you argue about now?"

Roxie shifted up into a sitting position, her back against the headboard, her gaze across the room.

Crystal waited. Waited some more. "Well?'

"What makes you think we argued?" Roxie glanced at her, then nodded. "Knoxville Academy will offer Jesse a position for next year."

Crystal sat upright. She looped her arm over her sister. "Are Maine and moose and snow and subzero temperatures so important you'd give up Jesse?"

Roxie had returned to staring into the distance.

"Jesse's reasonable. School teachers can work on the tundra."

Roxie's sunny laughter told Crystal she'd broken through her sister's malaise.

"He came around, didn't he?"

Roxie smiled. "I think so." Her face brightened, and she peered at Crystal. "How'd Mama and Daddy take to your quitting school?"

Crystal quirked her lips.

"Don't worry about offending others, Crystal. These are your dreams. If we don't chase our ambition when we're young ..."

Crystal waited for Roxie to finish.

Roxie slapped her forehead. Winced. "I'll be glad when I become un-stitched."

"When will they be removed?"

"Five more days—if Mama and Daddy let me live that long." Roxie paused Her lips moved as though she mulled over ideas.

Crystal was about to pick up her book again when Roxie spoke. "You did tell them Pearl skipped college to become a pastry chef."

"You, of all people, know Pearl can do no wrong for Mama and Daddy." Crystal ducked her head. "Of course, one has to be able to read to go to college."

Roxie punched Crystal's arm with a light hit. "A mocking word coming from you?"

"If you want to stop me from dissing our big sister, your punch has to pack something other than a mosquito swat." After a pause, Crystal exhaled a long breath. "Our folks did come around to Pearl's culinary dreams."

"I think they fell in love with Malachi."

"Don't blame them. He's an adorable teddy bear. Me? I don't have a beau for them to love." Crystal's voice dropped. Her wistfulness sounded pathetic.

"You're going to find the perfect man," Roxie said. "A prince who will carry you off to—"

"The Grammy Awards."

Roxie's laughter echoed Crystal's own. Roxie fingered a lock of Crystal's hair. "You are going to have a huge recording career. I know it. Do *not* kowtow to convention. *You* act on what you believe in. You're worth every success."

"Roxie?" Pain and love and worry for her talented sister overflowed Crystal's heart.

"Hmm?" Roxie wrapped a tendril of Crystal's hair around her finger.

"You need to act on what you believe in too. You have the same stellar talent as the rest of us."

She grimaced. "You've eaten my baking. Heard my lessons on the French horn."

Crystal stared at her sister. Willed her silence to make Roxie see the truth.

"My talent lies in counting ticks on deer and analyzing biotrophic elements in marshes."

"No." Crystal put on her sternest frown, made her eyes bore into her sister. "You have the most brains of all of us. You have patience. Photography. Biopolitics."

Roxie stuck her tongue out at Crystal.

"Chutzpah."

"Hoots-pa?" Roxie giggled. "What's hoots-pa mean?"

"Cheekiness, nerve, audacity."

"I've learned this trait from the best." Roxie kissed the top of Crystal's head.

"Who?"

"My little sister."

"You'll see this in action tomorrow. I'll be Nashville bound despite our folks' anger. Danica's too caught up in getting married to pursue our goals. Left to her, we'll be playing in honky-tonks or busking on street corners. She believes her brilliance and looks will nab her a contract. Me? I'm going to knock on every door and hit every club. If we don't have a number one album by next year ..."

"There's always music business. I hear UT—"

Crystal reached over Roxie for her novel. "You continue to tease, and I'll rip out your stitches one by one."

"That's my sister. Full of hoots-pa."

Roxie watched Crystal read. She wished she were more like her sister. Nothing ever daunted her or dampened her cheerfulness. Happiness swamped everyone who hung out with Crystal for a minute. Her sister's warmth and calm, even with her parents' disapproval of her decision to drop out of college, infected Roxie. Her eyes grew heavy. *Crystal will achieve what she wants.* Roxie dozed, then her eyes opened. *She'll never get Jesse, though. I love him. I'll make him change.*

Jesse paid little attention to the familiar winding roads into Townsend. Instead, he focused on Roxie's kisses. Recalled the warmth of her body next to his. They'd marry. Sooner rather than later.

He'd make her want to stay in Tennessee.

He smiled. She always came around.

Chapter 12

The sun peeked over the mountains. Though a light frost coated the ground, the sunny day promised comfortable hiking weather. *Valentine's day camping.* Jesse couldn't hide his grin as he and Roxie climbed out of his car at the trailhead to Morgan's Bald on Friday morning. Hiking beat going to class. Three days alone with Roxie. Jesse would change her mind about the Smokies.

"A weekend photoshoot. You gave me the greatest gift." Roxie drew him into a hug and kissed him.

Her mouth, warm and sensual, drew him closer, made Jesse want to share a tent rather than lug a second one seven miles up to the bald. Her breath tasted sweet like honey and cream. Why couldn't they sleep together? They were engaged, so as good as married. Desire tightened his arms around her. His fingers stroked her nape. Her skin silky. He bent to kiss the hollow there. Scents of roses or another flower he'd never be able to name begged him to linger.

Roxie jerked away, but she smiled. "I hope lots of people camp at the site. I think I'm going to need chaperones."

"According to Geoff, the whole world sleeps together. A crowd would think we were strange if we slept alone."

Roxie's smile faded. She stepped to the back of the car and banged on the trunk. "Open. If we don't leave, we'll never get to Morgan's Bald. All the good spots will be gone."

Jesse popped the trunk. "The campground is seven miles up. We should be there in four hours. Last night's campers will be gone. Tonight's crew won't show up until mid-afternoon. We'll have the pick of the place."

Roxie rummaged through her photography pack. "I can't believe you promised me all the photography I wanted."

"Two whole days."

While clutching her camera, she turned to Jesse and kissed his cheek. "Thank you. I needed a weekend in the wild. Too much college stress." She picked up her camera and adjusted her all-purpose zoom lens onto the body. "And you get to carry our supplies." With a grin, she slung her equipment over her back, grabbed her hiking poles, and strode toward the trailhead.

Jesse leaned against his car and watched her walk away. Not ten feet from him, she paused and knelt. Focused her lens on something.

They'd be lucky if they made the seven-mile trek by midnight. Crawling along the trail, photographing what? Squirrels? A hopeful spring flower poking its head out of the frozen ground early. His legs twitched and begged him to move. Fast. Not this weekend. He rubbed his neck, and a smile worked its way across his face. At least he'd be with Roxie.

Warm breezes drifted over Nashville's Cumberland River. Even at eleven p.m., Crystal didn't need a sweater. Sipping her seltzer and lime, she stretched her aching legs as she sat on a bench on Jack's rooftop. Beyond the deck, the river caught wisps of city lights. The wind brought a scent of spring begging to crawl up from the south. At nearby tables, patrons chattered. Merriment tinkled in their voices. A few fans had stopped by and raved about the set the Girls from the Hollow finished fifteen minutes earlier.

Crystal's band had hurried off to party or home to bed with their beaux. Danica, after bragging about her performance—sometimes her ego drove Crystal nuts— headed with Mike to Knoxville to work on their wedding. Crystal's jaw tightened. She'd quit school on faith, but after one month in Nashville, dreams of a career had faded. They had no club lined up for next weekend and had exhausted all their leads on agents. *My folks were right. Should've stayed in school.* Crystal sipped her soda and gazed into the dark night. The Ghost Ballet, the sculpture across the river resembling a red roller coaster split in two, should've been named Broken Ghost in the Hollow. Maybe her joke about busking on street corners would prove prophetic.

"Mind if I join you?" A man, maybe thirty-five or forty-years old, smiled down at her. Gray streaked his dark hair, but his smile made him look young.

"Sure." She shifted her chair. Company would be nice.

The man settled into the seat next to Crystal and handed her a card. "I'm Kyle Davenport."

Crystal took the card and stared, then stared at Kyle. Did her heart beat? Was her mouth closed? She swallowed hard and croaked a question. "From The Davenport Agency?"

He nodded. "I wanted to talk to you since I heard your demo."

Her heart, remembering to do its job, skittered. "When did you hear us?"

"Last month."

"Why didn't you call?" Crystal clamped her mouth shut.

"I wanted first to check out the band and see how serious you were," Davenport said. "I represent—"

"The best of the best. Billie and Nan, Washbasin Gentry ..." Crystal shuddered. She sounded star-struck and overeager. Surely this agent understood how flummoxed she was. He was *the* Kyle Davenport.

"After I heard your sets and saw several performances, I needed a chance to talk to you alone."

"Me?"

Kyle nodded then sipped from a Glencairn glass what looked like bourbon. "I want to sign you as a client."

Crystal straightened. She grinned so wide she had to look like a circus clown. "Oh, my! Fantastic. When can we meet and go over the contract?"

Kyle sipped again. He put his glass down on the table behind him. He held up his hand.

"What?"

"Here's the deal. I didn't call the group because the contract is up to you."

"Me?"

"Yes." He leveled his eyes. "*You* are the force behind the band—"

"Everyone pulls her weight. Danica works hard. Abilene—"

"Let me finish. You're the real deal. The big talent."

Why did her heart sink?

"I'll meet with the group *if* you fix the focus from your lead ... Danica you said?"

Crystal nodded.

"From Danica to you. Your lead has the chops and skill, but her ego will destroy the group before you get off the ground."

"She ..." Danica's bragging from earlier gnawed at Crystal.

"We can call your group Snow in the Hollow or use your full name and keep the band's name, seeing as you've established a platform. We can change the name to Crystal Snow and the Girls from the Hollow." He looked into the distance. "Though the last group name is cumbersome. I like Snow in the Hollow."

What do I say? My dreams, but ...

"You ..." Davenport shifted and leaned toward her. "... young lady, should be the focal point."

Crystal's mind tumbled. Chances like this were rare. If the band failed, she'd have to return to UT defeated. She didn't want a career managing music. She craved making the music, playing her fiddle. Singing. But Danica had organized the group. She ran everything—made all decisions, albeit with Crystal's business knowledge. None of her friends would go for Davenport's deal. Especially Danica. Everyone would hate her, and—

"Don't let a misplaced loyalty ruin your career. I know musicians. Your friends would stab you in the back if they had the chance to record without you."

"No. You don't know—"

He held up his hand to silence her. "To be successful in my work, I have to understand artists. You have the potential for a great solo career. From what I've seen, though, you're humble and loyal, so I think working as a group would give you more potential. The original talent of the crew is Crystal Snow. If you went solo, we'd hire a backup group or use studio musicians." Davenport sipped his bourbon.

Silence settled around Crystal. She looked toward the river, but she could feel Kyle Davenport's eyes on her. She turned toward him. Met his eyes. "I'll have to talk to the girls." *This will end our chance with the Davenport Agency.*

"I wouldn't sign you if you didn't discuss the conditions. The band's a team like a beautiful engagement ring. You're the diamond. They're the setting."

A waitress came around asking for orders.

"Another round for me and the lady."

For me? He wants to continue our conversation?

"You are beautiful ..."

Crystal clutched the bodice of her tee.

"No. This isn't a pickup line." Kyle reached to his waistband and unlatched his phone from the carrier. "He fussed with the cell's screen and pointed to the people on the screen. "My kids. April, twelve; Max, ten; and my wife, Angie, who is due any day now with our surprise baby." He chuckled as he stared at the phone. "We thought our surprise child was menopause, seeing as we're hitting forty." Kyle placed his phone face down on the table. His tone turned from doting to serious. "No, I'm not out for a booty call. You are beautiful, and society eats up beauty. Looks sell. Your fiddling talent? Insane. Talent's the thing that carries the load, and the song you composed? Exquisite. I sat in the audience on the first night you performed—"

"You were here?"

He nodded. "I watched two other gigs. Your band members took more of their cues from you. Even Danica. If you are the focal point, I'll sign the group. If they don't agree, I'll sign you alone."

"Perhaps you haven't noticed ..." She nodded to the crutches propped against the table. "How can I be the focal point?"

"What do you mean?"

"My disability—"

He held out his hand and frowned. "Don't go there."

"You said beauty sells."

"True. In the music business, no one cares if you can't walk or are disabled in some other way. Think about Stevie Wonder. Andrea Bocelli. Django Reinhardt. Brian Wilson. All brilliant musicians battling physical and mental disabilities."

"Mental?"

"Wilson. Had a schizoaffective disorder. Talking about mental disorders, Mozart was a piece of work."

The waitress returned with their drinks.

"Your disability doesn't diminish who you are. Doesn't destroy your gift. Talent like yours is rare. If your band doesn't recognize your worth, doesn't agree, you need to go solo. The world needs you."

Crystal sipped her soda. *Needs me?* She lifted her head, and the breeze caressed her face. She looked at Davenport. "Me?"

He nodded.

A shiver coursed through her. Somehow, she'd convince the band. "Let's do this."

"You have my number. One way or another, I want to sign you."

Crystal raised her glass to Davenport's. "Deal."

Kyle Davenport clicked his glass against hers. "Here's to a happy, long, and prosperous career." They clinked. Davenport chatted about his family.

Crystal caught bits of his conversation as rocks formed in her stomach. *How am I going to break this news to the girls?*

Sunday morning dawned frosty in the mountains and much colder than the previous day. Roxie lay in the foliage and steadied her camera on the tripod. She adjusted the exposure. Without her thinking about what she was doing, her fingers flew over the camera's controls. Beyond the campground, a mother bear emerged from her den in the hollow of a tree, about six feet up. Roxie's breath hitched as she hit the remote shutter release. The camera clicked like a machine gun—albeit a quiet one. A bear. Out in February? Not usual, although they didn't always snooze away the winter. Was the bear a mama or papa?

A motion from the stump caught Roxie's attention. What? No! She angled her camera and shot. A cub. The sow lifted the cub in her mouth, scooted down the tree and waddled off.

Roxie clicked, adjusted settings. Shot again.

If her exposure worked, she'd own the picture of a lifetime.

Yesterday, they spent a full day waiting for good photographs of some wildlife. True, she had fun canoodling with Jesse, but her reward? Now. Here. This moment. Jesse's gift to her ... She shifted her position. How could she repay him? He promised her another day here. Divine.

A hundred feet behind her, Jesse's tent zipper rippled in the campsite.

She turned. Put a finger over her mouth.

Jesse didn't see. "Want me to start breakfast?" His voice sounded loud in the forest.

"Shhh."

Mama bear perked up. Dropped her baby and faced Roxie who snapped a few more shots. The sow's light muzzle stood out beneath dark eyes. Mama bear held her pose.

Jesse's footsteps through the brush crunched. The noise louder than dawn's bird song.

The sow lifted her cub and scurried deep into the overgrowth of rhododendrons and vanished like a ghost into the mist.

Roxie sat back on her heels. Her head drooped.

"See anything good?" Jesse stood over her oblivious to what he'd done.

"Until you woke up."

"Bear?"

Roxie stood and pointed. "Better. The sow carried her cub—a rare thing."

"Wow. Sorry I missed the show."

"The campgrounds are growing too noisy as spring approaches." Roxie folded her tripod with the camera still attached. "Mama is worried. Maybe there's another cub in the hollow." She stood and took a step into the thicket.

Jesse grabbed her arm. "You are not checking on a bear's cub. Are you crazy?"

"But—"

"She'll kill you."

Roxie's shoulders slumped. He was right.

"I'll cook breakfast. Maybe the smell will bring them back."

She gazed at Jesse. So handsome. Smart. Outdoorsy. Worried about her. She couldn't stay mad the way her heart stuttered whenever he came near. He was so perfect. Most of the time.

He returned to camp quieter now, but too late for her photoshoot.

Ten minutes later, hot coffee warmed Roxie. She cupped her hands around the tin mug and savored the aroma. She sipped, and the bitter tang warmed her mouth and chest. Which pleased more—smell or taste? Did one have to choose?

Jesse stirred water into powdered eggs and poured them into the hot pan.

"Being outdoors in the cold makes those fake eggs almost as good as real ones." Hunger chased the last of her irritation at losing her shots. She did have the rest of the day, and if mama had a second cub, she'd be back once quiet returned. Roxie thumbed through the playback on her camera. "Look, Jesse!" She held up the camera.

Jesse took it from her hands and studied the image. He squinted and grinned. "The baby's so tiny. Still so distinct against the light muzzle of the sow."

"Do you know how unique this shot is? The exposure looks good. *Nat Geo* worthy."

He kissed her head as he returned the camera. "You ought to go into wildlife photography."

"Too competitive. I'd like to make a little money from my career."

"Didn't you final in some contest?"

"Semifinaled." *Why doesn't he remember?* "Wild World."

"When do the results come in?"

"April first."

"What's the prize?" Jesse sat across from her.

"A photo tour in Alaska."

"When you win, you'll find your dream." He scooped food onto her plate. "Seeing as you nabbed your shots, let's pack up and see if we can hit the next trailhead. I think Thatcher's Trail is five miles up."

What? Roxie's heart stopped. "Given the seven miles we hiked yesterday, we'd have to slog twelve miles back to the car today. Too much." She salted her eggs and shoved a forkful into her mouth.

"If we leave within the hour ..."

The food stuck in her throat.

"We can make Thatcher's in two hours. After we summit, our trailhead is downhill, so we can make good time back down the mountain."

She said nothing as her heart sank lower.

"Roxie? Are you listening?"

"You promised a camping photoshoot."

"You said you got great shots. We have one day left."

Roxie sipped coffee to help her swallow. In the back of her mind, she heard Jesse gab about hiking. She only saw new cubs. So young.

"Roxie?"

She threw up her hand to silence him. "What?" Annoyance colored her voice. *Why is he bugging me?*

"I asked a question."

"I didn't hear."

"Do you ever listen to me?"

Roxie shoved bacon into her mouth. The salt dried her mouth more.

"Geoff tells me the trail is easy. We can cover the five miles—"

"But the babies—"

"Knowing a sow is hibernating a hundred or so yards away is dangerous. You took great photos, so we can hike now without worrying about them."

"You didn't want me camping alone to take photographs."

"Dangerous alone."

"You promised me this time to explore the animals of the Smokies. Told me bear and coyotes and wild hogs lived here. Even panthers. If I discovered them, I'd quit obsessing about moose—"

"But I'm bored."

"I want to stay here. You promised."

"I want to hike. Get miles under my belt."

Campers in the next site wiggled out of their tent. They glared in Roxie's direction.

She hissed. "Why is everything about you?"

"Because if I don't fight for me, you won't."

Roxie's heart broke. Valentine's day today. His gift reneged as Jesse now thought about himself. Stay in Knoxville when they married. Give up moose for bear. Hike fast and not savor the journey. She blinked back tears as she shoved the breakfast away. *Do we have anything in common?* She rose and scraped her plate into their garbage bag and packed her camera.

Jesse couldn't hide his smirk. The tilt of his lips and the tightness around his eyes meant one thing. He started to dismantle the tents.

This morning proved one thing. The two of them wanted different things. All they did was fight, more so since they got engaged. He wanted to move. She wanted to study. He wanted the Smokies. She wanted the Adirondacks or the Alaska Range. She wriggled the cubic zirconium off her finger and stepped over to Jesse. She extended her clenched fist.

"What's this?"

"I'll be off trail. Enjoy your hike. You can find me here when you're done."

"Roxie."

She dropped her ring in the dirt in front of him. "We aren't right for each other."

She turned and strode along the animal path she'd found earlier.

Chapter 13

After church, Crystal scurried into the apartment they rented in Hendersonville. The half-hour commute from Nashville was worth the low price—if a two-thousand dollars a month rent was a low price.

Wind blew through the door with her. How could the weather have turned so cold so quickly? Last night she sat on Jack's terrace in a T-shirt. Today, she had to wear her pink hoodie.

She shivered. The wind blowing off Old Hickory Lake rattled the windows. Her sister had to be loving her stay in the mountains—frigid temperatures and hot fiancé.

Crystal threw her purse on the coffee table and knocked on Leanne and Abilene's door. No answer. The door wasn't latched, and it opened a hair. The perfectly made beds proved her friends hadn't come home last night. With Danica back in Knoxville, Crystal had the Sunday alone. She'd hoped to dial Danica in on a group conference call this afternoon. Everyone needed to be together. No way did she want to repeat the news about the Davenport Agency signing them if she took the lead. Once was more than enough.

Tension pounded in her temples. An artery would burst soon. She didn't want to be alone with the news unshared. The unsettled issue rattled her too much. The thought kept her awake half the night as it was. Her heart pounded when she thought of becoming the focal point, especially with her inability to walk unaided. What if Davenport's change ruined the group's dynamic? Worse. Everyone would hate her. They'd claim she stole the position because of her ego.

She slumped onto the couch. Danica had found their apartment two weeks ago. She signed the lease, and the four of them crowded into the four-room apartment made the place affordable. If they broke up and went their separate ways, who'd pay the lease for the next year? How could she go crawling back to Mama and Daddy and tell them they were right, and she shouldn't have dropped out of school?

I'm getting ahead of myself. Maybe everything will work out. I choose to hope.

She tapped her fingers on her legs. The rest of the day—the lonely day—stretched before her. She needed to be with someone. Shivering in the cool apartment, she shoved her hands into the pockets of her sweatshirt and fingered the junk tucked into the front pocket. She pulled out an old tissue and a scrap of paper. After stepping into the kitchen, Crystal tossed the tissue. The other scrap looked like a note. When had she last worn this hoodie? She unfolded the paper to make sure the note contained nothing important. The writing looked unfamiliar.

Lisa Simpson? Vernita Barnes? *I remember.* Her aunt and grandmother. Lisa had scrawled a phone number and address. Crystal had promised to keep in touch.

Why did she forget?

The afternoon hung cold and empty before her. Maybe they'd like a visit today. She wandered back to the living room and slumped on the couch once more. She googled the address written on the note. Lisa and Vernita lived in Fidelio, Kentucky, an hour from here. Six weeks ago, they told her Vernita had little time left to live. What if she had waited too long, and the woman had died?

Crystal rubbed her temples. An Advil wouldn't relieve her ache. Something more than a headache pounded her. She cringed in guilt as she fingered the note. Vernita's plea to see her if she'd found forgiveness in her heart felt as fresh as if she uttered the words today. No way would Crystal want to die forgotten and alone. Or at least, not sure if those you apologized to had accepted your apology.

Should she call? No. What if no one wanted to see her? She'd still be stuck alone here. If she drove to Kentucky, she'd be moving. She'd have a mission. A purpose other than breaking up the band.

No. Think positive. Roxie always believes the worse. I always yell at her. I'll believe the band will accept Davenport's idea.

Fifty minutes later, Crystal pulled into the driveway fronting a brick ranch house. She sat in the car and stared. A small lawn, brown from winter, and a neat garden trimmed the house. A breeze blew daffodils, the one hint of color. Aside from the dancing flowers, all was still—no movement in the living room. No car in the driveway. No sign of life. She was too late. She bit her lip and shifted into reverse. Back on the street, she braked. No. Running away solved nothing. Dead or alive, she needed to know, to let Lisa realize Crystal cared. Maybe Vernita still lived? Her grandmother would welcome her. They wouldn't have given her their address and phone number if they hadn't wanted to see her. She pulled back into the driveway. With hesitant steps, Crystal lumbered to the front door.

On the doorstep, she swiped her sweaty hands on her jeans. How could she sweat when the temperatures hovered at the freezing point? Should she knock? She still had time to run back to Hendersonville.

She glanced at her car and inhaled a deep breath as she made up her mind.

Roxie trudged down the mountain behind Jesse. Back to his car. *Let him run. Move. 'Get miles under his belt.'*

Jesse disappeared over a downed log and around a curve.

She shifted her camera pack on her back. The straps dug into her shoulders and the fast clip down the trail winded her. She plopped down on the log and dropped her pack. She needed to breathe. No way would Jesse leave her stranded. He could wait in the lot until she arrived.

Why is my heart breaking?

She picked a tick off her hiking pants and bent over to grind the bug against a rock. Instead of sitting upright, she buried her head in her lap.

Why do I love him?

He's gorgeous.

Not a good reason. Her last boyfriend, Mark, wasn't handsome, but for a high school kid, he devoted himself to her. Why did she ditch him?

Too doting.

Jesse's smart. So is Mark. Loves the outdoors. *Mark.* With bullheaded Jesse, everything became a battle. Like the ride home from Pearl's wedding or living in Knoxville and not Maine, this hike. Jesse always promised. Little time ever passed before he reneged on his promises. Did she love him because of his unpredictability?

Tears burned her eyes. They wanted opposite things. No. They needed opposites. They'd never have a love like Mama and Daddy. Those two complemented each other—different, but they shared the same goals.

If destiny wanted her and Jesse together, he'd come back once he realized she didn't follow. He'd sit close to her and let her savor the beauty in the world he loved. They'd return to the car at a slower pace—one where breathing was possible. They'd compromise. They wouldn't walk at her turtle waddle. Not at his jackrabbit sprint.

She sat. Waited. Lingered longer.

Jesse didn't return.

Crystal rapped three times on the door with the pretty stained-glass inset. Footsteps pattered inside. Her heart pounded.

The door opened a crack. "Crystal? Is that you, Crystal Snow?" Barely had Crystal nodded when her Aunt Lisa pulled her indoors and into a bear hug, her body warm after the cold February afternoon. "You are an answer to prayer."

Crystal stepped away and blinked several times. *Me? God's answer?* Crystal couldn't focus as Lisa's hands still held Crystal's shoulders as though touching her magnetized Lisa.

"My mother's been praying you'd come see her. You and Roxie." Lisa's hands slipped along Crystal's arms and gripped her hands. She tugged her into the living room. "Let me take your coat."

"I'm not too late? Vernita hasn't ..." *How do I ask if her mother had died?*

"Soon. Hospice says Ma has a week, maybe two, left. Today, she rallied." Lisa frowned. "A rally often signifies the end. Never mind my gloom. Come. She'll love seeing you." Lisa led Crystal across a neat living room with few furnishings. Spare but sophisticated. She pulled Crystal into a darkened room.

"I don't want to wake her."

"She sleeps all the time. Every time she wakes up, she asks about you."

The *tap-tap-exhale* whirr of an oxygen machine mimicked breathing. The air smelled of urine and decay. Under pink sheets and a floral comforter, Vernita's thin body lay on her side.

"Are you sure we should wake her?" Crystal touched Lisa's arm.

"I have no doubt." Lisa leaned over her mother. "Ma, you have a visitor."

The frail body stirred, and eyelids opened as though they pushed up a hundred-pound weight. "Crystal?" Vernita's voice was huskier than six weeks ago. She raised her hand.

Crystal grasped the cold flesh of a hand so thin she could count each bone. Was there any muscle left?

"Sit." Vernita dropped her hand. It flitted like a dying bird against the mattress.

The insistent tap of Vernita Barnes's hand compelled Crystal to sink on the bed's edge. A fecal odor joined the other oppressive smells. Crystal gagged. She choked the feeling back. *Five minutes. Then I'm gone.*

Silence, except for the swish of the oxygen concentrator, settled for several minutes.

Maybe pray with her then leave? Crystal stirred to ask.

"I've been begging the good Lord for one last time to see ya." Vernita coughed. Using a tissue, she wiped bloody spittle from her lips.

Crystal shuddered. The sight of mucus mixed with blood tossed her stomach. *Thank you, Lord, I'm not a nurse.*

"Ain't got much time left. Wanted to make sure you forgived me."

"I have. Though I don't have anything to forgive. Roxie remembers the one time we visited you in jail. I was so young I don't remember the visit."

"Too hard to ... talk. You tell me good ... things 'bout yer life."

Crystal had to carry the conversation but how? She opened her mouth. Her tongue thickened. No words formed.

The click click exhale sounds of the oxygen kept up its inexorable pace.

"Say ... anything." Vernita closed her eyes and her chest rose and fell. "Nothin' fer me to tell. I ain't done nothin' but lie here ..."

"My band's been playing gigs ..." *Would she know the word gig?* "Performing in local clubs in Nashville."

Vernita's head nodded a mite. Her eyes stayed closed.

"We're living outside of Nashville now."

Vernita's eyes fluttered but remained closed. "You and your sister?"

Crystal shook her head. *Wait. Can't see me shake my head.* "No, Roxie's in school in Knoxville. I live with my bandmates."

"Feels good to know you's near."

"We may not be in Nashville for long even though we have a year's lease because ..." The warm room grew oppressive. Crystal unzipped her hoodie and took the fleece off.

Vernita said something.

"What?" Crystal bent close to Vernita's lips.

Vernita mumbled something sounding like why.

"An agent offered our band a contract, but he wants me to be the star, and I can't be because of Danica, she's our lead ... *Slow down, Snow. Calm your nerves.* She inhaled. "Sorry. I didn't mean to dump on you. You have enough to worry—

Vernita's fingers flickered over Crystal's. "Tosh, girl. I'm meetin' Jesus. Ain't got to worry 'bout nothin'." She folded her fingers around Crystal's and lay her hand on the bed.

Crystal smiled, and her heart settled. Vernita's icy hand warmed in Crystal's and comforted her. Guilt about not coming sooner fled as God's grace melted her spirit. She arrived in time. She studied Vernita whose breath became more regular. *Is she asleep?*

"Listen to me, girl." Vernita's eyes popped open—so not asleep.

Crystal nodded.

"If them girls knows what's right, they'll sign that there contract. That there agent's the expert. He knows talent. I'd say the same thing if this din't concern you. I'd say the same if he wanted one of them others to be the lead. Mark my words. Might be ..."

Crystal lifted her head and waited for the rest of Vernita's sentence. After a few minutes, she figured the woman had finished. She shifted to stand. "I should—"

"Might be God's blessing for *you*. If'n that agent wanted one of them ladies to lead, they'd throw the rest of the band under the old donkey cart. My advice—" coughing cut off Vernita's words.

Crystal grabbed a tissue from the bedside stand and wiped Vernita's lips. The tissue came away with threads of blood. Crystal's heart sank, but the retching feeling didn't attack her this time.

"My advice. Pray. Listen to the man upstairs. Do what he wants. If I had ..." Again coughing cut off her words.

"Shh. No more talking." Crystal caressed Vernita's head. She stood to leave.

Vernita grasped her hand with more strength than her

fragile form implied. "Stay till I sleep?" Her eyes begged.

Crystal sat. She watched as Vernita's eyes closed. Watched the irregular rise and fall of her chest. Crystal ached to leave. Everything felt awkward. What right did she have to sit here? She didn't know her purported grandmother.

As you do to the least of these—

"Show me your talent. Sing."

Crystal jumped at Vernita's voice. "Sing what?"

"Somethin' purty." Vernita's eyes shut once more.

For the next hour, Crystal sang every hymn she loved.

Once she saw that Vernita slept, Crystal stepped into the living room. "Thank you for letting me visit, Lisa."

Lisa stood from the easy chair where she knitted. "I'm the one to thank you."

Crystal stepped toward the door.

"Wait." Lisa leaned forward like she wanted to dash after Crystal. "Can you sit a minute? I've got tea or soda or coffee."

Crystal looked toward the dark sky. "I don't want to interfere. Your family will want dinner."

"No one's home but me."

Alone with a dying mother? Crystal took a place on the sofa across from the easy chair. Topics of possible conversation fought in Crystal's mind. *What to talk about?* She smiled at Lisa.

"Todd, my husband, is helping my oldest boy fix the roof on his garage. The other boy's in college." She fiddled with her knitting for a few seconds. After a moment, Lisa tossed the yarn aside. "I need to apologize."

Crystal squinted. "How so?"

Lisa licked her lips. She let out a long sigh. "When I tried to adopt Roxie, I should've taken you."

"I'm happy with Mama and Daddy. They—"

"Wait." Lisa inhaled and studied her lap. At last, she looked up. "I'm not going to be poetic with my words. Please don't interrupt. I'm not insulting you or anyone even though I sound like I am. This is an admission of my own selfishness. Your disability was problematic for us. I judged wrong, and I didn't look beneath the surface. When I had the chance to adopt you both, I took Roxie because she wasn't crippled." She held up her hand as though she understood Crystal was going to argue. "I know crippled is the wrong word to use today. Back then, we used words like gimp or lame or crippled. Whatever. As years passed, I realized, had you come with us in the adoption, Roxie would've been comfortable and happy. She would've taught me how to care for you. Because of my decision, I lost both of my brother's girls. Worse than my pain, I caused Roxie big issues of abandonment. I'm sorry." She leaned against the easy chair as though her confession or apology or guilt emptied her of all strength.

What to say? Crystal caught Lisa's gaze and locked hers on Lisa's. "You didn't cause Roxie's issues. Our biological parents, their death ..."

"I didn't help her any. I should've."

"I love my mama and daddy. Roxie does too. All things work together for good, and things worked out well."

"Your sister hates us."

Crystal scoffed. "My sister is intense, but kind and compassionate and talented and beautiful. My best friend. She had night terrors when she was young. Over the last few months, they resurrected. I think she has to find forgiveness for events out of her control, and the things done to her that people meant for good."

"You'll tell her how sorry I am?"

"Of course." Crystal rose. "I do need to go. I'm glad I

got to see Ver ... my grandmother before she passed."

Lisa walked her to the door. She blinked several times, but a tear slipped down her cheek.

"What's wrong?"

"Why do we repent only when we're going to lose everything? I hated my mother until I took her in. I coveted my pretty little niece and ignored the other sweet child. Sometimes, I wonder ..."

Crystal stood on the stoop and waited for Lisa to finish. When she said nothing more, Crystal laid her hand on her aunt's forearm. "God's never late. He restores the years the locust devoured. He gave you time."

Lisa's tears turned to sobs. "Don't forget us."

"Never." After releasing Lisa, Crystal returned to her car. She looked at her aunt illuminated in her car lights. So sad her grandmother reconciled with everyone so late in life. Fortunately, she made amends before she died. Crystal shivered in the cool night. How could she love this woman after two brief visits? Her visit was supposed to ease her own loneliness. Make her decision easier.

Would her band mates throw her under the donkey cart?

She'd experienced their artistic anger and pride. Subjected the girls to her own. What did she want—peace or a career?

Or friends?

She couldn't lose her friends.

Chapter 14

Neon lights flashed in the darkened windows as Jesse pulled into Nicky's Tavern. He pulled next to a white pickup and turned off the ignition. Darkness, cold, and a half-empty parking lot promised a desolate evening. Country music drifted out of the bar. Seems even the crooners were losers tonight. They had cheating wives, dead dogs, and beer.

His one hope? On Sunday nights, Nicky's hosted dart tournaments, so Geoff would be here. He needed Geoff tonight.

As Jesse stepped to the bar, the malty smell of beer permeated the place. Tonight, regardless of his father's alcoholism, beer begged him to drink and forget. He flagged the bartender. "A Hops-cut." He swiveled in his bar stool to scan the room.

Geoff stood with a group of guys in an alcove to the left of the door. He lifted his fist clutching several darts and nodded toward Jesse. He turned and threw an outer bull. The soft thunk of the remaining darts drifted across the room half-full of patrons. Fifteen minutes later, Geoff strode up to Jesse and called to the bartender. "Give me a Smoky Amber. Put my brew on Chad's tab." He turned to Jesse. "Hey, man. Thought you and Roxie were hanging today. Ain't it lover's day?"

"Ended early." Jesse glanced toward the dart board where another group started a new game. "You did well."

"Second place. At least I don't have to buy the round." He sipped his beer. "Want to join us?"

Jesse looked at the guys crowding a table by the door. To play a few games with the guys, to laugh, lost in laughter and friendship, he'd forget.

Geoff pulled up a stool next to him. They sat and drank for a few minutes in silence. "You never hit Nicky's any more. Roxie acting up again?"

Jesse hiked a shoulder and slugged back a gulp of beer. *Slow down, Maxwell. Don't want to get drunk.*

"What happened?"

No hiding anything from Geoff. "We split up."

Geoff shifted toward the bar and stared at his glass.

"Doesn't surprise you?"

Geoff shook his head. "What're you going to do?"

Jesse drummed his fingers on the smooth finish of the bar. They left little patterns on the damp wood. "Time to move on."

"Time to find someone who'll ..."

Jesse scoffed and punched his buddy's arm.

"I don't know how you stay celibate. You're weird. Or do you like ..."

Jesse laughed outright. "No. I'm into chicks, and I'm cool. God's in control."

"You know Roxie's sister has the hots for you."

"What are you talking about?"

"She's a looker." Geoff raised his eyebrows.

"If me and Rox can't work things out, how will Crystal and me? She's loyal to her older sis." He gave a sardonic grin. "And a slower hiker."

"Love changes loyalty. So, what caused the breakup this time?"

"All Roxie wants to do is lie in the brush—"

"Sounds good." Geoff winked.

"Do you only think about sex?"

"Don't tell me you don't."

"Roxie lies around and watches chipmunks or snails or the blossoming of a lady's slipper. She does make Crystal look like a sprinter."

Geoff scanned the room. "Look." He nodded toward a couple of girls a few seats down. "They're on the prowl. See the black-haired chick? She should be a swimsuit model. Chat her up and see what happens."

Jesse took another slug of beer.

"They're not Christian, I know. Why not make Roxie jealous? Teach her a lesson, and go after another chick. Works for me all the time. If these babes don't interest you, make a move on Crystal. You like her better anyway."

"No, I don't."

"You grin every time you mention her. I can recognize lust. I'm an expert." Geoff laughed.

Jesse sipped his beer to hide his chuckle. *Shouldn't find him funny.*

"Find another girl. Roxie'll see what she lost. Besides, sometimes, the new woman beats the one who ditched you."

Jesse fingered his beer. *Make her jealous? With Crystal?* His lips twitched. *Never.* "Let's join your friends."

Geoff raised a hand to the bartender. "Another round."

Jesse shook his head. "I'm good."

"Come on, dude. We need to party."

Jesse chewed his lip. To get a buzz on would ease the pain of losing Roxie for good. Had to be for good. If they stayed together, he'd go crazy."

"Give him a Smoky Amber, will you?" Geoff called to the bartender.

Maybe one more. One can't hurt. Jesse picked up the glass the barkeep slid over to him.

With beers in hand, they joined Geoff's friends. As they bantered, Geoff's advice ricocheted around Jesse's mind. *Crystal?* Warmth flowed through him. *I like his plan* ... He scrunched his eyes closed. *No. Never. I can't.*

A little after ten, Crystal let herself into her apartment. Dishes littered the sink, so Abilene or Leanne or both were home, though the door to their shared bedroom was closed and the lights off. A soft glow drifted from under the door to the bedroom she and Danica shared. She hadn't come back from Knoxville, had she? Not with all the wedding planning for June's shindig. She eased into her room. "Roxie! What are you doing here?"

Crystal's sister turned reddened eyes toward her.

As fast as she could work her reluctant legs, Crystal hurried toward Roxie and flung herself on the bed. She grabbed her sister. Roxie's tears on this weekend meant one thing. "What's wrong?"

"Jesse and I are through."

Crystal pulled Roxie to her and ran her hand over her hair.

Roxie's shoulders heaved, and tears dampened Crystal's shoulder. Her poor sister—and not just about Jesse. Whenever someone loved her, Roxie found a fatal flaw because he liked *her.*

Crystal pulled away and gazed at her pale sister. How many times had Crystal held her beautiful wreck of a sister. "Do you want to talk?"

Roxie nodded but said nothing.

Crystal sat up and edged against the headboard while Roxie turned on her back. With an arm curled behind her head, Roxie stared at the ceiling. "We ..."

tangled lives

Crystal waited. *Lord, help—*

"He wouldn't let me photograph the bear."

A smile worked its way to Crystal's lips. She bit back the grin. "Photograph a bear?"

"Umm-hmm." Roxie appeared unaware of how out of the blue her statement sounded. "Last week, he promised me a Valentine's photoshoot, all weekend, however long I wanted."

Crystal remembered. In the days leading up to the shoot, Roxie talked nonstop about Jesse's gift. She wanted him to see what she loved as much as to learn why he relished the Smokies. If they understood each other's desires, they'd compromise somehow.

"You hiked up to Morgan's Bald, right?"

"Friday, we cut classes and hiked to the bald. We set up camp and explored the area. No good shots." Roxie wriggled upright and held up her hand. "Don't start a lecture."

"I'm not saying anything."

"We had separate tents."

Crystal winked.

Roxie's smile said the worst of her emotional rockslide had passed. "The animals hid all day Saturday. Nothing interesting lives in the Smokies."

"The bears and hogs and panthers would dispute your statement."

Roxie swatted her sister. "Brat. Anyway, Sunday dawned crystalline ... a bear climbed out of her den." Roxie smiled.

"*Her* den?"

"The critter was a sow, so I have to use the pronoun *her*. The word *it* sounds inanimate. *He* is the wrong gender for a sow. The light matched a photographer's dream. The sun glowed soft, but bright enough to expose the subject ..."

Crystal's mind drifted as Roxie talked about the technicalities of exposure or depth of field.

"Jesse made so much noise getting up." In no chronological order and with few breaths taken, the story spilled out. "Seeing as I had beautiful photographs of mama carrying her tiny cub, Jesse demanded we hike five more miles to the Thatcher trailhead. His change of plans forced me to understand. We'd never be right for each other. He wanted to move. I wanted stillness. He needed the Smokies. They bore me." Pain showed in Roxie's eyes. They shimmered with unshed tears. "I love him, Crystal."

"I know you do."

"Almost everything within me wants to marry him."

"Almost everything?"

"We fight at cross purposes. Always. I can't love East Tennessee like he does. He deserves more love than I can give."

"He doesn't love you the way you deserve."

"But I ..." Roxie hung her head and blinked several times.

Crystal understood the searing gouge in Roxie's heart. Her own crush on Jesse often sent her to her room crying, and now, Crystal prayed she was over her infatuation. In high school, she'd spent many nights awake while jealousy burned inside her heart because some boy that she liked preferred her friends. Boys wanted to be her best friend, never her lover. They didn't see her. They noticed her braces and awkward gait.

The sisters sat against the headboard in silence. Crystal looked away, her heart heavy. Her sister loved Jesse. Crystal didn't understand why. Both adored the outdoors. Jesse's looks would melt Medusa, and her pretty sister made them a photogenic match. Their similarities ended there. If opposites attracted, their relationship magnetized them. Their bond would destroy them in the end.

"Tell me about your day. Why were you so late coming home? I must've waited close to ..." Roxie turned toward the bedside clock. "After eleven?" She grinned and wagged a finger at Crystal. "I waited two hours for this party girl to come home."

Crystal stuck out her tongue.

"How'd last night's gig go?"

"After our show at Jack's, the band went wherever they go. I sat on the back deck. Wasn't there fifteen minutes when Kyle Davenport joined me."

"A guy? Romance?" Roxie perked up as though only love mattered.

"No. A recording agent."

The last signs of sorrow evaporated from Roxie's face. She threw her arms around Crystal then shifted to a cross-legged position. Roxie leaned in toward her sister. And her smile? Pure Roxie. "Tell me."

"We can sign with the Davenport Agency—"

Roxie clapped. "Fantastic—"

"There's more."

"Why aren't you dancing with joy?"

Crystal chuckled and tapped her braces.

"Your hardware never stopped you from dancing before. What's wrong about the offer? Why so glum?"

"Kyle Davenport wants me to be the lead. He claims I'm the focal point."

Roxie leaned back, her face solemn. "Danica will dispute with him. The other two won't care as long as they can perform and party. Danica though?"

Crystal stared. Light and dark twined in the patterns the light made on the ceiling. She moved her head, and the patterns shifted with the change of perspective.

Roxie tapped Crystal's head. "Composing again?"

She swatted Roxie's hand away. "Studying the shadows on the ceiling."

"Those silhouettes will become a composition," Roxie said. "Now answer my questions."

"They don't know yet."

Roxie shifted back against the headboard once more and nudged against Crystal.

Roxie's warmth flooded into Crystal's arm and flowed through her veins. Like chamomile tea, her touch soothed.

Roxie stared at her. "Do *not* let your sweet 'everyone comes before me' personality make you lose your chance. *You* worked hard and sacrificed more than anyone—"

"No, I haven't."

"Where's Danica today?"

"Planning a wedding."

"Did she quit school to pursue her recording career?"

Crystal ducked her head and found her hands interesting.

"Change her wedding plans?"

Crystal's head jerked up. She gave Roxie *the* stare.

"Abi and Leanne both were drunk when I got here at nine. Two party girls. But you," Roxie leaned forward, "you have done everything. Gave up school. Pounded the doors of every agency. Encouraged the practices. Have the most talent—"

"The other—"

"I'm not saying the other three don't have amazing gifts. They do. Abi's bass playing rivals McCartney's or Mingus's. Leanne's drumming is better than yours was when you were little."

Crystal rolled her eyes.

"Your gift, though, shines like ... like I imagine the aurora borealis does. If I ever see the northern lights in real life."

"You'll see them when you head to Alaska."

"Yep. When I win the *Wild World* contest, I'll get a free trip. But I don't think the northern lights shine in May."

"Not with twenty-four hours of daylight."

Glee or anticipation twitched in Roxie's lips — something other than despair.

"Doesn't the trip head out in May?"

Roxie nodded.

"Graduation's on the eighteenth. Finals happen in the first two weeks."

"I'd have to win to go for free. Free's all I can afford with grad school on the horizon." Roxie melted where she sat. "However, *if* my baby sister signs a contract and earns a billion bucks ..."

They laughed.

"I'm taking a shower. Using your toiletries." Roxie left the room.

"What's mine is yours."

"Your roommates believe that too."

"We share. We're in the Girls from the Hollow Commune."

"The platinum record commune."

Crystal bit her pinky nail and looked away. *Right. If I ever get a backbone.*

Jesse opened his eyes and rolled over. The room lit from a streetlight was unfamiliar. He moved and bumped into something. Not something. Someone. Floors creaked in the nighttime chill, yet sweat coated him. His heart raced and not from his hormones as they had in the last hour. *What have I done?* He stared at the woman beside him. Dark hair splayed over the white pillow. What was her name? Addison? He grimaced. No. He squeezed his eyes shut. Madison. Her name is Madison. He sat up and slipped on his boxers. Jesse inhaled a deep breath to steel his nerves. The room smelled of what? Sex and beer and all things he should've avoided.

"Hey." Madison opened sleepy eyes. Her tousled hair looked sexier than when it had been combed and tamed. "Loving and leaving me?"

Dear Lord. Forgive me. What did I do? The room spun. Four beers—three too many. No. Four too many in a bar he should've avoided. Now?

Madison grabbed his arm. "Stay a while."

If he were a cad, he'd crawl back into bed, but he had to get out of here. What if Roxie found out? Crystal?

Memories of long hair covering his face, warm skin and natural curves smelling of sweat and flowers, a body he hungered for last night. Right now? He fought the urge to vomit.

Madison glared. Her eyes, dark in the night, stabbed him. Such a pretty woman. Not as beautiful as Crystal or Roxie. Their opposite—dark and sexy and free-spirited. Long black hair, high cheekbones now dabbed with mascara.

"Come cuddle." She looped long arms around his neck and pulled him to her.

Her warm body called him. He swallowed down his desire.

He had to be a cad. "No." His heart reeled as though it lost its rhythm, and he stumbled to his feet. "I made a mistake. I'm sorry. This was wrong."

Madison lurched upright. The sheet clutched to her naked chest trembled with her breathing. Her eyes narrowed and her jaw worked. "You ..."

A staccato sound like curses followed him as he clutched his clothes to his chest and strode toward the bedroom door. He couldn't hear because his ears rang, his face first cold, then hot.

A book crashed into the back of one knee and buckled his leg. Jesse grabbed the doorframe as he nearly crumpled from the reflex. Beyond the bedroom, he staggered into his jeans. At first, he tried to put both feet in the same leg. He stumbled. Got the jeans on. As he strode from the apartment, he pulled on his tee. The night would be long and painful. Crystal claimed no sin was too big for God to forgive. Somehow, he had to believe this.

Roxie returned from the bathroom and found Crystal sitting in bed reading her Bible. "No Lovecraft or Koontz?"

"Jehovah just burned up Nadab and Abihu because they offered a sacrifice, and they shouldn't have. Scarier than anything those authors write. Can you imagine being engulfed in flames coming out of nowhere? Can you feel the pain and fear? How about their father? Aaron had to be wracked by horror and grief." Crystal stared off. Her fingers tapped against her legs.

"Are you composing a tune about Aaron's sacrilegious sons?"

She nodded. "I'd imagine their agony causing them to repent. Aaron, though—how he must've grieved. I can hear the fiddle starting in the lower register, rising in frenzy, have the joy of redemption and end with an adagio—both sad and at peace because of the justice of God."

"Good grief. I take a shower, and you compose an opera."

"Hand me my music paper." Crystal pointed to her desk. "I need to write the melody down while the idea is fresh."

"Have you checked the clock? Midnight has passed." Roxie handed her the well-used pad and settled next to Crystal as she scribbled.

"Gotta write when inspiration hits." Fifteen minutes later, Crystal dropped the notepad and slipped under the covers. "You better go to sleep. What time's your class?"

"I'm not going to school tomorrow."

"You? Cutting class?"

"Stearns's class starts at eight. He's more boring the second time around. Jesse's in my section of campus in the morning. Maybe I'll hit my afternoon session. Or hang with you."

"I have a suggestion."

Roxie curled her arm under her head and closed her eyes. "Go on."

"I saw Vernita and Lisa today."

"What?" Roxie's eyes popped open. "Why on—"

"Found their address in a sweatshirt. They gave the info to us back in January. Vernita will die any day."

"That's too bad. But why did you visit?"

"They wanted me to."

Roxie closed her eyes.

"They want to see you."

"Why on earth?"

"They need you to know they're sorry for the pain they caused. They want you to know they care about you."

"You told me. I know." Roxie turned over. "Goodnight."

Roxie lay still, tried to even out her breathing, to make Crystal think she slept. Why did those two women terrorize her?

Chapter 15

Jesse peered through the window of the door into Stearns's classroom. No Roxie. She must be out of his line of sight next to the wall. The students he saw tapped away on their laptops. Their focus seemed to be on the prof, their expressions serious, as though every word Stearns spoke deserved to be preserved. That, or they were emailing friends. He checked the time. Five minutes until class ended. He leaned against the wall across the hall and fiddled with his phone. The screen couldn't hold his attention. After his night with ... *whatever her name was* ... he felt dirty, vile, unworthy of Roxie—all the while desiring her more.

Noise jarred him back to attention. Streams of students fled the classroom. Given Roxie's take on Stearns's reputation, fleeing best described the undergrads' escape. Jesse watched. Waited. Stearns stepped out and turned off the light. No Roxie.

Jesse's shoulders slumped. Not like Roxie to cut sessions. Even Stearns's. He lifted his phone and texted her.

JESSE: You cut class. I need to talk. Call me.

His thumb hovered over the send icon. *Last night. How can I ...?* He backspaced and erased the text. Didn't want Roxie to think he was desperate, even though every nerve in his body craved her. Time to move on. Maybe Madison? He squinted. *Addison? What the heck did she call herself? What kind of Christian am I? Christian? No, what kind of human being?* The hall grew quiet. Students hurried outdoors or settled into nearby classrooms. *What is wrong with me?* Five minutes later, he strode down the hall. *Hadn't Crystal's mantra been 'No sin is so great God's love can't erase'?*

If only.

Last night's sin, Geoff's nagging, Crystal's warning at the wedding. They were right. He needed to move on. Forget Roxie. Her mercurial personality sometimes eclipsed her compassion and loving nature. He halted. Drugs had killed Roxie's parents. Pearl, eight years old when they died, was left to take care of her sisters. Then Roxie's biological aunt attempted to adopt her. She brought Roxie home accompanied by night terrors. He curled his hands into fists. He had to help his girl heal. How? Everyone had scars. He wished he were enough to erase hers.

Seated in her sister's car, Roxie crossed her arms and stared at the countryside flying by her window. "I don't know why you talked me into this."

"I didn't. God wants you to bless Vernita." Crystal gazed in Roxie's direction. "Besides, you cut school. Let Jesse suffer when he doesn't find you."

"What makes you think he's looking for me?"

"He's Jesse. This is what Jesse does."

Roxie bit back a grin.

"Quit smirking."

"Shouldn't you keep your eyes on the road?"

Crystal glanced at Roxie. "I am."

tangled lives

The car drifted onto a rumble strip.

"Yikes. If you're watching the road, why are we crashing?"

Crystal righted the vehicle and grinned.

They drove in near silence the rest of the way. Within the hour, they pulled up in front of a modest brick house. Roxie climbed out of the car in front of the trim yard. The lawn showed hints of green as spring began its slow advance. Daffodils dressed in yellow sunshine proclaimed their reason for being here. The flowers looked so happy and flourishing in their new life. Joyful flowers, here for a moment. In a month, the inexorable heat would begin its assault, and these flowers would give way to ticks and mosquitoes.

The door of the neat ranch flew open before anyone knocked. Lisa Simpson, dressed in jeans and peach sweater with her light brown hair pulled back into a tight ponytail, looked as prim as Roxie remembered from six weeks ago. Lisa threw her arms around Crystal. "I'm so glad you came back. Mom took a turn. She ..." Lisa looked away, then stepped back from the door. "Come in. Please."

Roxie followed as Crystal stepped into the home, as immaculate and spare as the outside. Nothing out of place. Roxie's heart pounded. The orderly home resurrected memories from the few months she'd stayed with her aunt. Systematic. Regimented. Controlled. She wished she could control her life right now. Aside from the clean, spare living area, nothing was familiar.

"This is my son Spencer." Lisa pointed to a man about Crystal's age. "My husband, Todd, is at the grocery store. You missed Theo. He left an hour ago because his wife has to work, and he needs to take care of his kids." Lisa rubbed her forehead and offered an apologetic smile. "I'm babbling." She focused on Roxie. "Mom wants to see you

167

with all her heart. Guilt from your five-minute contact in jail a billion years ago won't let her rest. She wants forgiveness. Come." She held out her hand.

Roxie stared at the offered hand, not wanting to touch the woman who stole her from her parents all those years ago. She grimaced. Not stole. Wanted to adopt her.

Lisa dropped her arm. "This way." Lisa and Crystal disappeared into a darkened room off the hallway.

Roxie's stomach twisted. Like winding the chain while sitting on a swing when she was little, once her tension let go, her world would careen. She stood in the living room. *Mama would cringe seeing how rude I am.* Guilt gnawed her, little rats eating her from the inside. Lisa and Vernita needed kindness, not rejection. *I of all people should understand her need.* She glanced around. Spencer had disappeared.

Resolve straightened her back. Roxie forced one foot in front of the other. Her steps felt as though Velcro lined the soles of her shoes. In the bedroom, curtains had shut off the outside light. The small space, as neat as the living room, smelled of stale air and human decay. The rhythmic thumping of an oxygen machine, along with the stench, crowded the space.

Crystal had lowered the bars of the hospital bed and sat on the edge of the mattress. Her fingers trailed the contours of Vernita's cheek as she lay inert.

Were they too late?

Crystal bent over and kissed her cheek.

Roxie's stomach clenched, and she stepped back. Why couldn't she be like Crystal? Why did this lady—smelly, on death's door, but human and in need of love—repulse her? She had to be more like her sister, so at peace with the sick woman. Roxie glanced around, but Lisa had stepped away. By the bed in the overheated room stood a rollator and a commode. On a water-stained pine table, all sorts of cleaning supplies stood in formation like little soldiers—wipes, sanitizer, water, pill bottles, skin barrier cream. Roxie took a step toward Vernita. Hesitated before she sat on the seat of the rolling walker near the bed.

Vernita opened her eyes. Her head strained upward, and heavy breathing filled the room.

"Move down a little, Rox." Crystal shoved the commode away from the bed. "I don't think she can see you."

Roxie shifted the rollator, swallowed the lump in her throat, and smiled. "Hey, Vernita."

"Good to see ya." Vernita closed her eyes as though uttering the four words exhausted her.

Roxie half rose to flee, but as if the heat of the room, or guilt, or God, weighted her until she settled more heavily and stared at the floor. "I'm sorry ..." She wanted to say she was sorry Vernita was dying, but words sounded ... wrong. "I'm sorry I was rude to you when we talked last month." Her forehead crinkled with her unexpected words. "I was wrong. Forgive me." Her voice cracked on the last words. Without a doubt, she was sorry. Her hands shook. She clamped her fingers tight to keep them still.

Vernita lay unmoving.

Just her luck. She repents, and Vernita sleeps through her apology. Wait, had Vernita's breathing stopped? Panic set Roxie's heart pounding. *Please, God, let her be sleeping. Not dead.* Roxie leaned forward and listened for an intake of air.

Vernita's chest rose and fell. Her eyes fluttered.

Tension fled Roxie's shoulders. When Vernita awoke, Roxie would repeat her apology.

"'Sss-kay." Vernita wasn't asleep. "You was little. I skeered ya. Do you forgive me?"

"Of course." Without any conscious decision, Roxie slipped off the walker and knelt by Vernita's side. Several tears slipped down Roxie's cheek. She couldn't dash them away as her hands gripped Vernita's chilled fingers. "You're more than forgiven. If God's forgiven me all I've done, who am I, or what kind of woman would I be, if I held a grudge for more than fifteen years?"

A small smile lifted the corner of Vernita's lips. "Tell me purty tales 'bout that beau of yers."

"We broke up."

"Why?"

"We want different things." Roxie's voice cracked. "Still breaking up is hard." Her shoulders lifted, and she ducked her head as though to hide. Mama said Roxie did this all the time as a child. Said the posture made her look like a turtle. How she wished she could be a turtle and duck into a shell and never face the world again. Roxie gripped Vernita's cold hand tighter. She wanted to will warmth into the dying flesh.

"Don't you be sad about your feller." Vernita took several large breaths. "All my life, I hankered fer a man. Any man. Thought I needed one. Never trusted my own worth. The result ..." Vernita closed her eyes again, and once more the click and swoosh like an exhale of the oxygenator fill the room.

Roxie glanced at her sister.

"The result ..." Vernita once again proved she hadn't fallen asleep. "Was two children by two men I didn't know. My son ruined his life. Three babies never got to see the world 'cause of abortions. I was a fool. No man's worth the price of your soul." She gasped for air but wiggled a finger as though to wait for more wisdom. "If'n you can't be happy alone, ain't no man gonna make you whole."

Roxie's eyes widened. *Poor woman. No wonder she was such a mess. Abortions? Different fathers? Drugs?* She blinked as the words of her judgment registered. When you fisted your hand to point a finger at someone, three other fingers point back to you. *Forgive me.* "You did nothing wrong to me. Why do you need my forgiveness?"

"'Cause I damaged you. Words cut deeper than knives. Words are almost as damaging as the abortionist's knife." She took in huge gulps of air but still clung to Roxie's hands with surprising strength. The oxygen machine continued its pace as though timing the pause as Vernita struggled to speak. "One piece of advice."

Roxie leaned close to better hear. Vernita's shampoo, lavender, the scent of the Snow girls' youth, wafted up. Roxie's heart constricted until a warmth of love forced her heart to fill and to quiet.

"My advice is yer worth more than a feller who ain't got sense to cherish you. Believe me." Vernita fell asleep for real.

They sat for minutes. Raspy breathing and a clunking oxygenator filled the space.

Crystal gathered her crutches. "Ready to go?"

Roxie continued to kneel by the bed. She hadn't been ready to come here. Now she didn't want to leave. She whispered. "Everything you thought you did to me, to us, is forgiven."

Vernita didn't move.

"I hope you heard me." Roxie bent and kissed Vernita's temple, the skin almost as chilled as the woman's hand. This woman, her grandmother, didn't have much time left on earth. Roxie lingered and caressed Vernita's hair, thin and fine, but like silk. At last, she stood and joined Lisa and Crystal in the kitchen where a man she assumed to be Todd unpacked groceries.

"Thank you," Lisa said.

"Let us know when ..." Roxie couldn't finish the words.

Lisa nodded. Tears clouded her eyes.

Crystal's sister sat beside her in the car without speaking or moving. Talking seemed sacrilegious somehow. She peeked at Roxie who stared straight ahead. The car whizzed down roads now looking familiar.

Men. Vernita's words haunted her. How jealous she'd been of Roxie. Over the years, her infatuation over Jesse elevated him to idol status. She lusted over him. She coveted Jesse. Lust and covetousness, big sins in the big ten. Men dominated her friends' lives. Leanne and Abilene slept at the fellows' apartments regularly. Mike governed Danica's life. She talked about him more than their music. Her need for a man's love overshadowed Crystal's world, but why would she need one so bad she'd forsake the things important in life?

Roxie loved Jesse. With all her heart and soul, she loved him. Still, their relationship tore her sister apart.

Pearl had waited a long time for Malachi to come along. Her best friend Violet had helped Pearl raise her son, Journey, for six years. She had turned down all sorts of men who wanted more than friendship. Her sister waited for Malachi even when she didn't realize she waited for him specifically.

What do I want?

Like turning on the proverbial light bulb, her desires crystalized.

Later, back at the apartment, she waved Roxie off. Now the moment of truth. Crystal flexed her fingers to relieve the tingling. She stepped into her home.

Abilene and Leanne lounged on the couch watching *Brother Where Art Thou?*, a bowl of popcorn between them.

"Welcome home." Leanne wiggled closer to Abilene and patted the cushion next to her. "Join us. We started the movie five minutes ago. We'll restart it. No one ever complains about watching George Clooney over and over."

"Can we talk?"

Leanne straightened and shoved the bowl of popcorn onto the coffee table. "You sound serious. What's wrong?"

Even though Crystal tried to squelch her smile, her lips lifted and her spirit grinned. "Nothing." She took a deep breath. "At least, I hope nothing."

Abilene clicked off the TV and leaned forward.

Crystal sank onto the chair across from them. As she laid her crutches down, she worked on composing herself, but thoughts tumbled, and her grin demanded its place on her face. She looked up. "We have a chance for an agent."

Both girls whooped.

"This is good news, so why so anxious?" Leanne asked.

"There's a catch."

"An agent with a catch? No snafu will ruin getting an agent, so spill the beans, girl." Abilene rested her elbows on her knees. Her eyes pierced Crystal's.

Crystal licked her lips. She needed to rip the bandage off, so to speak, and tell them. "The Davenport Agency will sign us if ..." She stuttered to a stop and stared at the two pairs of eyes gazing her way. *So much for ripping off the band aid and getting this over with.*

"If?" Abilene's stare still held Crystal's eyes.

"If the band ..."

Leanne squared her shoulders. "For heaven's sake, Crys, you don't have stage fright, so why are we scaring you? If the band what? If you ditch us?"

Crystal held her breath. Leanne's words were too close to the truth. She exhaled. "No. If the focal point of the band ... if I'm the lead."

"No problem." Abilene clapped. "When do we sign?"

"Wait a minute." Leanne scowled. "How'd you double deal Danica? She created our band."

Abilene scowled at Leanne. "No. *We* are the band. We do not belong to Ms. Danica Vaughn."

"Who found our apartment? Arranged the gig at Jack's that gets Crystal the record deal?" Leanne turned back to Crystal. "So, how'd you worm your way into the lead?"

"I didn't. After Saturday's concert, Kyle—"

"Oh, first name basis?" Leanne's voice sneered.

Abilene reached over to Leanne. Her soft voice told Crystal she saw through Leanne's pique. Abi would talk sense into Leanne. "Let her finish. You know Crystal better."

Crystal mouthed a thank you to Abilene. "Kyle Davenport approached me. He said ..." She swallowed hard. "This is hard for me to say, even though it flatters me."

"Danica would have no problem bragging." Abilene laughed.

Leanne scowled at her.

"He said I was the natural leader and should be the focal point. He'd want to change our name to something like Snow in the Hollow. The agency would sign us if we accepted this slight modification. In reality, not much would change. I'd sit center, do more vocals, although he wants the fiddle as the highlight, and I can't sing and play at the same time. Little would differ."

"I have no problem," Abilene said.

"I don't like the idea. What will Danica say?"

"Maybe she'll agree," Abilene said.

"Right." Leanne still scowled.

"If not, majority rules." Abilene faced Crystal once more. "When does the agency need to know?"

"We have time. First, I'd like to see what Danica says."

"If she says no," Leanne said, "we'll have a tie."

Crystal shrugged. "Let's see."

Abilene hurried to her bedroom and returned with her laptop. Crystal joined the others on the couch where they FaceTimed their friend. The computer rang and rang.

An instant before the program would've disconnected, Danica came into view. "You caught me in time. Mike and I were leaving for our last caterer's food test. What's up? We have to be fast ... we're late already."

"Good news-bad news," Abilene said.

"Good news first." Danica's phone bounced as the scenery changed behind her. "I'll talk while Mike drives."

Abilene and Leanne looked at Crystal. "An agent offered us a contract." She spit out the words.

Danica whooped. The phone jiggled then stopped. She approached Mike's car. "With this news, how can bad news follow? When do we sign?"

Crystal's throat dried more.

Abilene and Leanne stared at her.

After a deep swallow, Crystal related the conditions.

All movement of Danica's phone stopped. The face transmitted back to them scowled. "You." Her mouth tightened. "You little traitor. After all I've done for you."

"We all—"

"Shut up, you Judas. Your idea is the lamest one you've ever had. You and your ego. A lame lead? How can you move around, give us signals, lead us? You can't even walk." The connection ended.

Crystal froze, her eyes fixed on the image of the three of them staring at the disconnected screen.

"I guess we have our answer." Leanne lifted her chin, took a breath, then exhaled. "We carry on as the Girls from the Hollow." She strode into her bedroom. The door clicked shut.

Abilene sat without moving for a moment. She shut the laptop's lid and took Crystal's hand.

Crystal shook off her grasp but still stared straight ahead. She heard one word over and over. Lame. Lame. Lame. Her gaze drifted to her legs. No one ever held her use of crutches and braces against her until now.

"Our negotiation isn't over." Abilene rested a warm hand on Crystal's shoulder.

She looked up and nodded.

Her roommate ran a hand through her spiked hair. Her brown eyes spoke compassion. "No majority. We'll work things out. Danica's under stress."

Crystal stood. The heft of her crutches, the independence they gave her comforted. "Thanks. I need some space."

In her room, she sank onto her bed. What would she do when Danica returned? They shared a queen size bed.

A text pinged. Danica.

begin text

DANICA: I think you better find another place to live. Until I marry, this is my apartment.

end text

She fell back on her bed. *Okay, Ms. Danica Vaughn. Figure out how to pay the rent without me.*

If she calmed herself, God would direct her paths. Maybe tomorrow Danica would come around. If not? Lots of people lived under bridges. Even recording stars.

Chapter 16

Roxie's eyes popped open as her heart beat against her chest, leaving no room to breathe. The dream. She didn't scream this time. At least, Roxie made progress. In this morning's dream, the head had hands as cold as Alaska's glaciers. They grabbed her. The ice froze her as if Elsa from her favorite childhood movie *Frozen* had touched her. In her dream, death stalked, but not her. Who?

She blinked. Her heart stilled.

Death wanted Vernita. Her grandmother.

Roxie stared into the dark willing sleep to claim her. After a few minutes, she threw off her covers and tiptoed into the kitchen. Her roommates slept, as sane students did at four a.m. She put water for tea on to boil and then dressed.

With a tea bag steeping, she sat at her desk to catch up on the two classes she'd cut yesterday. She logged onto her computer. As the website loaded, she watched the light seep into the world outside, making the night's blackness more gray than ebony. The skeletal limbs of the trees brushed against her window. The sorrowful sound echoed her mood.

Crystal would sign her contract any day now. With Jesse free, would Crystal claim him? If they got together, would she lose her sister—her best friend? How could she hang out with Crystal if she dated Jesse?

Jesse? Why couldn't he compromise? Why couldn't they work out their problems? More important, why did she love him?

Roxie buried her head in her hands. *Lord, somehow you have to help me let go. Lisa, Vernita, Mama, Pearl, none of them did a thing wrong to me. Yet they haunt me. Why do I believe I'm worthless?*

A tap at her bedroom door made Crystal look up from the Bible on her lap. "Come in."

"Coffee." Leanne held up a cup.

"Thank you." Crystal took the brew. Its earthy aroma tempting.

"Join us for breakfast?" Leanne nodded toward the kitchen.

"I'm good. Thanks." Crystal sipped as she turned back to the Bible.

Leanne didn't leave. "You know, Danica didn't mean—"

Crystal glared at her roommate. "Maybe she did."

"Things took an unexpected twist. She had to feel blindsided. Her wedding's coming—"

"Whatever." Crystal waved a dismissive hand. "Out of the abundance of the heart, the mouth speaks. I'll find a place to stay and be gone before Danica returns, even though I've paid my rent until the end of the month." She looked back at the words in her Bible—Leviticus and what the Israelites could and could not eat. No spiritual support here, and a snoozer to boot.

"You belong here. I'm sorry about my attitude last night. I was arrogant."

Crystal focused on the page as though not being able to eat a camel or rock badger mattered to her.

"Shock made me ..." Leanne's voice lowered. "No, shock is the wrong word. I didn't consider who you are, your character." She took a huge breath. "I would've signed under Davenport's conditions without fretting about everyone else. I've never known you to be self-absorbed. Please accept my apology."

Crystal peered at Leanne. She'd stepped back into the doorway, her eyes downcast. Her roommate meant what she said.

"Don't make any decisions. About moving. You belong here. We belong together." Leanne turned as to go, then faced Crystal once more. "Don't decide about the contract. We'll work things out." The door clicked shut.

Crystal closed the book but drank the coffee. Out in the kitchen, the soft voices of Leanne and Abilene drifted through the door. Crystal strained to hear their conversation, but she made out no intelligible words. Her suitcase sat by the door, and she itched to move. She shifted her legs over the edge of the bed and opened the drawer in her bedside stand. She picked up the tan and sage business card belonging to Davenport. She fingered the paper and stared at the print. Email or phone call? Her band members complicated the signing. Talking in person or over the phone would make the issue clearer. Perhaps Kyle Davenport got to his office by eight? She crossed her fingers and dialed the number.

"The Davenport Agency." The bright voice of the receptionist cheered Crystal's heart. She'd sign today like Leanne, by her own admission, would've. For sure, Danica wouldn't hesitate to sign—other members included or not. Crystal would worry about the others later. "This is Crystal Snow. Mr. Davenport offered to represent me." She paused. Recalled Leanne's soft voice and downcast eyes. Remembered Abilene's unwavering alliance to her.

"Are you still there?" the receptionist's sweet voice brought Crystal back to the present.

She'd have faith. "Can I speak to him?"

"I'm sorry. Kyle's father had a heart attack last night—"

"I'm so sorry." Her throat constricted in an undefined emotion. Grief? Disappointment? Sorrow for Davenport? "Did his father—?"

"No. Thank heavens. His father will recover, but he's having bypass surgery today. Mr. Davenport should be in next week."

Crystal's heart sunk. She wanted the deal settled. Be done worrying about Danica. Surprise Leanne and Abilene with Davenport's plan to reorganize the group.

Tapping echoed over the line. "I see he wanted to meet with you. How about we make an appointment?"

Crystal nodded. "Whenever you have an opening, we're ready."

"Next Monday at eight a.m. Will that do?"

"Perfect. Thank you." When they disconnected their call, Crystal tapped the appointment into her phone. She sipped her coffee, cold like her anger. Abilene had been open to the deal last night. Leanne brought her coffee and apologized. Still, Danica proved problematic, and Crystal couldn't stay here whether she had two more weeks on her rent or not.

Roxie. She could live with Roxie while she found some place close to Nashville. Maybe if she bunked with her best friend, she could help Roxie see how important she was to Lisa and Vernita and Mama and Daddy and Pearl and to Jesse. Roxie and Jesse loved each other like Scarlett and Rhett or Katrina and Petruchio.

Roxie couldn't believe in herself. Her sister fought for everyone else, never for herself.

What to do now?

Swiveling off her bed, she tossed a few clothes—wide-legged pants and long skirts into her overnight bag. She rolled her suitcase into the kitchen.

Abilene straightened at the table. "Going to ..." Her gaze drifted downward, and she frowned. "Going to leave?"

"You heard Danica. I've got to find a place to live."

"Leanne told you we don't want you to go."

"Danica and I share a bed."

Leanne turned earnest eyes to Crystal. "I'll swap rooms. Danica and I get along well. We're both egotists."

Crystal pursed her lips as she thought about Leanne's suggestion. The idea sounded good, but ... "Thanks, but I need space."

"My offer is firm. Take some time." Leanne stood and reached for Crystal's roller bag. "Let me help you with your suitcase."

Crystal threw her a smile. "I'm good."

Even though Roxie shared an apartment in UT with two other girls, she had her own room. No way could she permanently live at Roxie's and still work on her career, seeing as Knoxville was almost three hours away. Maybe Davenport knew of an affordable place.

Affordable? Not anywhere near Nashville.

Fifteen minutes into her drive, a text arrived. Pearl. Crystal tapped her Bluetooth messages, and the automated voice read out her text.

begin text

PEARL: Guess who's having a baby? Woot. Call me later. Backlogged at the bakery.

end text

Crystal grinned. A niece or nephew would arrive soon. How divine.

Her latest composition, "Aaron's Lament," played in her head. Not the crazy, destroyed by fire melody, but the adagio. The resolution. She improvised lyrics as she drove. Pearl's good news was a harbinger of positive things to come.

When stressed or sad or confused, walking lifted Roxie's spirits. Today, despair felt as heavy as August's humidity. Her feet fought every step she took as she wandered along Phillip Fulmer Way on the UT campus near Jesse's hangouts. Her backpack tapped against her back as she scanned the passing students, hoping one would be him. At nine a.m., he'd be finishing a run. She stopped plodding and leaned against Neyland stadium. If she lingered, would he show up? Roxie sank onto a bench nearby and tucked her legs beneath the bench. She watched students scurry by, ducking against the breeze off the Tennessee River. After two hours of trudging along the river and the campus, Roxie needed to hit the library.

With a heavy sigh, she stood. Stearns's research paper needed to be finished by next week. For once, the idea of entering Hodges Library held no allure. Stearns's subject matter bored her beyond endurance. As soon as she knocked out this paper, she'd work on her favorite course, Ecology and Management of Wildlife Health.

As she stepped onto Volunteer Boulevard and approached the stately brick library, her phone pinged. She checked her text and smiled. *Pearl's pregnant?* Hundreds of babies and bottles and diaper emojis follow her sister's message. Obviously, the news delighted Pearl. Roxie's finger hovered over the keyboard to respond. She looked up. *Jesse? Near the library? He never* ... Wait. He and a pretty girl with long black hair and exotic features were lost in dialog. Roxie stood under the trees bordering the pedestrian walkway and stared. The two stood facing each other, their sides facing her. She couldn't read their lips. *Who?*

If she entered the library, she'd have to pass them. She smiled. *Give him something to think about.*

Who was she that she unnerved Jesse? Their relationship followed the general course of her life. Roxie pivoted and ducked down the Johnson Ward Pedestrian Mall. Her breath came hard, but not from her brisk stride. *How could he?*

The library was now out of the question. How would she finish her paper?

Coffee.

Instead of Hodges, she'd hit Catalyst Café, the latest coffee shop on Cumberland Avenue. Along with craft coffees and teas, the café sported high-back cushioned chairs. If she was lucky, one would be empty. The high backs would offer a place to screen off the rest of the world. A cocoon in the midst of a throng. Seeing as Catalyst's sofas surrounding a square, distressed table were so popular, she'd never get a seat there. Everyone loved Catalyst, which catered to all types, even the gaming geeks. One corner of the shop held strategy games and chess boards. They coaxed students to linger. Despite its name, Catalyst didn't propel students on with their lives. Loitering students bought lots of coffee and pastries.

Catalyst would be her study buddy today. After all, between last semester and this one, she had all the notes she needed for Stearns's paper.

She turned down Melrose Street and slowed. The thought of Jesse resurrected. Had he found someone new already? He claimed he loved her, but had he moved on to an exotic-looking woman.

Addison—or was her name Madison—Jesse couldn't keep her name straight, strode across the library's courtyard straight toward him. He should've figured she was enrolled in UT. Only students hung out at Nicky's. He glanced around for a place to hide.

Madison marched up to him. Although her eyes narrowed, a small smile played across her pretty, full lips. "Stalking me?"

Jesse smiled. His muscles softened, and despite his conscience telling him to run, he leaned in toward her. His voice lowered. "No. Seeing you approached me, how am I the stalker?" He reached for her shoulder, then dropped his arm as though burned.

The girl's smile broadened showing perfect teeth between lips that asked him to kiss her.

"Again, I'm sorry about the other night."

Madison or Addison rubbed her arms and stepped a bit too close. "I shouldn't have gotten angry with you. I flirted and invited you up to my room. I don't indulge in one-night stands." Again, her laughter sounded like wind chimes. "I guess I should say—one-night-standups."

Jesse shut his eyes for a long moment. "Me, too. I don't believe in ... or shouldn't believe in ... sex outside of marriage. Alcohol and ..." He inhaled crisp air and relaxed. "Your sex appeal is intoxicating." He leaned close and smelled the flowery shampoo she used. "Madison."

Her smile sparkled in her eyes.

He got her name right.

"Then why did you this time?"

"This time what?"

She frowned. "Have a one-night stand. With me."

Jesse licked his lips and searched for words. "Because ..." He couldn't say he was lonely or brokenhearted. He leaned in close—so near he could kiss her cheek with ease. If he wanted. "Because you're irresistible."

"Oh, flatter me some more." Madison took his elbow. Her finger trailed down his arm. "I never saw you on campus before. Are you heading into the library? We could study together."

"Library?" He laughed. "My ex's sister Crystal says Hodges was the last place she'd look for me."

"Crystal? You mentioned her last night. Does she go to UT?"

He shook his head. "Crys is looking to make a name in music."

"Tough road."

He pursed his lips. "Not for her. She's gorgeous. A virtuoso fiddler. A brilliant businesswoman."

Madison tilted her head. "Is Crystal your girlfriend too?"

"No way. Why do you ask?"

"Your eyes sparkle every time you mention her."

Jesse looked away wanting to hide his eyes—not show this woman, Madison, his soul.

"What's your major?" Madison's fingers lingered on his wrist and started his heart pounding once more.

"Education. I'm working on my masters in phys. ed and health. Graduate in May. I finished my morning run ten minutes ago." He nodded in the direction of the sports' complex. "I never saw you on campus either."

"In January, I transferred from Roane State to UT's forensic anthropology program. I want to explore my culture."

"Cherokee?"

Her smile answered him. "What gave my ancestry away?"

Black hair, coppery skin, beautiful cheek bones and eyes. "Lucky guess. I'm heading to the new coffee shop on Cumberland. Want to join me?"

"Sure." Madison looped her arm through his.

Jesse wanted to pull away, needed to avoid temptation, but the softness of her torso pressed against his side tugged him closer. His arm brushed against the softness of her curves. Heat climbed up his neck. In Catalyst Café, he'd sit across from her. Not next.

Inside the coffee shop, Roxie settled into a padded chair in an alcove adjacent to the pickup counter. She arranged her brie and bacon sandwich and large, black coffee next to her computer. With her laptop's lid raised, she opened her Word document and retrieved her outline and research on the ethics of water distribution. She groaned. She lived in Tennessee. Would move to Alaska. No water issues in either place.

Shifting between documents, she lost herself in work.

"Why don't you find a comfortable seat? I'll wait here for our coffee."

The voice. Every muscle stiffened in Roxie's body. She could pick out Jesse's voice anywhere—in a concert crowd, whispered in the forest, and definitely by the counter behind her. She started to turn toward him.

"We're in luck, Jesse," a husky female voice called behind her. "The comfy couches opened up."

Roxie slunk down in her chair and prayed to be swallowed up. Until a few minutes ago, students had hogged the couches surrounding the coffee table six feet behind her. She chanced a peek. The beautiful, dark-haired girl from the library sat behind her. She fussed with a mirror and applied lipstick.

"Caramel latte and a large nitro cold brew," the barista called.

Nitro cold ... Jesse's favorite. Roxie hunched her shoulders. No way did she want to look like a turtle in front of this girl. She softened her pose and stared ahead. Saw nothing. Facing Jesse would destroy her. How could she escape without them seeing her?

"Here you go." Jesse spoke behind her. Dare she peek again?

"Thanks, Jesse. I shouldn't drink so much sugar, but Catalyst's caramel lattes are worth the calories."

"You don't need to worry about calories."

Flirting? No. She and Jesse broke up on Sunday. Two days ago. He couldn't have moved on already. Roxie had to be mistaken.

"So, about Sunday night." The girl paused like she sipped her coffee or embarrassment silenced her. "Like I said, I don't hop into bed with strangers, but you're different."

Roxie shoved her hand over her mouth to cover her gasp. *Jesse slept with her on Sunday night? They had broken up hours before.* Anger rolled up Roxie's throat. She slammed her computer shut.

"I'm a new Christian. Sex is for marriage."

Roxie scraped the chair back. It teetered before righting itself once more. She glared at Jesse who sat on the couch adjacent to the dark-haired girl.

Jesse's jaw dropped. "Roxie!" He jolted to his feet and took several steps toward her.

Roxie held out her hand to stop him. "Some Christian. A fight. We had one fight. Like we haven't reconciled after more serious altercations. Maybe we would've reconnected." Her hand swung out. The sting from her slap abated her tears but stoked her anger.

Jesse palmed his cheek. "No. We wouldn't have reconciled. We're toxic together."

With narrowed eyes, she glared into his. "You made sure of that." Dizziness twirled the room. She grabbed the chair back and clenched her teeth against the scream growling in her throat. "You," she pointed a finger at the dark-haired woman. "What a ... hussy. Bragging about sex—to my fiancé, ex-fiancé —so all the world could hear?" Stiffening every muscle, she turned and scooped up her papers and computer. Summoning dignity—or what she hoped passed for dignity and control—she tucked each into their place in her backpack. She wanted to clutch them to her chest and run. She couldn't give Jesse the satisfaction of seeing her upset.

Jesse's hand clasped her shoulder. "Roxie?"

She shrugged off his touch and squared her shoulders. "Don't. You. Touch. Me." Without looking at him—seeing his face would destroy her—she hoisted her backpack over one shoulder. Summoning the last of her dignity, she walked out of the café holding her head high, leaving her coffee and breakfast sandwich on the table.

Outside, control crumbled. She turned back toward the main campus. Her body begged her to run. She darted back down Melrose Avenue. When she reached Tyson Alumni Center, her legs refused to hold her. She sank onto a bench under bare-limbed trees, and her grief doubled her over. The tears she'd held back since she first saw Jesse and the girl outside Hodges overcame her. She cried until sobs hiccuped her chest. Deflated, she leaned against the back of the bench.

Why did she love him?

Why did he cheat?

She stared at the stately yellow alumni building with its pillared portico and beautiful colonial classic architecture. She loved UT and its collegiate atmosphere. Every building held history and style. Today, the regal campus mocked her. Told her she wasn't worthy. She glanced at her phone. Ecology and Management of Wildlife Health would start in fifteen minutes. Lectures and notes would numb her mind. Losing herself in the wild world would help her escape her sorrow. She picked up her pack and took a step. Stopped. *No. Jesse hadn't cheated.* They were through. Still were. Yet, why'd he sleep with the pretty girl so soon after they split? He claimed he didn't fool around anymore since he converted. Perhaps he kept his celibacy because he didn't love her. Jesse didn't desire *her*. Found nothing sexy in her. She stared into the distance as another sob shuddered.

"Are you okay?" An older woman turned toward Roxie. She stretched out her arm as though to console her.

"I'm okay." Roxie lifted a shoulder.

"Can I help?"

Roxie gazed into eyes wide with compassion and forced a smile. "I'm good. Broke up with my guy. Nothing time won't heal."

The stranger's eyes glowed as though she understood. "I've been there. You're right. Time's not the healer, though." The woman pointed toward the sky.

"Thank you." She offered a small smile. When the woman walked off, Roxie lifted her eyes skyward. *Jesse's kind and handsome and smart.* Those traits would never sustain a relationship. He was also self-absorbed and too interested in other women. She scoffed. Especially her sister.

She shook her head and strode to class.

Jesse slunk back onto the couch next to Madison. He closed his eyes and took a deep breath. *Nothing's hidden that won't be revealed.*

"What an awkward moment." A warm body nestled next to him. Madison's closeness soothed.

He nodded.

Madison took his hand. With a sharpie she'd produced while shock and guilt slobber-knocked him, she scribbled numbers on his hand. "Here's my contact info, in case we have any chance together."

He stood as she walked out of the café. Roxie and he would destroy each other. Crystal was right, and he should've believed her, but he'd hoped to marry soon. Why?

His motives were wrong. They were natural. Biological. Instinctive. Why did God make sex so difficult?

Crystal would know.

Chapter 17

Crystal pulled up to Danica's home, an unassuming tri-level house trimmed in brick on an acre lot. All the way here, Crystal expected her resolve to dissolve. Still, anger or exasperation or the need to make her closest friend, outside of Roxie, understand the band needed her, Danica, as much as anyone. She turned off the ignition. Barely had she clambered out of her car when the front door flew open.

"What do you want?" Danica stood on the stoop, her arms crossed.

"You."

Danica's eyes narrowed. She didn't approach.

Crystal walked toward her. "Can we talk about the contract?"

"Your double-dealing?"

Crystal looked around. *Okay. We talk here.* "I didn't finagle my way into the lead. Davenport approached me—"

"You didn't tell him his suggestion was a nonstarter?"

"His deal was acceptable. I'm going to sign. Leanne came around, so she and Abilene are on board. The band is incomplete without you."

"As background noise?"

"If you think you'd be background noise, then you believe Abilene, Leanne, and I don't add a thing to the group."

"Don't put words in my mouth."

"Those are the implications of your words. If no longer being the focal point makes you unimportant, the three of us are inconsequential."

Danica's eyes bored into Crystal. Any colder and ice would encase her.

Anger tightened Crystal's throat, but she struggled to keep her voice calm. "The other two and I discussed our situation with both the housing and the contract. Together, we reasoned the deal would be the best route for the four of us. All of us talked out our reservations of the reorganization. They're party girls and have no interest in faith, yet they sought wisdom. You though? For a Christian, your arrogance is ... inappropriate."

Danica gnawed her lips. Perhaps she was reconsidering her stance?

"On Monday, I have an appointment at Davenport's agency to iron out details—easier in person than via email. You have until Monday to join us."

"Don't hold your breath." Danica pivoted. She paused, and her shoulders stiffened. She faced Crystal once more. "I'll be back in Nashville on Monday. Be out of the apartment by then." She stormed into her house. The wood door slammed behind her. The screen, anti-climatically, clicked shut a few seconds later.

Crystal ground her teeth as heat coursed through her. *Who was this woman?* She'd seen the ego when Danica referred to the group as *her* group. The apartment was *hers*. She took the headline in everything they accomplished.

What's wrong with you? She stared at the closed doors of Danica's family home. She'd imagined different outcomes. First, she prayed Danica would listen to reason and also hoped she'd rescind her eviction notice.

In her car, Crystal rubbed her tense muscles. Leaning against the driver's seat, a melody bubbled up. The music, as always, worked magic on her mood. Danica's pride would destroy her future. Her pride wouldn't ruin Crystal's. She started her vehicle and smiled as she backed out of the driveway.

Danica did have six days to change her mind.

She pursed her lips, knowing she should pray for Danica.

Maybe later.

No one ever locked a door. Crystal let herself into her sister's apartment fifteen minutes later. Except for the bedrooms and bathroom, the apartment was one open space. After grabbing a Dr. Pepper from the fridge, Crystal flopped onto the couch and tapped open her phone. *Apartments—Nashville area.* She perused her options. Not many, and she'd have to gig in the restaurants on Broadway. Play her heart out to diners who didn't listen. She bit her fingernail. She could always busk on the streets.

She giggled softly as she imagined herself sitting on a stool in front of her open violin case filled with pennies and quarters. What would she play? "Jolene" was ever popular.

Her anger over Danica's attitude had faded like the darkness at dawn. So too would the worry of finding a suitable place to live. Now was the time to push forward, make her dreams come true. She'd burned all her safety nets. While young, healthy, and—she smiled as she recalled Davenport's words—beautiful, she'd work her performance.

The lyrics to "I Feel Pretty" played in her mind. She hummed along. She was pretty, and witty, and oh so talented. *Take that, Danica.*

Why couldn't Roxie believe the same about herself? If she believed, the pain her sister felt would fade too. Roxie, though, lived so in the present. The way things went today was the way they'd always be. God alone could change her, but, apparently, he wasn't in the mood.

She laid her head against the arm of the sofa and scrolled through her social media accounts.

Roxie and Jesse. Her sister had posted a picture of them starting out on Friday. Man. Jesse was cute.

And free. For real.

Two things would keep Crystal away from him. First, a relationship with him would kill Roxie—if Roxie's own relationship with Jesse didn't kill him first.

For the most part, Vernita spoke truth. She didn't need a man to be complete. After all, as Davenport said, she was talented and *beautiful*. Crystal shifted upright and dug out her notebook. The music she imagined on the way back from Danica's resurrected. Never had anyone created a bluegrass-downhome-tango. Somehow, she'd make the music work.

An hour—or was it two?—later, the door to the apartment flung open. Roxie dashed to into the living room. She tossed her bookbag on the table and plopped down next to Crystal. "You have no idea what an answer to prayer you are—albeit one I never uttered. Why are you in Knoxville?"

"To visit my sister."

"Apparently, you plan to visit for a while. I saw your suitcase in the back seat of your car."

"Danica evicted me. I need to find a place to live."

"She *what*?"

Crystal poured out the details of Danica's double-dealing.

"Why aren't you pitching a fit?" Roxie's eyes hardened, and she lifted the notebook from Crystal's hands. "I'd be cussing—the mild darns and shoots—still those words are cusses according to Grandma Cora. Instead, you're writing music."

"I can't stay angry at things I can't change. Besides, music makes a way for me to work out issues."

"Aren't you paid up on rent for two more weeks?" Roxie asked.

Crystal nodded.

"You have a right to stay in your apartment."

"Remember? We share a bed."

"If sleeping next to you bothers her, she can move to the couch."

Crystal wrinkled her forehead.

"Don't be a wuss, little sis. You are as worthy as Danica. Besides, you said the other two want you there."

"They do. Leanne offered to swap rooms."

"See. Drummer girl solved your problem."

"Maybe."

Roxie hopped off the couch and grabbed a Dr. Pepper and bag of chips then settled cross-legged facing Crystal. "Jesse found another girl already."

Crystal straightened. "What? I've never pictured him as fickle."

Roxie hiked a shoulder. "He slept with her Sunday night."

"He *what*?"

"Start composing. If you're as angry as I, you'll write the bluegrass equivalent of *The Ring Cycle* or 'The Song That Never Ends'."

Now isn't the time to tell Roxie she created half the problem. Let her blab.

"What am I going to do?" All traces of humor and anger and self-righteousness evaporated.

They sat for a few moments.

"Here's my advice," Crystal said. "Finish school. Head to U Maine in the fall. Your dreams matter. You matter. Roxie Star Snow is important by herself, not because some guy likes her."

"Some guy?"

"Think of your history. Not with Jesse, but Mark and Jimmy, going all the way back to Deacon Mills."

The laughter spilled out of Roxie. "Mills? How old was I?"

Crystal shook her head. "Don't know. This is Mama's tale. She hated the man for months because he blamed the death of her daughter and her husband on a sin he believed Mama committed. You used to run into his arms when you were little. I think next to Jesse, he was your longest crush."

"He snuck me Bubba-Rubba-Gum. Mama hated the gum. Said I stuck the goo in my hair to hide it."

"Seriously, remember what Vernita said, you don't need a man to be complete. You and Jesse ..."

"I figured if we broke up, you and he would get together, not some unfamiliar dark-haired beauty."

"I could never. You love him, even if ..." They sat in silence for a few minutes. Crystal grabbed her crutches. "Help me get my gear?"

"No." Roxie stood. "You are going home. Claim your spot, and let Danica accept the consequences of her pride."

"Roxie?" Crystal's forehead tightened. "I need to stay—"

"No. You. Don't. Get a backbone. Go home."

"You sound like Mama."

"Seems neither one of us have learned Mama's lessons." Roxie held up a finger. "I need to remember I'm worth something." She held up a second finger, then pointed it at Crystal. "You need to stand up for yourself."

"Maybe we're twins?"

Roxie's pretty smile creased her eyes. "Your talk about not needing men makes you sound like Vernita. See her three times, and she becomes as much your grandmother as Grandma Cora."

"A fourth grandma's a good deal—Grandma Cora, Grandma Snow, Ma Jaynes, and now Vernita."

Roxie took Crystal's shoulders. "You will go home tonight. Hendersonville will keep you close to the clubs and Music Row. You'll be able to visit Vernita and Lisa—"

"What makes you think I want to visit Vernita?"

"Because you're Crystal. Let's hit Calhoun's for a late lunch before you go. I'm starved."

At seven, Crystal returned to an empty apartment. After stuffing her leftover meal from Calhoun's into the fridge, she yanked her roller bag into her room. Something was wrong. She glanced around the small bedroom she and Danica shared. All of Danica's personal effects were gone.

Had she come back and moved out?

No. Not Danica's style.

Abilene's stuffed teddy bear sat on Danica's side of the bed. Her Alexa smart speaker and copies of *Tattoo Today* were on the end table. Crystal opened the closet doors. All of Danica's clothes had been replaced with Abilene's.

Her friends hadn't listened to Crystal's words. They'd listened to her heart. As she sank onto the bed, she couldn't stop the grin spreading across her face. Roxie had been right to send her home. She wrapped her arms around her shoulders. She was home, and she had a whole lot of hope to hold on to. *Thank you, Abi and Lee.*

Crystal had unpacked when someone tapped on the apartment door. "Coming." She hurried through the living room and opened their door.

"Jesse."

Her heart somersaulted. *What is he doing here?*

"Can I come in? I need to talk."

She heard the advice she'd given Roxie. She had to follow her own.

Jesse stood on the front stoop. "I know you're not expecting me. If your roommates are in, we can go someplace. Eat? I need to talk.

"Abilene and Leanne are out. I'm stuffed from lunch. What do you want?" Crystal's voice sounded cold, unlike her.

Jesse glanced around. "Roxie and I—"

"I know. And you slept around hours later."

"Please. Can we talk?" His brown eyes held worlds of sorrow. She couldn't let him in. "Your wisdom, your ... love. Crystal, you have the answer to my problems. You've always been wise. Loving." His heart raced. Seeing her lifted chin and flinty eyes, her anger protecting Roxie, perhaps he'd always loved the wrong sister. *No. Stop. I can't lose Roxie and fall into any woman's arms. No rebounds.*

Crystal stepped aside, still holding the door.

Jesse longed to see her smile. This wasn't like her to not welcome him.

"Have a seat." Crystal pointed to the kitchen table.

Jesse slunk down.

"Can I get you anything?"

He shook his head.

Crystal sat across from him. She said nothing for several minutes.

The awkwardness gnawed him, and he had to make himself breathe—deep, even breaths. He twitched his fingers. *Say something, Crystal.*

Crystal leaned toward him. Her frown told him he'd get no comfort. "Roxie told me everything—from the aborted

Valentine's photo shoot to the Valentine's Day sleepover you had with a dark-haired girl."

If he could melt, he'd liquefy right now. Every nerve begged him to hide. His fingers gripped the table's edge. For a moment, he wanted to crawl under and hide.

"So, why run here? Think I'm going to hop into bed with you too?"

His mind flashed the image of them together. The thought came too fast to tamp down, and it sealed his tongue.

"Well?"

"No." He sounded too defiant. "Never. You aren't the kind of woman to betray your ideals. So, no. I'm here because you've always been the wise person—the one who understands."

She stared. Said nothing.

Seeing the revulsion in her eyes seared his core. To be hated by Crystal would be a punishment too hard to bear.

"Am I not good enough to sleep with?"

He shook his head. "Where is this talk coming from? You're not snarky."

"You know I've loved you since you and Roxie started dating. You've lasted longer with her than any other guy."

"So I've been told. Repeatedly. I should've listened to you. Slowed down our relationship."

"You should've delivered what you promised. A whole weekend lying in poison ivy being devoured by ticks would've reassured my sister you loved her for who she was. Instead, you force her to follow your whims."

"I didn't—"

"Yes, you did. You know her story—middle child, old enough to know her parents didn't care about any of us and left us to be raised by Pearl—who didn't even know her real name until she was eight. Her biological grandmother told Roxie she was a retard." Crystal smiled her innocent smile. "Called me a cripple. Vernita was right about me. Fortunately, I was too young to understand or remember." Her smile told Jesse she laughed at herself. "Then Lisa adopted Roxie." Crystal's tone softened, and her sweet character peeked through her words. "When Roxie slid into her reclusive, silent self, like the child Mama found in the dilapidated, abandoned house, Lisa brought my sister back to Mama and Daddy. To Roxie, she wasn't good enough for Lisa. Even though she wanted to come home to us, she believed Lisa hated her."

"I know—"

"No, you don't. If you did, you would've behaved differently."

"I—"

"Listen to me."

Jesse bit his lip and gave a curt nod.

"At home, Mama had another foster child, and her favorite goat was in the middle of a complicated birth, consuming our mother's attention. All this time, Roxie was too little to understand. No one rejected her. She was loved by Mama, Daddy, Lisa, Pearl. Me. I don't know how to reach her. I'd always hoped you'd break through, but you always ..."

"I always what?"

"Always want your way."

"No, I don't." Anger flared like a lit book of matches. Jesse ground his teeth. His heart vised and became too tight to pump blood. *Women. Who understood?* He stood.

"Sit down, Jesse Maxwell."

"Don't tell me what to do."

"Then goodbye." Crystal shifted her chair back.

Jesse plopped down. "I don't always want my own way."

"The job at Knoxville Academy?"

"But this position is a dream come true."

"And Alaska isn't Roxie's dream?"

"But Alaska's so far from family."

"Alaska has been her focus as long as I remember. She told you a zillion times about her aspirations—long before you fell in love."

"There're mountains here."

"They're not Alaska. There're no moose or grizzlies or wolverines or northern lights."

"Someone has to give up their dream."

"Plenty of schools around Alaska. Only one last frontier with tundra and the aurora borealis and a wilderness where no one has ever walked."

Jesse hung his head. Crystal. At adoption, her parents gave her the middle name Joy because of her personality. This joyful woman never had much of an issue speaking her mind. She said what she wanted and believed people would come around. They would accept her. So different from his Roxie Star.

"You know she loves photography. She agreed to the camping trip to try to love the Smokies as much as you do. You reneged on her gift."

"I didn't. She got good shots of a sow and her cubs. I thought she had what she wanted, and I believed Roxie would compromise."

"Maybe there were more bear pictures. Maybe stalking the black bear would make her compromise, but you quashed her chance to see richness here. You insisted she hike. Fast. No pictures. Coming back from Florida—"

"Enough." Jesse's bellow frightened him. He wanted to punch something, or someone.

"No. Coming back from Florida, the two of you fought. You were so wrapped up in yourselves, you forgot me at the truck stop."

"I—"

Crystal stood. She propped her hands on the table and leaned forward.

"So, what do I do?"

"Anything you like. As of now? Your future does not include the Snow family." Crystal pointed to the door.

Crystal watched Jesse trudge out of the apartment. For the first time since she met him, she didn't care how he lived his life, as long as his future had nothing to do with Roxie.

Or her.

Chapter 18

On Monday, Crystal sat with Leanne and Abilene at a polished wooden table in Another Broken Egg on Commerce Street. The industrial-looking café sported gold-colored heating ducts and stainless-steel lighting fixtures—very trendy and popular. This morning, Crystal didn't care about the atmosphere or the fabulous brunch items. She raised her virgin bloody mary. "Here's to a career making our *own* music."

Abilene and Leanne lifted their full-throttled cocktails. They clicked glasses.

Abilene sipped her tequila sunrise. "I can't believe Davenport's already searched out venues for us—before we even signed."

"At the Ryman, opening for Washbasin? How does that happen?" Though Crystal understood. If God opened the door, human imagination couldn't fathom the opportunity.

"He knew a good deal when he heard us." Leanne's face flushed, and her eyes glistened. "He has good tastes."

The waitress arrived and placed a plate of shrimp 'n grits in front of Crystal. She looked down at the food. Hungry five minutes ago, now her appetite fled. While the waitress slid plates of crab benedict and a skinny omelet in front of her friends, she peeked at her phone. Danica hadn't answered her texts.

"Praying?" Abilene asked.

Crystal jumped. "Not yet."

"She's still fretting about Danica." Leanne shoved a slice of omelet into her mouth and leaned across the table toward Crystal. Her movement plopped her signature braid over her shoulder. "Don't you always tell us we have to accept the consequences of our decisions? We left the contract open so we could add her. Nothing more we can do."

"Amen." Abilene waved her fork in the air. "And I ain't fretting none. My crab benedict is divine."

Leanne chuckled and playfully punched Abilene's arm. "Amen and divine. I think you're getting religion too."

Crystal cut a piece of shrimp. Anxiety fled as the crisp sweetness of the shrimp exploded in her mouth. She'd done everything possible to entice Danica back—visited her, called, texted, and convinced Kyle Davenport to add her to the contract should she change her mind. The time had come to quit worrying about everyone else's happiness. They had to accept the end results of their choices. Danica, Jesse, and Roxie. Crystal was done being Ms. Fix It for the three of them.

The food tasted so good Crystal wanted to lick the last morsel of brunch from her plate. More than flavor, she wanted to stretch this occasion with Leanne and Abilene.

Leanne leaned back in her chair. "I'm not ready to go. Let's order coffee."

"I'll drink to that," Abilene said.

Crystal smiled. Abilene drank everything and to anything. Soda. Wine. Milk. Coffee. Usually, though, the liquid was more adult.

She and her friends chatted for another half hour. At last, Leanne stood. "I'll go convince Richie to reserve a space at our studio." Her wink hinted about her method of convincing. "Maybe they can fit us in, so we can record 'Aaron's Lament.' Why does Davenport want to sell that song when we have 'Barefoot in the Hollow' ready to go? He signed us because of 'Barefoot.' "

"Don't care." Abilene said.

Leanne shoved up from the table. "We're on our way. Richie said his company could start working on a stage production as soon as we signed."

"Aren't you rushing things, Leanne?" Crystal asked.

"Again, I quote you." Leanne made air quotes. "If we don't step out in faith, God can't work. After fronting for the opening of Washbasin Gentry, we'll have our own tour."

"How much does his firm charge?" Crystal bit her lip. "We're low on cash." *Especially if Danica moves out.*

Leanne batted her eyes once more. Her cute nose wrinkled like a bunny rabbit. "Faith, Crystal. I'll get the price down."

After hugs and another fifteen minutes of chatter on the street, Crystal drove to her apartment to put the final touches on the song she'd started when she tried to move in with Roxie. She turned her key to unlock her door and found it unlocked. *Did we forget?*

Danica stepped out of Crystal's bedroom. "I'm gone one week, and not only have you not left, but I've been moved out of my room." If her scowl shot .22 bullets, Crystal would've been dead.

"Seeing as you're angry with me, we thought—"

Danica stormed into her new room and slammed the door.

Crystal leaned against the kitchen sink. A carving knife lay in the dish drainer. Her fingers itched, and she picked up the knife. She smiled as she saw herself chopping off Danica's head and shoving the noggin into the freezer.

Maybe then Danica would come to her senses. One of her novels showed her how to dispose of the dismembered body parts, making them impossible to find. Koontz had worked out the flaws of the murder in his novels, so she'd avoid the mistakes his villain had made. She wished she were the type. The problem would be solved. She dropped the knife.

She ran her hand over her head. Why shed any more tears over infantile behavior? Let Danica be. Seeing as God let us choose our own way and learn from our mistakes, she'd let Danica reap the consequences of her own actions.

When do I listen to myself? Crystal stepped into Danica's room without knocking. "We're going to talk."

Danica lifted folded clothes from her suitcase on the bed and laid them in the dresser drawer. "Maybe you. Not me."

I should've let Danica throw her tantrum.

"Shouldn't you be packing? I told you your lease was up." Danica slammed the dresser drawer and faced Crystal.

"First, the four of us have to scrape together our pennies to make rent here. Without me, the three of you will be homeless."

"Without *you*? Like you hold us together."

Crystal bit back her laugh. Danica's mocking falsetto sounded more like a whining child than an irate adult.

"Wipe off your smirk." Danica crossed her arms, but her scowl added to the humor of her childish attitude. "Everything revolves around you."

Crystal sank onto the bed and stretched out her limbs. With her legs, she nudged the suitcase closer to the edge. Smiled. *Do I dare push it over?*

"If not for you, we'd still be a band."

A chuckle erupted. *Why am I finding her tantrum and lack of logic funny?*

"Why are you laughing?"

Crystal clenched her lips to keep from snickering too loudly.

Danica jabbed a finger at Crystal. "Watch your legs. You'll knock my suitcase on the floor."

Crystal leaned against the headboard and propped her hands behind her head.

"Make yourself at home."

"I am. This is *our* home."

Danica zipped the suitcase.

"Notice the pronoun I used. Our."

Danica jostled the bag under the bed. "Maybe if you got up—and out—my bag would fit better."

"Maybe if you sat, we could talk things out."

Danica left the room.

Crystal waited.

Five minutes later, Danica returned. "Still here?"

Crystal looked around the room as though searching for something. "I'm still sitting in your room, so I guess I am. Now sit and talk."

Danica sighed and stayed by the door."

"Don't be comfy." Crystal nodded toward the extra space on the bed. "Your spot awaits should you tire of standing and being a grump."

Danica shrugged and leaned against the doorjamb.

"As you know, we signed our contract today. Davenport thinks he can get us an opening spot with Washbasin Gentry."

Danica's eyes widened, and she appeared to fight back a smile.

Crystal quirked her lips. "Well, an opening act before their *real* opening act. Sort of a warm-up for the warm-up. Better yet, do you know where we'll perform?"

Danica said nothing.

"That's right. The Ryman Auditorium, original home of the Grand Ole Opry. Hosted Minnie Pearl, Dolly Parton, Johnny Cash, and now Snow in the Hollow."

Danica straightened and looked as though she'd leave.

"I'm not done, Danica Vaughn."

Danica resumed her stance leaning against the jamb.

"Washbasin's Grammy nomination is good for us—even as the opening for the opening." Crystal slid around on the bed and dangled her legs over the edge. She leaned forward. "Danica, our band needs our lead guitar, not to mention our main lyricist. We'd be a better group if you played the guitar."

Once more, every muscle in Danica's face tightened her features.

"Your tension ages you, Danica."

Her friend still said nothing.

"This attitude isn't like you. I've never seen your ego ruin—"

If Danica's eyebrows raised any higher, they'd hit the ceiling. "My ego?"

Crystal inhaled and softened her voice. If she kept calm, Danica's fire would die. "Yours."

Danica said nothing.

"As a Christian—"

"Don't throw my faith in my face." Danica stormed out of the room.

So much for the old proverb, a soft answer disintegrating wrath. Crystal stood. *Danica's problem.*

Jesse strode past Strong Hall on UT's campus. Cars streamed down the busy road, and students loitered in late winter warmth. The cool, sunny weather felt wonderful after his run. He needed Catalyst Café and a double large cold brew nitro. A dark-haired girl dressed in a Tennessee orange hoodie sat on a bench under the trees a few feet away. His heart skipped a beat, and he stopped walking. "Madison?"

The girl turned, and Madison smiled. Her glossy, full lips begged him to kiss her. She stood and approached. She sauntered close. Madison's perfume, with hints of vanilla, took him to a safe place. He couldn't step away. "What brings you to my stretch of campus?"

"Coffee."

She slipped her arm into his. "Fine minds. A caramel latte had been calling me before you walked by."

Jesse started to pull away, but her arm tucked into his lured him in. *What harm is there in sharing a coffee?* His thought wasn't a question but a hope. "Join me." They walked arm in arm, but he couldn't look at her. He focused on the ground.

Madison, still linked to his arm, brushed against him as they walked in silence. The quiet didn't feel awkward. If he kept his distance, maybe he and Madison could have a platonic friendship like he and Crystal. Her torso drew closer, and his heart kicked up a notch. Madison's proximity didn't entice him like being near Crystal always did. Crystal was almost irresistible. Being Roxie's sister helped him sidestep his attraction.

"I haven't seen you around for a while."

"Went to Nashville."

"For a show?"

"No. I needed to talk to Crystal."

Madison stopped. The motion halted his step.

"Something wrong?"

She shook her head. "Do you realize, every time you mention Crystal's name, your voice sparkles?"

"No, it doesn't."

Madison widened her eyes and pulled him along once more.

Crystal knew the title of the song she started after her confrontation with Danica at her home in Knoxville. She scrawled the title on top of her latest revisions. "Tangled Tango." Hot and passionate in a tango rhythm with a bluegrass twist linked Roxie and Danica and her in their interwoven conflict. She needed Danica's help on the lyrics.

Danica.

Her roommate moved around the kitchen and living room area. The noises she made no longer sounded angry.

Crystal picked up her violin and played from the beginning. She stopped and erased the notes, rewrote a more staccato rhythm, and played again. Hunger and lack of movement drove her into the kitchen even though the angry roommate still roamed there.

"A new song?" Danica frowned. She didn't look toward Crystal. Her eyes seemed what? Indifferent? Distant? Not the warm, friendly Danica who'd shared the same room until yesterday.

"I need lyrics."

"What did you call the piece?"

"Tangled Tango."

Danica sank on the stool across from Crystal. "I like what I heard. Play the whole piece."

Hope bathed Crystal as she returned to her room. Once inside, she allowed her grin to surface. *Danica's thawing.* Back in the kitchen with her fiddle, Crystal composed her face making sure no vestige of her smile remained. Sitting on a bar stool, she bowed the melody. A soft staccato bounced off the strings, then as though the fiddle stumbled, the rhythm shifted, and the notes took on a fire that suffused anger and love and conflict into the kitchen. A final shift slowed the tune to a bluegrass musicality.

Her roommate's face lost its angry visage. Danica's fingers tapped on the table.

Crystal stopped. One look at Danica, her eyes far away—the look she used when lost in creation—let hope resurrect. "You have lyrics?"

Danica stiffened and stood. "Nice piece."

Crystal picked up her fiddle and played once more. After a few minutes, she lay the violin on the table with a soft clack.

"Your melody's an earworm." Danica hummed the song. Her fingers tapped her thigh.

"Why don't you write down what you're thinking?" Crystal leaned forward and gnawed on her lip. *Will she come around?*

"Aren't tangos a mite sensuous for a Christian?" Danica narrowed her eyes as though glaring, but a softness seeped through.

"While you're up, get me the bread and pb&j fixings."

"Get them yourself." Danica stepped toward her room. Stopped. Without turning, she spoke. "Reminds me of ..."

"What?"

"A very catchy piece." Danica stepped into her bedroom, and the door clicked behind her.

Crystal hummed the tune as she slathered peanut butter on one piece of bread. She dobbed the jelly on top of the irregular coating of peanut butter. Roxie would scowl and tell her to spread the peanut butter in a smooth, even layer. On the opposite piece, she should cover every inch of the bread with an even layer of the sweet jelly. Roxie claimed Crystal needed crunchy peanut butter, not smooth. Crunch would add extra peanut flavor. Nope.

Not for Crystal. Crystal slapped the second piece of bread on top and grabbed the knife. Roxie insisted sandwiches needed to be cut diagonally. Crystal sliced her pb&j crosswise, parallel to the edges. *Good thing you're not here, Rox. You'd be nagging me on the fine art of sandwich making.* Thoughts of her sister and their traditional sandwich-creating teases made Crystal sense her best friend's presence.

Danica's ego wouldn't plague Crystal if Roxie were here. She hummed loudly as she poured milk—not the rich sweet goat milk her family still loved more than the bovine water. They resorted to cow's milk when Mama sold her herd of goats to become a full-time vet tech. Still, milk satisfied. Daddy always said, "Be happy with what you have. How can we slap God in the face considering the abundance of his blessings?" Daddy's wisdom stuck with her like peanut butter. She improvised lyrics as she peered at Danica's room. *Earworm, eat your way into her heart.*

She scrolled her texts as she bit into the sandwich. *Lisa?* Her heart sank. Lisa's mother died. They'd only reconciled a year or so ago, and now Vernita was gone. Crystal glanced at Danica's door. *Why does pride and offense eat up so much of our lives?*

She texted Roxie.

begin text

CRYSTAL: Vernita passed away last night. The wake is Saturday at Mason's Funeral home, 12-4. Come with me?

end text

After five minutes of waiting, Crystal assumed her sister sat in class. Roxie always answered texts unless she was in the middle of an exam.

Maybe she was being tested.

tangled lives

Vernita died? Roxie continued typing her notes after the quick peek at the text flashing on the top of her computer screen. *Too bad. And no thank you. No wake. Don't have connections with the Harrison-Simpson crew.*

Her professor enumerated the anthropogenic factors in wildlife health. She needed to concentrate, but the message icon on the bottom of her MacBook showed she had an unread message—the one that had flashed across her screen. She clicked the icon, opened the message. She shut the app. The message indicator disappeared, enabling Roxie to concentrate on class.

Jesse sipped the last of his cold brew and shoved the cup aside. Keeping his eyes on Madison, he leaned his forearms on the table in Catalyst. "Now you have the full story about me and Roxie. Making matters worse—if possible—Crystal reamed me out about how I treated her sister. I guess my friendship with her has ended too."

"Ended with Roxie, yes. I don't see Crystal staying angry, not the way you describe her." Madison ran her finger along the back of Jesse's hand.

He pulled away, but her touch sent electrical shocks down his spine. Jesse stood. "Class calls." Jesse tossed his cup like a basketball player making a long shot. The container plopped into the garbage.

Madison walked her trash to the garbage can. She turned toward the door Jesse now held open for her. "Thanks for the coffee."

"Hey, Saturday, want to do something?"

"Darts at Nicky's?" Her hip bumped his as they walked out onto Cumberland Avenue.

He thought of his drunken mistake. Wrong place and too much beer tied him to Madison. Nicky's wasn't a great choice. "Darts sound great."

Chapter 19

On Saturday morning, Roxie's eyes opened wide as the nightmare receded. Lying in bed, she wrapped her arms around herself. No terror accompanied the dream. Maybe Vernita's passing brought a healing, as if her physical presence on earth tormented Roxie. She lay back down and savored the heavy quilt lying over her like Mama's arms.

"My little Star," Mama would say when night terrors assaulted Roxie. "Nothing to fear when God is in the room."

Roxie gazed around her bedroom as though she would see God. Or Mama. She rolled on her side and checked her phone. Eight. Should get up.

By now, Mama would be cleaning up breakfast dishes. Daddy would be mucking the horses' stalls. Jesse would be running.

With the thought of Jesse, her heart squeezed tight like clothes through an old-fashioned ringer washing machine. She sat up and the snippets of the morning's peace vanished. Saturday morning and nothing to do.

Not nothing. Crystal's nagging chased the last of the peace away. Her sister claimed going to the wake would bring closure to her chronic nightmares and heal her. She had time to go to Fidelio, Kentucky, and attend.

For what? Five minutes of mindless chatting after a three or four-hour ride there. Another four hours back to Knoxville. No. She didn't need healing. Her night *non*-terror proved the point. Vernita's passing ended her torment. Now all she needed to do was to forget Jesse.

What was he doing today? She hadn't seen him since her last visit to Catalyst Café. Without him, Saturday loomed empty. She needed animals. Only nonhuman creatures accepted you as you were.

The zoo.

Roxie grinned. She hadn't been there in a year. She'd take her camera. Zoo Knoxville would open long after the mid-morning sun eclipsed the best light for photographs. The light would wash out the shadows and blow out the highlights. She peeked through the window as she sat on the edge of the bed. Bright white cumulus clouds decked the sky bringing out a robin's egg blue. The color always soothed her. Perhaps the picturesque cloud cover would soften the sun's harshness. With a little luck and Lightroom tweaking, she could create a good photo.

Two hours later, at feeding time, Roxie arrived at Zoo Knoxville. She wandered the paths and found herself standing in front of the zebra pen. This morning, the striped ungulates roamed their spacious exhibit. Scents of elephants a few exhibits down blew her way. Little kids would hold their noses because of the stench. Her? The earthy smell made her feel alive. She closed her eyes and imagined herself on safari. She'd call being immersed in wildlife heaven. *If Jesse … No!* She set up a tripod.

In the middle of the habitat, a mama zebra munched hay while her foal bumped her udder to make her mama let down her milk. The baby stopped nursing before Roxie could affix her 800 mm zoom to her Nikon body. The heavy lens needed extra stability, and she worked the brace to hold the lens in place.

Once set up, a cloud shielded the scene from harsh light. Peering through the lens, the zebras appeared to be next to her, so close she felt she could reach out and run her hand down their bristly manes. The mare looked up, her beautiful head in profile. Roxie shot. The mare shifted her head, her nose nearly touched her baby. The shutter clicked. Again.

"You came with full hunting regalia."

Roxie jumped at the voice and turned. Squinted. The fellow wearing the navy-blue shirt and slacks of a zookeeper looked familiar. Dark hair and brown eyes. His top lip, like a cupid's bow over the full bottom lip. Gorgeous. His name badge. Kenji. *Where do I know him from?*

"You don't remember me." His smile revealed beautiful straight, white teeth. "Kenji Barrister. I met you during your sister's gig at Jacks on the River last month."

"Of course." She held out her hand.

He glanced at it, then peered into her eyes as though hesitant to shake. He held up both of his hands sheathed in latex gloves. "Been cleaning the pen. You don't want to grip my digits."

"Been there."

"And will be again when you're off into the wilderness studying God's creatures."

Roxie smile. "Good memory."

"Your fiancé here?"

Roxie ducked her head and raised her shoulders. She stopped herself before she reached full-turtle posture. *Stop hiding, Roxie.* Her sister's voice sounded so clearly in Roxie's head she could swear Crystal stood next to her. She jerked her head up and squared her shoulders. "No longer engaged."

"Why?" Kenji's face looked concerned. Shocked. "I'm sorry. Not my business."

"We were wrong for each other."

"But you loved him."

Kenji's words weren't a question. He understood.

She smiled.

"I'm sorry for you two." Kenji's eyes sparkled. "I lied. Not sorry at all." He leaned closer.

A child knocked into Roxie's tripod. She and Kenji lunged for the camera at the same moment. Kenji's arm looped around Roxie's back. His chest brushed her shoulder as he grabbed her gear. Neither pulled away. Everything felt what ...? Right. His arms, his closeness, made her think this was a part of the healing she felt in her morning's dream.

"Hey?" Kenji peered at her face. "No more stitches. Wound looks good."

Roxie felt where she'd bashed her head a month ago. "I can feel the scar."

"Should fade."

She gave a half smile. How she wished to linger.

"Join me on my lunch break?"

Roxie ran her hand over the barrel of her lens as she gazed toward the zebras. *What harm?* "I don't know. Having broken up a week ago."

"I'm not asking you to marry me, or even date me. I'll meet you at this bench," he pointed across the path, "at noon. I have a whole hour, and I promise I'll wash." He wiggled his fingers.

"In that case ... see you at twelve."

"If you'll excuse me, I've got to go check on Maribel and Zuzu."

"Maribel and Zuzu?"

tangled lives

Kenji pointed toward the Hartmann's Mountain Zebras she'd been photographing. "Maribel's the mare, Zuzu the foal. I need to vaccinate Zuzu."

Roxie picked up her heavy equipment. No way should she meet Kenji. He was ... too cute? Too soon after Jesse ...? Too right?

Five minutes later, she stepped down the concrete steps to the gorilla exhibit. The creatures had a beautiful and huge outdoor area to roam, but they congregated in the glass enclosure. She set up her equipment, but the dark lighting at the gorilla exhibit, along with the smudges on the glass, made photographs impossible. People clambered in her way for better views. She didn't blame them. The baby gorillas wowed everyone. The silverback, twenty-two-year-old Bantu, fathered a passel of babies who now swung from platforms or rode clinging onto their mothers. Bantu sat with his back to the window as though embarrassed to be gawked at by all these strangers.

Roxie understood his feeling. Immerse her in her world of animals, and she'd turn her back to the humans who ruined nature. *If I could chat with Dian Fossey.* Too bad poachers found their extermination of gorillas more valuable than Fossey's life. Murdered at the age of fifty-three.

Her parents' ages.

Instead of wriggling through the crowd here, Roxie wandered down the bamboo-lined path. Light spilled in patches through the vegetation or through the lazy clouds. She inhaled the smell of the clean, green chlorophyll of the bamboo. Crowds thinned and the peace of being alone in the middle of a popular zoo filled her. Where to go? The lemurs.

Two hours passed watching the primates swing. A zookeeper talked about their habits. Roxie knew most of what the woman said but found her speech fascinating.

"The diets of lemurs …"

Roxie's stomach grumbled as the zookeeper talked about fruit. *Hungry.*

Lunch! She checked her watch. Noon. If she hurried, would Kenji still be waiting by the bench?

In Mason's Funeral Home, Crystal stepped into the small room reserved for Vernita Barnes. Up front, the few standing sprays of flowers attested to a sad life. So few flowers. The room too empty. Lisa stood by a simple coffin talking to a woman. Her sons and Todd sat in a group to the side. Heavy curtains hung from the windows blocking all vestige of daylight. The cloying smell of carnations set Crystal's nerves on edge. She clutched the grips of her crutches tighter. During times like these, the crutches comforted, gave Crystal strength. *Run, Crystal, you have time.* She let out a breath and loosened her grip. The action chased away the thought of running. Ten minutes. All she needed was ten minutes to pay her respects. Vernita deserved someone to care. Once done, maybe she'd drive home. See Mama.

Mama. Meredith Snow was an elixir. Her presence made everything good. Crystal would tell her about Danica and the gig with Washbasin Gentry—at *the* Ryman Auditorium—and Roxie's fiasco over Jesse. The latter wouldn't surprise Mama. She'd frown and say something like *poor Roxie.* Once more, Mama would talk about the bad timing of Roxie's childhood traumas over her first five years of life. She would sigh in sorrow over the hurt on this quintessential middle child. Sometimes Mama sounded more like Daddy, the social worker. Mama would know how Crystal could help her sister.

The woman who talked with Lisa headed toward Todd. Crystal flexed her hands to shake out tension. She hated wakes and didn't know Lisa well. Maybe Roxie had the right idea, and Crystal should've skipped this.

Lisa looked up. Even across the room, her smile signaled joy at seeing Crystal.

No. This is right and just and good. She stepped up to her aunt. Her jaw twitched. The words stuck to her dry, thickened tongue. What to say? She stammered. "I'm sorry." She leaned in and kissed Lisa's cheek—easier than hugging around crutches.

Lisa took her arm. "Come. Be comfortable. Sit."

They settled in two folding chairs in the front of rows of empty seats.

Lisa stared ahead as though studying her mother. "The part that stinks, that hurts the most, is I knew her for one year. My grief is more about the years my mother wasted." She dabbed her eyes. "At least she changed, came to faith." Lisa laughed. "Kind of an annoying faith, dragging me all over creation to help her make amends."

They sat in silence until awkwardness made Crystal reach for her crutches. She readied her farewell.

"My brother, Danny, wasted his life too."

Crystal sank back into the chair as Lisa talked once more.

"Your father never changed. Never reconciled with God. I spent so much time angry at Mom and Danny, I forgot how precious they were in God's sight. Hatred colored my life. A shameful fact."

What to say? No words would heal. "Our pasts happened. Our histories will never change, although they can transform our future and work for good."

"So wise for someone so young." Lisa stood and reached out a hand. "Come, look at my mother, then talk with Todd, Spencer, and Theo."

Crystal stood by the head of the casket. She felt large and clumsy and tongue-tied. *What does one say? I don't know these people*. Vernita looked dead. Why did people claim the dead appeared peaceful when they lay in state? Vernita's head lay on an ecru, satin pillow. Her long, gray hair was held in clips, and in lifeless hands, she held a small New Testament. She scanned the scant flowers and cards. The empty mass card holder. Peace settled over her. She'd loved Vernita when her grandmother needed love the most.

Released from the viewing, she stepped over to Todd and his sons. "I'm sorry for your loss. She looks peaceful." *How stupid I sound*. Crystal sat, and an awkward silence followed. *How does one talk to strangers you should've known?* Roxie was right in one thing, they knew little about each other, and Vernita's passing would sever their ties.

After they exhausted their small talk, Crystal said goodbye and stepped into the cool February afternoon. Sunlight bathed her, washed away the gloom from the wake. Early yet. Not even one. What to do?

Pulling out her phone to check her calendar, she found a message. From Jesse.

begin text

JESSE: Call me. Important.

end text

Her heart stuttered, and her finger hovered over the keyboard. She dropped the phone into her purse. If she hurried, she'd be in Jacksboro in time for dinner.

Crystal pushed her dessert plate away on the coffee table. The moment she showed up at home, Mama called Grandma and Grandpa Crabtree, Ma and Pa Jaynes, her late husband's parents, and, of course, Aunt Sunny and her gang. The Snow tradition said if one member celebrated, everyone had to join in. Had she given Mama and Daddy time, they would've invited their entire church, their work colleagues, and the UT football team.

She climbed into her car sated. She smiled as she savored the day. She had a contract with an agent. Family. Love.

And a text she hadn't answered.

Crystal turned on the ignition and reread Jesse's text. She slid the message to the left, hit the trash can icon. She didn't need any drama. Danica caused enough. She didn't need Jesse. He—and Roxie—had to grow up. Had to figure out life on their own.

Chapter 20

Crystal closed her eyes and leaned against the backrest of Leanne's car. Her roommates soft chatter, a susurrus like the wind in the pines. Their murmurs reminded her of Mama's lullabies sung at the end of a long day after playing with goats and horses and eating homemade ice cream. The week had ended, and they'd finished their rental of the recording studio. Their demo included "Aaron's Lament," "Tangled Tango," and three of their older tunes that Danica had no input on. She threatened copyright infringement.

Now the sound techs would work the final magic. Within the week, their album would rest in Davenport's hand. Pure contentment. Peace. The depths of her heart told her this demo would nab them a recording contract.

Phrases about Richie and Conner and her roommates' love lives drifted to the back seat in snatches. Love oozed in their voices, but unlike days past, no jealousy inched its way into Crystal's heart. Roxie was on her way to falling in love with Kenji, leaving Jesse free for her, but for the first time since Crystal met him, she had no desire. Vernita's advice rang true. *If I can't be contented alone, no man will make me happy.*

One man mattered—if, indeed, God identified as purely male. Didn't the Bible say in his own image he created humans? The writer of Genesis stated male and female he created them in his own image. God transcended everything human. Even though the deity was inscrutable, crafting music gave her an inkling of what God felt when he designed the world. Out of nothing, beauty.

"You coming, or are you going to dream in the back seat all afternoon?" Abilene slammed the passenger door.

"Beautiful dreamer." Leanne crooned as she loped to the apartment.

Alone in the car, bathed in potential, Crystal lingered. Why did God bless her so much? Mama found her. She married Daddy. Davenport signed her. Her faithful friends enhanced her life. Her stomach rumbled and reminded her none of them had eaten since breakfast. What time was it now? She clambered out of the car and hobbled into the kitchen. As the door clicked behind her, she stopped. Crystal looked from one roommate to the other. Leanne, clutching a crumpled paper in one hand, stood over Abilene who slumped on the kitchen bar stool.

"What happened? Did someone die?" Crystal asked.

Leanne held out the note. "Someone's dream."

Crystal took the paper and unfurled the note from Danica.

> I need to say this in a note. If I had to speak my mind, I'd say things I believe deep in my heart. Those caustic thoughts would burn. I have no intention of hurting y'all as I've been hurt. I'm moving back to Knoxville. Good luck paying the rent for the apartment I found. Perhaps your Grammy Award will make ends meet. As for me, God's leading me to a solo career. When one door closes, he opens another. I have to use my talent, or I'll lose the gift.

Crystal's diaphragm contracted, and she sank onto a kitchen chair.

"How do we pay the rent?" Tears threatened Abilene's voice.

"Maybe we all move out." Leanne's anger sizzled in her husky hiss. "Let the ... let Danica pay up the lease. The contract's in her name. She enjoys reminding us about this. As she reminds us of all she's done for the group."

"She claims the band is hers." Abilene's jaw clenched so hard the muscles pulsed. "Danica told me if we went on without her, we'd have to change our name. Like she didn't pitch a fit when Davenport suggested our change."

Crystal chewed on her lip. *Am I angry? No. Sad?* She took all the possible steps to reconcile with Danica, and she had prepared for this possibility. No. She wasn't angry. Disappointed, yes, and dismayed about Danica's witness.

She looked at her friends and leaned back in the chair. "Her decision won't ruin our success. We've done everything we could to convince Danica. We've all called her. I drove out to Knoxville, and she didn't have the decency to invite me into her house. We stood on the front lawn like strangers. Reasoning with her and leaving an opening for her to join us didn't move her. I don't know what's going on. I've seen her ego which is as big as ours—"

"Hey. Speak for yourself." Leanne laughed. "Hers is bigger than of all of our conceit combined."

Abilene slapped Leanne's arm and smiled. Tension slipped out of the room.

"We can't do anything more, and no way will I allow Danica's bitterness to ruin our success," Crystal said. "She loses. Not us."

"I never expected our sweet Crystal to move on without everyone happy." Leanne raised a hand and high-fived Crystal, then slunk onto an adjoining chair. They sat in silence until Leanne's stomach grumbled. "I'm hungry."

"We can tell." Abilene turned and looked toward the stove. "After six. We all should be starving."

"Do you mind if I go to Richie's?" Leanne asked.

"I expected as much." Crystal looked up at Abilene. "I'm assuming you'll be with Conner."

"How can we leave you alone at this time? Our demo's finished, and Danica's tantrum left a hole in our band." Abilene said.

"I'm a loner. Maybe I'll write a song. Call the tune, "Danica's a Jerk.""

Leanne and Abilene bit back smiles until Abilene snorted. Crystal and her roommates laughed until they cried.

After wiping away their tears, the two left. Crystal pulled leftovers out of the fridge. Faith. No one pleased God without faith. The verse used to bug her. No faith meant no connection with God. No connection meant no way to find faith. A tortuous circle until one day—she was maybe thirteen—she understood. If she didn't believe, didn't accept her value despite her limitations, how could anything God did for her be grasped? If not grasped, she couldn't enjoy his blessings. Not acting in faith would be like Mama handing her a bowl of ice cream made from goat's cream. If she'd never tasted the homemade treat because she didn't believe goat's milk tasted delicious like Mama said, she'd never have experienced the delight of the gallons she'd eaten.

She arranged the leftovers from their favorite Chinese restaurant, Golden Ginger, on a plate, set it on the microwave turntable, and hit the reheat icon. The microwave hummed.

Believe. Only after believing can you see what God's given you.

Danica has to believe she's valued even if she isn't the primary focus. No one could dump this fact into her head.

If she didn't believe, there was nothing anyone else could do.

The microwave chirped. She opened the door and the aroma of ginger wafted from her lamb dumplings.

Spicy dumplings. She closed her eyes and inhaled the aroma of her favorite seasoning. The image of her dinner shifted to dark hair and eyes of another spicy dumpling.

Guess I'm not as over Jesse as I thought.

Jesse sat shoulder to shoulder with Madison at Nicky's watching the dart game on Friday night.

Geoff stood behind a cute coed with rainbow-colored hair. He held her hand, gripping a dart, as he pressed closer than necessary behind her. "Face the wall. Not the board."

The girl arched her neck and looked over her shoulder into Geoff's face. "Like this."

Jesse felt the sexual tension as he watched. His own heart thrummed against his rib cage, and his gut ached.

Geoff tugged her closer, his lips next to her ear and whispered something. She giggled.

Jesse's buddy on the prowl did not provide an interesting evening. Itching to move around, wanting to annihilate his own lust, he turned toward Madison. "Want to shoot pool?"

Madison smiled and stood. At the table, she racked the balls and executed a break shot. She sank the number eleven ball into the corner pocket.

Jesse stood back and watched, a bit awed as Madison pocketed three other balls. Roxie didn't care for pool and had never mastered the game. Madison's skill gave him few chances to play. Sadly, pool was the only action she liked. Madison never wanted to walk or swim or hike.

Heaven forbid he suggest she join him for a run. Roxie tried but was so slow, he quit asking. He, not her. Why didn't he understand what he did to Roxie? All Madison loved was dinner out, shopping, and sex.

He had given in to the latter a few more times. The struggle to behave like a Christian slipped out of his grasp from her continual closeness, her perfume, her makeup. Abstinence was an impossible task. The Bible had to be updated.

Why did God demand the impossible?

If impossible, he needed to end his relationship with Madison.

Near the end of the third game, Geoff ambled over to Jesse and Madison. He'd looped his arm around the pretty rainbow girl. "Amira and I are heading out. Do you mind?"

Madison sidled up to Jesse. Her scent of vanilla surrounding him. "No. We'll be hitting my place once I whoop Jesse one last time." She turned her pretty face and gazed at him. Her hooded eyes smoldered, so he thought they'd catch on fire. Her lips parted. Her breath, a mixture of alcohol and fruit from the red wine she favored when she "wasn't drinking."

His blood heated, and he stepped away. *No. We're not.*

Geoff winked. "Have fun." He and Amira walked out of Nicky's, their arms wrapped around each other. Geoff's hand slipped into the back pocket of her jeans drawing Jesse's eyes to an area of Amira he didn't need to imagine.

Time to end things with Madison. I can't go on like this. How many times had he tried? Apparently without success.

Madison's hip pressed against him as she chalked her cue stick. His resolve weakened. *Break up tomorrow?*

Madison turned toward Jesse and looped her arms around his neck. She kissed him. The full, warm lips pulled him in. He burned as the kiss deepened. If he weren't standing in the middle of Nicky's, he'd lose all control. He broke loose.

"I'm tired of pool. Want to head to my place?"

Yes. Breath battled against his tightened chest and strained against his ribs. "No!" The word came out too loud. Jesse shrugged out of Madison's grasp.

"Am I so repulsive?"

No, no, no. Jesse inhaled to slow his heart. "You're too attractive. But ..."

She crossed her arms and scowled. "Is this a 'you love me but are not *in* love with me' moment?" Her voice dripped sarcasm.

"No." Honesty set him free. He didn't love Madison. Like Roxie, she was wrong for him. Unlike Roxie, he'd never love her. "We can't sleep together anymore."

"Are you gay?"

He scoffed. He'd failed so easily so many times with her. "You don't understand. I'm a Christian—a really bad Christian, but still, I believe what the Bible says. Our relationship is wrong. I'm not being fair to you. I'll drive you home, but this is our last date and my last time in Nicky's."

"Don't bother." Madison grabbed her purse. "I'll find my own way home."

Jesse watched. Worry troubled him. Should he call an Uber for her so she could get to her apartment safely?

She settled at the bar, one stool down from some fellow. She turned her head and eyed the stranger. The dip of her head and her smile said, 'I'm available.' Madison wouldn't be alone. Safe with a stranger, though?

He'd been a stranger once. Jesse straightened his back. God didn't force him to act against his will. He'd allow Madison to solve her own problem. At this moment, he was going to solve his own.

Kenji dropped Roxie off at her apartment. His kiss tingled to her toes. If only she were married. She had to find someone soon. They broke apart as she studied him in the porch light. He rivaled Jesse in looks. Dark hair and eyes, like Jesse. Loved the outdoors, like Jesse. If she had a checklist, he'd click all the points. Why didn't she love him?

"I'll call you later in the week." Kenji kissed her forehead and trotted back to his car.

Roxie waved as he drove off, then let herself into her empty apartment. Roommates still out. By eleven, she settled into bed and grabbed her phone to check her texts. The cell had been vibrating in her pocket all night, but people who paid more attention to their phones than to the person they were with aggravated her.

She answered most texts with emojis or one-word answers until she read Crystal's.

What? Her text needed to be answered with a phone call. She hit Crystal's contact. The phone rang once when her sister picked up. "Why did Danica move out?"

"Hello to you too." Crystal's laugh told Roxie that Danica's fit didn't bother Crystal as much as Roxie thought the action should.

"I told you in my text."

"Why now when she could be included in the contract? Snow in the Hollow is a good band, and knowing you, everyone will be front and center in turns. Recording companies would be run by idiots if they didn't sign you. What kind of fool is she?"

"Don't say fool."

"Don't quote Scripture. I didn't say *raca*. I used an English synonym for the Aramaic term."

Crystal groaned.

"Why is she so ... idiotic?"

"Aren't all of us?"

"Speak for yourself." Roxie laughed.

"You're retaking Stearns's class. This action nails you into the idiot category."

Roxie growled. "Why do I love you?"

"I'm pretty and talented, and when I make millions, you'll get a share."

"There is that."

"Pride overworks our sense of self. We think we deserve more than we have, and so we lose all we have. Danica lost control of her ego."

They chatted for an hour. When Roxie hung up, only one line of conversation stuck. "We think we deserve more than we have, and so we lose all." *I didn't deserve Jesse.*

Too late for do-overs.

Not too late for corrections, though. She had to call Kenji.

Chapter 21

In mid-March, spring arrived in full force. The waters through the Smokies ran fast, and kayaking called Jesse. He phoned Geoff. "Hey, bud, time to knock off an item on our bucket list?"

"Skydive?" Geoff laughed at his stale joke.

Jesse would never jump out of a plane. Everything else was fair game. "No. Shoot the Sinks."

"Almost as good."

"Grab your kayak. I'll pick you up in fifteen minutes."

An hour later, Jesse pulled his truck into the last parking spot at the Sinks. He clenched his teeth as he loosened one ratchet strap holding his green and Geoff's red kayak to the bed of the truck. So many people gawked at the rapids flowing through the section called the Elbow—the sharp bend rounding the Sinks. He drew in a deep breath to settle his nerves. *This crowd? Witnesses to my foolishness?*

"Looks like we'll have a cheering session." Geoff worked a ratchet strap on the other side of the truck bed.

Jesse threw the straps he loosened into the truck bed and stepped to the back of the truck. "How cold's the water, do you think?"

Geoff hauled his kayak off the truck. "Under fifty, for sure."

"The chill will keep my brain functioning when I drown." Jesse laughed to hide his shiver as a breeze funneled between Meigs Mountain and the Little River.

"Chickening out? I've shot rougher rapids."

Jesse turned toward the crowds gawking at the rock-lined cascades where the Little River made an S-curve under the bridge on Little River Road. Raging water slewed between giant boulders. Trees and mountains extended beyond the narrow gorge. Years ago, logs had jammed the river bend. Loggers solved the problem by dynamiting the jam. The results were a magnificent cascade through towering boulders and a river with an altered course. Spring rains and runoff created torrents today. They'd have ample room to navigate around the boulders and the one passage through the cascade to calmer pools.

Jesse studied the river, and his head spun as he saw the well-known signs dotting the river's edge. Danger. Drowning Risks. No Swimming. These never deterred the kayakers determined to prove their mettle.

Or they never daunted the crazy kayakers.

"Dreaming ain't gonna get the deed done." Geoff tossed Jesse his wetsuit. "Suit up, dude."

The men stepped off trail and stripped off their jeans and tees down to their diving shirts and shorts. Shivering in the cold they wriggled into wetsuits and water shoes. Back at the truck, they locked their clothes in the cab.

Jesse trembled even as the neoprene warmed his skin. His dry mouth begged him to back out, but he wasn't a coward. He and Geoff had trained. Had planned their route and their techniques of navigating this challenge as they conquered other icons of the Smokies. While hiking Middle Prong or up to LeConte or the Tennessee portion of the Appalachian Trail or Mount Cammerer or Rocky Top where they sang UT's theme song of the same name, they bragged about how they'd maneuver the class V rapids here.

They'd already kayaked the whitewater of the Obed, 'Devil's Jump' up on the Plateau, and other rapids. Never anything with water so high. So fast.

"Not chickening out, are you?"

Jesse shook his head.

"As I said earlier, dreamin' won't shoot the Sinks."

Jesse grabbed his kayak. "Let's do this."

They portaged across the road and upriver until they found a suitable spot in quiet water about a quarter mile upstream. After slipping on life jackets, they adjusted their helmets.

Geoff hopped in and shoved away from shore.

Jesse's stomach twisted. A voice inside his gut said to back out, but Geoff was already streaming down river. *Too late.* He shunted off from shore. His kayak wobbled as the water grabbed him and raced midstream. He inhaled as he gained control, then blew out his breath. If this was the easy stuff, what lay ahead? He paddled and righted his vessel. The kayak shot down the river.

Geoff, several yards ahead, his red kayak bright against the brown water, raised his paddle over his head. Jesse imagined his whoop as he hit the first of the rapids. Geoff dipped the blade back into the water and worked the river.

The rushing river roared in Jesse's ears. Water splashed over him in a light spray foreshadowing the rapids ahead.

Geoff hit the Elbow at the S-curve.

Rapids now seized Jesse's boat. Too frightened to panic, he paddled. Swifter water propelled him downstream toward death. He needed to back out of his stupid stunt. *The shore. Not too late.* Jesse made a stab for dry land, for sanity. Water raged against his vessel as he paddled toward shore. He dipped the blade, shoved against powerful currents. Every muscle in his arms strained and water cascaded over him. *The shore. Hit the shore!* The river had made up its own mind. Little River twisted his kayak and aimed it broadside for the Sinks.

No!

He stroked until he thought every fiber in his biceps would shred. *Not broadside, Maxwell. Don't*—Suddenly, he remembered he shouldn't hit the Elbow head-on. He shoved right.

Thrust left.

The main curve hit.

When Jesse reached the top of the Elbow, water surged over him. Froze exposed skin.

Cold. So cold.

He wobbled left. Water sloshed over the tilting kayak. Twisted it.

Righted.

More icy water. Ahead of him more raging torrents.

Paddle. Paddle. He breathed as he gained control. *Going to survive.*

Without warning, Jesse's kayak torqued right. Like the hand of a giant, the force of the rapids capsized his boat.

He went under. Flipped free of his vessel.

Jesse's shoulder slammed against a boulder. Pain ratcheted down his arm, the agony paralyzed his limb as he strove to push up. To surface. To breathe.

Water somersaulted him, and he bounced off another rock like a pool ball against bumpers. His arm regained movement—excruciating pain. Jesse shoved against the granite boulders like a rogue cue ball on a pool table. The rocks kept him submerged.

His feet hit bottom. He pushed up with his legs. His right one snagged under a rock. Currents pushed him downstream. The rock wedged him in place. Jesse struggled to free his foot as his lifejacket forced him up. Pain ricocheted along his lower leg.

He clenched his mouth tight against a gasp. The current torqued his leg and agony fiercer than any he'd ever felt tore through him. He had to pull free. Had to.

Using the last of his energy, he freed his leg. The agony ratcheted up his limb and through him. The pain made him dizzy, like he'd black out any minute.

His brain begged for consciousness. His lungs begged for air. Panic demanded he inhale. The current forced him under until water gushed into his lungs with a burning power.

Roxie sat in her living room bingeing on the Hallmark Channel. Without a man in her life—and she didn't miss Kenji at all, despite his being gorgeous—life was lonely without love.

She didn't look for anyone else. Two weeks ago, she realized she had to correct her course, so instead of dating anyone, she'd watch true love on TV.

Her phone rang. She paused the romance and lifted her cell. *Jesse's mother?* Her heart hammered. Joyce wouldn't call her unless something awful happened. Maybe Arlo crashed his car again—another DUI? She stared at her cell. Maybe Bradley? Her finger refused to push the answer button. *Voice mail's going to pick up. This can't go to voice. Can't.* She connected. "Is everything okay?" Her voice shook as if western winds blew in a March snowstorm.

Sobs answered her.

"Jesse?" A chill trembled every muscle, as she realized Joyce called about the one person she loved. Roxie choked for air. "Is Jesse okay?"

"No."

"Oh, Lord God." Her only prayer was to whisper the same three words over and over.

Joyce's sobs quieted. "I'm sorry. He's not …"

Not dead, oh please say not dead.

"He's hurt. Bad hurt, broken up. May not make it."

"Where is he?"

"We're at UT Hospital. He's in surgery, and things don't look good."

Roxie's heart stuttered. She clenched and released her fingers, trying to force her voice to work while Joyce cried on the other end. "What happened?"

"Geoff says they shot the Sinks. Jesse …"

Roxie hyperventilated as she waited for Joyce to continue. She and Jesse argued with fury when he wanted to whitewater kayak.

"Jesse took the turn over the rapids broadside. Went under. If a doctor from Ohio wasn't viewing the falls, Jesse would be … They fished him out … He wasn't …"

Roxie couldn't breathe as if the frigid spring waters clogged her lungs.

"He wasn't breathing, but still had a pulse. The doctor gave him CPR. Someone had emergency cell service."

Roxie closed her eyes.

"They cleared the parking lot waiting for the rescue helicopter. Medivac landed. Raced him to UT. Triaged him. Rushed him to surgery. Worried about hyperthermia, broken bones, under water too long, so he may be brain dead." The words rushed out of Joyce's mouth like the raging waters of the Sinks.

Roxie grasped her throat. Struggles for breath froze her thoughts.

"They've been working for an hour now. A doctor gave an update. Still not stable …"

Again, Roxie waited while her chest constricted like she had a heart attack. The pain sat on her sternum like one of the boulders Jesse had hit.

"I know you're not together any longer, but you're still my family. You two still love each other. His dad, brother, and I are in the waiting room in the surgical wing at UT now. Please come."

"No need to ask. I'll be there in ten minutes."

Still love each other? Hope resurrected as Roxie raced to her car, her sprint a speed Jesse would've been proud of. *Joyce says he loves me.*

Her driving speed would've delighted Richard Petty. *I need my sister.* After she crossed the Tennessee River and hit Cherokee Trail, the final approach to UT, she called Crystal.

The phone rang.

Rang again.

Answer, answer, answer.

Voice mail picked up. Seeing as the time was ten a.m. in Nashville, Crystal had to be available. Restaurants didn't open until eleven. Gigs at honky-tonks came at night. Crystal *was* available. She left what information she could as she pulled into the parking garage. Late morning. The car climbed each level of the lot. Higher. Higher. No spot and old people crawling in their vehicles searching for a place to park.

Sunlight cascaded over her as she hit the highest level, the one section exposed to the elements. She parked near the stairwell and elevator access of the nearly empty tier. Chirping her car locked, she ran to the stairs and flung open the metal door which clanged against the wall behind her. She'd run faster than an elevator. Down. Down. Down and out.

Crystal sat on her bed towel-drying her hair. They had to leave for their set at Margaritaville in an hour. She hummed as she tossed the towel to the far side of the bed and grabbed her comb. One benefit of no Danica was she had no roommate anymore. Abilene had returned to her single bed in Leanne's room. Abilene laughed and said if she shared a bed, she needed to cuddle. Crystal wasn't her type.

The downside of no Danica and her lack of rent was having to play the lunchtime crowds on Broadway for extra cash.

She ran her comb through her hair. Dreams resurrected as she worked the snarls. Davenport had submitted their demo for a possible contract to Tennessee Notes and Capitol Music. Capitol Music? She closed her eyes and smiled. Was signing with the big boys possible? Join the music stars at Capitol Music? She hummed and combed.

Life was good.

With the last snarl cleared, she tossed her comb aside and reached for her braces. Her phone sat on the bedside table. Maybe Davenport called? It was Saturday, but hey, without dreams, nothing happened.

She picked up her phone. *Roxie voice mailed?* Her sister never called unless something serious happened. Never would she leave a voice mail. Rox texted. Crystal frowned and tapped the icon. "Jesse's in UT. Surgery. May not make ..."

Her jaw dropped as she listened to her sister's panicked voice. Tears sounded in the timbre. Crystal's hand shook as she hyperventilated.

Sobbing garbled the rest of the message. All she heard at the end was that Roxie needed her.

This can't be. Crystal dialed her sister, but Roxie didn't pick up. After disconnecting, Crystal texted.

"Call me. I'm on my way."

She tossed her phone aside. "Leanne. Abilene. Come. Quick."

Abilene scurried into Roxie's room.

Crystal bit back the tears threatening. "I've got to go to Knoxville."

Abilene's brows knit together. "We're playing Margaritaville soon."

Leanne joined Abilene.

What to do? I have to go.

"What's wrong?" Abilene sunk on the bed next to Crystal. She gripped her hand.

"Jesse's in the hospital, and his chances aren't good."

"No!" Leanne's fist flew to her lips.

Abilene inhaled. "You need to go. For Roxie. For him."

"We have the gig." Crystal looked around the room but focused on nothing.

"Abilene's right. You have to go. We'll manage."

"How?" Even as Crystal worried, peace crept into her heart molecule by molecule. She hoped she could see Jesse before he ... no. He wouldn't die.

"No one listens to the musicians in these chain restaurants." Abilene chuckled. "I've been playing more lead guitar. I'll fake it. Won't sound like a fiddle, but tourists don't care."

"Go." Leanne plopped next to Crystal. She handed Crystal her left brace.

Abilene fished out a pair of wide-legged linen pants and a powder-blue tee. "You look more beautiful—if possible—in blue. Hurry. Jesse will survive. We'll pray."

In the corner of the UT waiting room, Crystal found Roxie seated in a plastic chair. Her head leaned against the wall, her legs stretched in front of her. Crystal hurried to her. As she slid into the next chair, Crystal placed her hand on Roxie's shoulder. "Rox?"

Roxie startled and sat up. "Sorry. I must've dozed."

"What's the news?"

"Right now, the worst is a broken femur and shattered tibia."

"Leg bones?"

"The tibia's here." Roxie ran her hand along her shin bone. "The femur." She tapped her thigh."

"A broken femur is serious."

"Nearly bled out from his break. He shattered ribs, cracked his clavicle, broke his humerus, and has a concussion." Roxie gave a rueful grin. "All those c-sounds make me sound like a songwriter."

Crystal fingered her sister's hair. "The concussion? How bad?"

"No one knows. The good thing about drowning in this weather is the cold preserved his brain. He didn't die and, hopefully, doesn't have a serious brain injury. They won't know until he wakes up. Thankfully, he's always been careful and wore a lifejacket, wetsuit, and a good helmet. He cracked the helmet in two, but it saved him. He's been in surgery for close to four hours." Roxie pointed to an LED board following the progress of those in surgery. "According to the last update, he had another hour or two under the knife. Nerve damage. Tibia so shattered they need a rod. If they don't fix it ..." Roxie looked away, her breathing rapid and loud.

Crystal pulled her sister to her shoulder as she surveyed the room. She spoke after a few minutes. "Where are Joyce, Arlo, and Bradley?

"After the report, they went to grab lunch or a coffee— or in Arlo's case, a beer somewhere. My stomach wouldn't let me."

"I need coffee. I saw a Starbucks in the lobby. Join me?"

Roxie yawned. Then nodded. "I've been falling asleep here—sort of an aftershock."

Crystal and Roxie took the elevator to the main level and wandered the curved, tiled hall. Lining the wide, white walls, cushioned benches invited people to linger. Down here, no antiseptic smells assaulted them. Friendly aromas wafted—hamburger from the cafeteria. Coffee from the green and white Starbuck's kiosk.

"Two hot mocha lattes with whipped cream." Crystal inserted her debit card into the card reader. After paying, she joined Roxie at the pickup counter. "Got us full-fat, lots of sugar. Since we need comfort, I ordered extra whipped cream."

Roxie smiled her thanks. She and Crystal waited in silence for a minute.

"I don't believe this." Roxie grabbed Crystal's arm.

Crystal followed her sister's gaze. The corridor held the usual characters—elderly couples walking hand in hand, families trying to corral children, a mom being wheeled toward the exit holding her newborn. Young men. A dark-haired girl about their age.

"How dare that floozie show up here."

"What are you talking about, Roxie?"

The barista called their names.

"Let's grab our coffee and go." Roxie's face reddened. Her eyes turned flinty. "I want to get back to the waiting room."

"What's wrong?"

"Nothing. I need to get out of here." Roxie grabbed their coffees and strode toward the elevator, not waiting for Crystal.

Crystal scurried after her sister.

"Roxie? Is that you?"

Crystal turned. The dark-haired girl she'd seen as they waited for their coffee strode toward them.

"Keep moving," Roxie hissed. She jerked her hands and coffee leaked from the covers.

"Slow down. I can't go as fast as you." As though to prove her point, Crystal stumbled.

"Roxie. Wait. I need to talk to you," the girl called from behind them.

Roxie skidded to a stop and spun around. She took a step toward the woman who called her. "What are you doing here?"

"Geoff told me about Jesse. How is he?"

Roxie glared. Her frown deepened, and the cups shook in her hand.

"Roxie." Crystal grabbed her sister's arm and steadied the sloshing coffee. "What's wrong?" She looked at the woman. "I'm Roxie's sister, Crystal." She glanced at her sister. "Jesse's condition is hard on Rox."

"For me too. Even though Jesse and I broke up, a day hasn't gone by I haven't regretted not trying to reconcile. I've started going to church with my friend to see if there's anything to his religious stuff."

"Faith isn't stuff." Roxie turned, took a step toward the elevators. *No. Won't run.* She pivoted toward the woman. "Madison, he's with me now. You best leave."

Madison's eyes narrowed. "Don't lie to me. I know you broke up. He said his decision was final." She looked at Crystal. "If anything, Jesse's moving on to your sister."

Roxie stepped forward, her eyes like flint. But her rock-hard glare wasn't aimed at the woman. She directed her scowl toward Crystal.

Moving on to me? The woman's words scrambled Crystal's thoughts. She'd seen Jesse once since the breakup when he came out to Nashville. She told him she wasn't interested and needed no man. She never answered his texts except to tell him to forget Roxie. "I don't know what makes you say such things."

"You're oblivious, Crystal."

Crystal's jaw dropped.

Madison toyed with her earring and studied the floor as though her thoughts were written there. At last, she looked up. "Jesse and I had a good thing going, but I didn't understand his religion obsession. I love him."

Roxie tossed the cup carrier at Madison.

Madison yelped and jumped back as she pulled her shirt covered in hot coffee away from her chest.

"Roxie!" Crystal couldn't utter another word. She worked her mouth trying to force out words.

Roxie pivoted and ran down the hallway.

Crystal stood frozen. She peered at the coffee, then at Madison. "I'm so sorry. I don't know—"

Madison waved her hand and silenced Crystal. Her voice gentled. "Don't be naive, Crystal. Jesse loves you. Always has, but your psycho sister trapped him. He won't go back to her. Maybe he won't come back to me, but I love him, and I'm going to stay by him until he heals." Madison strode toward the ladies' room leaving Crystal standing on the edge of a puddle of now cooled coffee.

Chapter 22

The door to the restroom opened. Roxie, sitting on the john, stuffed her fist into her mouth to stifle her sobs. Even though she hid in the stall, the woman would hear her distress. The last thing she needed was a stranger trying to comfort her.

What a fool. What did I do to Madison?

The water turned on at the sink. Paper unfurled from the automatic towel dispenser. More water. Paper. High heels clicked on the tile floor.

Tears turned to panic, and Roxie gnawed on her knuckles. *Will you leave? Please.* Roxie shifted on the seat, and the automatic eye flushed the toilet. She bounced off as images of E.coli, or worse, splattering her jeans made her cringe. The thoughts broke through her self-pity, and Roxie smiled in spite of herself. Here she stood, locked in a stall. Her hand reached for the latch. She held the bolt. Hesitated. Instead of leaving like an adult, Roxie leaned against the wall and peeked through the crack between the door and the support.

Madison scrubbed her clothes with a paper towel.

Guilt crawled up Roxie's spine, a spider making every millimeter of her skin crawl. Her hand trembled as she reached for the latch once more. She'd face her nemesis. Roxie stepped out.

Madison eyed her through the mirror. Her lips tightened.

"I'm sorry for what I did." Roxie closed her eyes and leaned against the support of the two stalls. "I have no excuse except pride." *Insecurity. Fear of rejection. Everything Crystal tells me.*

Madison glared into the mirror. Pure hatred glinted there.

"I'll pay for cleaning or ..." Madison's simmering silence froze Roxie's voice. She wished to be like Alice in Wonderland and shrink away, so small no one would ever find her again.

The door opened as another woman stepped into the room.

Madison squared her shoulders and walked out. Every movement sophisticated. Controlled.

After washing her red, swollen face, Roxie rubbed hand lotion from her purse over her skin hoping the oil would make her face less blotchy. Her shoulders slumped as she looked at her sad reflection in the mirror. Nothing would ever ease her pain or guilt or jealousy. Unable to stall—or hide—in the washroom any longer, Roxie returned to the waiting room. Staring straight ahead, avoiding eye contact with any of the anxious people waiting on their loved ones, she found a cushioned seat in a row of similar chairs facing the LED screen showing the progress of those in surgery. Jesse's ID indicated no advancement. She scanned to the left and right of her chair. His family hadn't returned. She assumed Crystal went home ashamed of her. What a fool she'd been. By now she had alienated everyone—Crystal, Jesse, his family. She picked up a magazine and flipped pages. Colorful ads, pages of print, articles, opinions spun past her eyes. After tossing one aside, she lifted another. *Popular Mechanics.* Scanned the print, saw nothing. People came and went, a tide of humanity waiting for operations to end.

A half an hour passed. Jesse's older brother, Bradley, stepped into the waiting room. He held his mother's elbow as though Joyce needed help balancing. Arlo didn't return. They slipped into seats on either side of Roxie. Friends. How good it felt not to be alone. Roxie turned to Jesse's older brother. "Where's Jesse's dad?"

Bradley quirked his mouth and tipped his fist toward his lips.

Roxie nodded in understanding. Jesse said so little about his family. Like her and her sisters, ghosts haunted him.

"Any news?" Joyce asked.

Roxie turned to Jesse's mother. "Not since you left." As though to prove her a liar, the LED board blinked, and Jesse's identification number moved from the category "in surgery" to "in recovery."

Roxie leaped to her feet. "He's out." She turned to pick up her purse and sweater. There, behind her in the corner sat Geoff who'd showed up at some point. Next to Geoff were Madison *and* Crystal. Pain rumbled deep in her chest like an alien pounding its way through you. After a long slow blink chasing away—what? Hurt? Jealousy? Shame? Roxie strode to the reception desk, hoping she looked determined and strong rather than like a sniveling child wanting to curl up in mommy's arms. "What's the news on Jesse Maxwell?" She pointed to the board. "I see he's out of surgery. When can I see him?"

"Who are you?" The receptionist looked up from her computer screen, but her fingers remained on the keyboard. Kind eyes glittered behind bifocals.

"Roxie Snow, his ..." What could she say? She'd speak in faith. "I'm his fiancée." The Maxwells now crowded around her at the desk, so close their breath brushed against her neck.

"I'm sorry. I can only give information to his next of kin." She looked at her computer and clicked her mouse. "He didn't name a fiancée when they admitted him. I can't give you any information." Her voice gentled from the businesslike voice she'd used when she first spoke. She looked over to the Maxwells, all business once more. "Can I help you?"

"We're Jesse Maxwell's family. I'm his mother, Joyce. This is his brother, Bradley."

The receptionist wiggled the mouse once more. "He's not in the recovery unit yet. I'll call you when the doctor's ready to give you an update." The receptionist looked at Roxie and shifted her gaze to Joyce. "Can we share information with his fiancée?"

"Fiancée?" Joyce glanced at Roxie, and a smile broke the tension of her face. "Absolutely. Roxie's the same as family."

For the first moment since Jesse's accident, Roxie breathed without a boa constrictor vising her lungs. Joyce called her family. Still loved her. After four years with Jesse, she should never have doubted. She turned and nearly bumped into Crystal, Madison, and Geoff. She bit her lip and strode away, taking a seat facing the reception. Joyce and Bradley talked to the others. Jealousy or self-loathing or despair muddled her brain. *Why can't I be normal? Why can't I believe?*

Crystal limped toward her and took a seat.

Roxie stared ahead. *Help me, Crystal.*

Her sister took her hand.

Please don't nag me.

Crystal said nothing.

Roxie's breathing quieted. Without speaking to her sister or even looking at her, Crystal heard. So like

God. She bowed her head. He loved her, Roxie Star Snow, unconditionally. Even though she threw coffee at Madison, fought with Jesse, refused to believe in herself, Jesus loved her with a bright, warm, unconditional love. Her pastor's sermons said God's love was greater than any man's. If Crystal's concern hinted at agapē love, how great was God's?

Five minutes passed. Joyce stepped over to Roxie. "We're going to meet the doctor now." She held out her hand. "You two join us."

Roxie sprung to her feet.

Crystal, still seated, asked, "Me too?"

"Absolutely." Joyce held out her other hand. "You're as much family as Roxie. Come."

Roxie glanced at her sister. Shook her nagging suspicions away.

A few steps down an adjacent corridor, the four of them crowded a tiny consultation room of pale green walls lined with upholstered chairs. They sat in silence, playing with their hands or staring straight ahead. The tension. Roxie forced an inhale, strove to breathe as deeply as possible. Air did not want to fill her lungs. The exhale brought no relief. She clenched her hands, loosened her fingers. She tried to rise. Crystal pulled her back. After fifteen minutes that felt like hours, the surgeon, who looked too young to be a doctor, entered and introduced himself as Dr. Wilson. He didn't smile.

Not good. Roxie opened her mouth to beg the doctor for good news. No words formed. She pinched her lips together.

He settled in a chair across from the family and leaned forward. "Jesse's stable for now. Unfortunately, the femur broke through the skin. He broke his tibia and shattered his ulna. We had to insert a rod, but the breaks didn't give us a good purchase for the rod. At the moment, we have his leg stabilized."

"At the moment?" Joyce's voice wavered, and tears clouded her eyes.

"If the bones don't stabilize, or he becomes septic, we may have to amputate.

"No!" Joyce stood. She crossed her arms and turned toward the wall. At last, she turned and faced the surgeon. "I'm a nurse. I've seen doctors fix compound fractures."

"Jesse's breaks are the nastiest I've ever seen. Let's not jump to worst-case scenarios. We may not need an amputation."

Amputate. Jesse runs. You can't

"He also fractured his right humerus. His four broken ribs and clavicle will make every breath painful. Medication will keep things under control." As though relieved he had finished relating the worst of Jesse's situation, the doctor's voice became less clinical. He sounded like he gave a rundown on the daily news—fast and less ominous. "The helmet he wore saved him from a serious concussion, but we still need to monitor him. We can't predict the severity of his brain injury."

"Brain injury?" Joyce slumped back onto the chair, every muscle melting. Her posture imitated Roxie's turtle stance when she had to hide from the world. "He'll be okay?" Joyce's eyes begged the surgeon to give a positive answer. Tears slipped from her soft brown eyes. Bradley held her hand.

"From most of the injuries."

"Most?" Joyce echoed like a child learning to speak.

"Besides the compromised blood flow from the femur, Jesse has a risk of infection causing sepsis."

"What does that mean?" Roxie asked.

"The thigh bone broke through the skin and ruptured blood vessels. A miracle kept him from puncturing the femoral artery and bleeding out. I don't use the term miracle often. The fact Jesse's alive is nothing less than the hand of God, because there's no natural or medical reason he lived."

Roxie trembled as though Jesse's hypothermia from his near drowning swamped her.

"What options do we have to save his leg?" Bradley's authoritative tone showed he was the only one in control of his emotions.

His resonant baritone calmed Roxie's trembling. His smile reassured her. Maybe Jesse had hope yet.

"If he stabilizes, we can send him to Dr. Bernstein at Vanderbilt in Nashville. Dr. Bernstein is an expert orthopedic surgeon. The best I've seen. He's one of three in the country who can stabilize these kinds of breaks using an Ilizarov frame—"

"A what?" Joyce asked.

"An Ilizarov frame is an external fixator. The halo rings are joined together with stabilizers to fix compound fractures. It's attached to the femur and tibia." The doctor pointed to his thigh and shin. "If anyone can fix the breaks, that doctor is Bernstein."

Joyce gnawed on her lips. "When will he be transferred to Vanderbilt?"

"Moving him right now could kill Jesse. We should know in a day or two if we can transfer him to Vanderbilt."

Infection wouldn't set in. Certainty flooded Roxie's soul. Without a doubt. Jesse was going to live.

"He's resting now." Dr. Wilson stood. "The next few hours are critical."

"When can we see him?" Roxie asked.

"He'll be in ICU in about a half an hour. Two visitors at a time. Five minutes. Jesse needs rest."

Jesse opened his eyes in a dim room. Monitors beeped. He shifted, but his leg, rigged in some sort of stabilizer sent shards of pain ripping through him. He turned his head. Mom and Bradley peered down at him. Their eyes confirmed how broken he was. No one needed to tell him. He felt every break and bruise, even as he felt dopey. Morphine or OxyContin or fentanyl muted the pain. Still, any movement made him want to scream.

Mom grasped his left hand. Her mouth moved, but she said nothing he heard.

"Dad would've been here. He's got a welding job, rush, you know how things go." Bradley stuttered and paused. "The customers needed the project finished yesterday."

Welding a beer bottle to his lips. Bradley didn't need to tell him. His brother's run-on babbling instead of his usual, steady speech said Dad was getting pie-eyed. Jesse had no strength to answer. He closed his eyes.

"We have to let you rest." Mom bent and kissed Jesse's forehead. She ran a hand over his head.

Jesse closed his eyes once more. Rustling woke him. Someone held his hand.

"Jesse," Roxie's soft voice spoke of their love. "Thank God, you're alive. I don't know what I'd have done had you died."

He smiled, and the action made his head throb. He praised the Lord for his life. A chance to do things right.

"I love you, Jesse. I'm sorry we fight. Let's never argue again. I need—'

He pulled his hand away with more strength than he thought he had.

Roxie straightened.

For the first time, he saw Crystal standing behind her. He smiled in spite of the pain. Light sparkled in her smile. Rox's sister exuded, what? Everything a Christian should feel, should be. Her faith and love tingled his toes, but his euphoria was probably the fentanyl. Crystal had clarified their relationship the last time they talked.

"Once you're better, we'll get—"

"Stop. Rox, stop."

Her lips twitched like she wanted to smile and frown at the same time.

Through his opiated mind, he recognized the thoughts flowing through her brain, but he had to tell Roxie the truth. God saved his life. Now he had to change. Be the man Christ wanted him to be. "Roxie, I love you more than you can imagine."

She grasped his hand tight in hers. Her eyes looked like hope. Like love.

He had to find the strength to continue before she mistook what needed to be said.

She kissed his forehead.

The soft kiss made him want to hold her. Love her. "I love you more than I can bear."

"Me too." She murmured as she ran a finger over his bandaged head.

How he wanted her touch. Her beautiful smile lit her eyes, blue as the summer sky. He tried to pull his hand away, but all he managed was to loosen his fingers from her grip. "Because I love you, we can't be together anymore."

Confusion clouded her narrowed eyes.

"We are going to destroy each other. Devastate our dreams." How his chest hurt. Pain meds had to be wearing off. He inhaled. Cracked ribs ratcheted the agony. Air wouldn't fill his lungs. Monitors beeped. Disinfectant churned his stomach. Love crushed his soul.

The clock ticked. Roxie spoke. "How can you say that? We've always worked things out. We—"

"Your time is up." A nurse interrupted her. "Jesse needs to rest.

Jesse lifted one finger toward the nurse. Hoped his eyes asked for a minute more. He had to speak, but breathing hurt. "We tried to make our relationship work. For four years. My love for you tortures me. Destroys your dreams. I want you happy." His body hurt too much to continue.

"But—"

Crystal tugged her sister, whispered something in her ear.

Shock showed in Roxie's wide eyes and parted lips. She shook her head. "No. You're wrong."

"I can't ..." Shallow breaths interrupted Jesse's words. He closed his eyes. *What hurts more the speaking or what needs to be said?* He opened his eyes and found Crystal. "You understand, Crys?"

Crystal nodded. "I'll make her see." She tugged Roxie's hand. "We need to let Jesse heal."

Roxie let her sister lead her out of Jesse's room and past the waiting room. She halted in the corridor and looked back toward the ICU.

"Jesse means what he said."

Roxie heard every note of empathy in her sister's voice. She glared her way. "No. You're wrong." She pivoted and stepped toward the elevator.

"Roxie, wait for me."

I won't listen. No. The elevator doors started closing. Roxie hit the button. They slid apart, and she slipped in.

Crystal hobbled toward them.

Roxie thought about reaching for the close button on the console. Instead, she opened the door and held it ajar.

Crystal stepped in. The doors glided shut, and the elevator descended.

Someone jostled Roxie.

Madison. Right behind her in a crowded space, Madison and Geoff stood in the same elevator.

Breathe, girl, breathe. Roxie gritted her teeth to squash the urge to punch Madison in the nose or to grovel for forgiveness for throwing coffee over her high-end clothes or to fall at her feet and beg her to leave Jesse alone. Instead, she stared at the elevator controls and tried to avoid the fact she rode with the woman who took Jesse from her. A manicured finger pressed the stop button. The elevator shuddered to a stop between floors.

"I have a few seconds to speak my mind, then we never need to see each other again." Madison's firm voice said she'd speak her mind.

Roxie reached for the controls to start the elevator.

Madison gripped her arm.

Roxie turned toward her.

"I don't understand your thinking. In Jesse, you had the perfect man, one who would give up everything for you." Madison bit a trembling lip. "Jesse refused to let me see him today, even though I waited hours. I, unlike you, can get the hint. We're through, even though we never really started."

Roxie tightened her muscles to stop her body's trembling. She must look like a terrified dog trembling at her owner's abuse.

Madison's eyes glanced Crystal's way. Her gaze softened and focused back on Roxie. "I'm going to save you from the heartache he inflicted on me. Jesse loves you, but if not for his adoration toward you, Roxie, he'd be with your sister."

Roxie opened her mouth. Shut it again. She sought her sister.

Crystal stood against the wall. She didn't look confused. Crystal understood the truth of Madison's words.

Something Roxie had realized many times. Something she always shoved into the recesses of her soul.

"Jesse will never move on his feelings for her because of you. If you want to be spared the heartbreak I'm feeling, find someone else. When you do, remember Jesse will always love you." She hit the start button. The elevator rumbled back to life.

At the first floor, the door opened. Geoff squeezed Roxie's shoulder as he led Madison past them. His fingers' pressure buckled Roxie's knees. The last of her broken pieces puddled at her feet.

Crystal tried to keep up with Roxie, but her sister's pace was a shade shy of running. Roxie disappeared down the curving corridor, so Crystal halted her sprint. *What would Roxie do?* If her sister was at their family home in Jacksboro, she'd mount a horse, grab her camera and head for the lake. Only in nature did Roxie find herself and feel God. In the city? Who knew where she'd hide?

Crystal didn't need to hurry. She'd find Roxie in time. Their phones had an app called Life 360. With the app, the whole family, except Pearl who always turned off the tracker, stalked each other—especially Mama's sister, Aunt Sunny. Aunt Sunny meddled in everybody's business and had no problem correcting their wrong moves. Sweet Aunt Sunny, a lot like her mother—Grandma Cora, meddling and loving. In her car, Crystal checked her phone. Roxie moved down Cherokee Trail. She would be heading home.

Crystal took her time. Let Roxie settle. At the apartment, she parked. Not bothering to knock, Crystal slipped into the apartment and headed for her sister's bedroom.

Roxie lay on her back. With a comforter tucked over her, she stared toward the ceiling. After a quick peek

Crystal's way, she once more studied the ceiling, making no other move.

Crystal crawled into bed next to Roxie. She unstrapped her braces and dropped them on the floor. She'd be here for however long Roxie needed her. Crystal wriggled under the heavy blanket and snuggled next to Roxie. Crystal took her sister's hand. To her surprise, Roxie let her run her finger over her smooth skin.

Roxie continued to focus upward as though the ceiling hypnotized her. "I should've realized."

"Realized what?"

"I always figured the attraction you and Jesse felt for each other was infatuation. My delusion blinded me. Jesse loves you."

"No, he doesn't." Crystal's heart hammered. She couldn't tell her sister she understood Jesse loved her. She couldn't hurt Roxie. "How can you—"

Roxie turned her head and smiled wanly. "I saw your face in the ICU. Saw the way Jesse looked past me at you."

"He loves you."

"I know." Roxie paused. In her silence, her body relaxed next to Crystal. "When we met, you were so young. Sixteen, weren't you?"

Crystal nodded.

"I remember the doe-eyes you gave him every time he came over. He used to tell me you were cute. Too young and still gawky." Roxie chuckled. "You were. Chicken Crystal we called you. All skin and bones, a long neck and flyaway hair."

"I hated the nickname." Crystal slapped her sister's arm as her face heated.

"Your fists made the issue known." Roxie turned toward Crystal and smiled her sweet grin. "Even when you were small and awkward, we saw the beauty you would become. Jesse told me every time he visited. I should've listened."

Crystal's heart-wrenching crush resurrected.

"His eyes lit up every time he talked to you."

Crystal relived the first moments she'd laid eyes on Roxie's latest boyfriend. She'd broken up with her high school beau Mark and brought Jesse to the homestead. That afternoon, Crystal had been riding Onyx when Jesse and Roxie strode out toward the barn. Roxie grabbed the reins. "Sis. Meet Jesse Maxwell, the man I love." Roxie turned to Jesse. "Crissy-Sissy is our baby sister."

Instead of leading the horse to the stable, Jesse swooped Crystal off and carried her into the barn. She leaned into his chest, tingled at the arms holding her. She felt like a Southern Belle. A heroine saved by a superhero. So in love. "For a while, yes, I had a crush."

"Now your crush has turned to love."

"No." Even as she protested, Crystal understood she never hid her love from Roxie or Jesse.

"During the wedding, you two spent so much time together, I complained to Jesse as we drove home. He claimed the wedding party monopolized me, so he had no one to hang out with. You meant nothing to him. You were a teeny-bopper, too young, my sister, et cetera, et cetera. I figured my man protested too loudly."

"That's why the two of you ditched me in the middle of Georgia like a rotten peach."

Roxie laughed. "Guilty." Her smile revealed Mama's nickname for her—Roxie Star. When Roxie loved, when she believed, she smiled like Vega—a bright and beautiful star. "Not our finest moment." Her brows arched, and she sought Crystal's eyes. "I'm so sorry for my jealousy."

Crystal put a hand over Roxie's lips. "I'll turn twenty in June. I've lived with you all my life. You think I don't know your heart?" They lay in silence as the rosy sunset faded and night deepened.

"Jesse and I are really over?"

Crystal didn't need to answer. She understood. Roxie didn't ask a question.

Roxie shifted. "Do me a favor?"

"Sure."

"Watch over him if they transfer him to Vanderbilt."

"You'll come visit."

"No." She sighed. "If we're through, I have to stay far away from him."

"No, you—"

Roxie put a finger over her lips. She nodded, and Crystal understood what her sister needed to do.

"I will."

"Promise?"

"Of course."

A tear slipped from Roxie's eye. She dashed it away. Another followed. Another. Soon she sobbed.

Crystal held her sister until all tears dried.

"I love him so much."

"I know, and he understands how much."

On Monday morning, an orderly loaded Jesse into an ambulance. They had told him he was stable, but the only stable thing about him was the pain. At the rate he gobbled oxy, he was going to turn into Crystal and Roxie's biological parents, unable to function without a fix. Hopefully, he wouldn't die in the woods, a needle stuck in his arm and left for the wildlife to devour like Roxie's parents had been. The docs at UT swore Dr. Bernstein could save his leg. But what good would that do? His bones were so shattered, he'd never run again even if they saved the useless limb.

At least, Crystal had promised to visit.

Knowing her adoration of her older sister, they'd only be friends. But they'd been close for four years. He'd accept friendship. No drama. No passion. No complications. Like an opioid, the thought settled his body.

Payback. Keeping his leg but being unable to run would be just desserts for all the times he pushed Roxie to move and move fast when they trekked outdoors.

His desires canceled hers.

Yep. Payback.

Crystal's phone rang early Monday morning as she battled traffic heading west to Nashville. *Davenport?* Her heart hammered, and she steered the car onto the shoulder. Good or bad, she couldn't be driving with whatever he had to say. Shifting into park, she answered.

"Kyle Davenport here. I have great news."

"I need a dose of good news right now."

"Bass-Line Music wants to sign you."

She opened her mouth to scream. Not Capitol or Tennessee Notes, but Bass-Line? Greats like Billy-Goat Evans and Nan Ferguson sang for them. Grammy nominees only, those two never nabbed a prize, but for sure, Snow in the Hollow would.

"Are you still there?"

She shuddered at her daydreaming while Kyle Davenport gave her the greatest news ever. "I am." She glanced in the rearview mirror to be sure she wasn't interfering with morning commuters.

"They want to rush the release of 'Tangled Tango.' They thought the demo was just about perfect."

"For real?"

"Indeed. They want to tweak a few numbers and need photos for the album cover. We've set up a few dates."

"I'm heading to Nashville now. I'll talk to the band. When do we sign?"

"I'll email the contract."

Crystal glimpsed a patrol car pulling in behind her. "I've got to go. I pulled off Route 40 to talk, and now a cop is checking up on me."

"Route 40 during rush hour in Knoxville? No need to park on the side of the road. You should be stopped on the highway."

"Not quite so bad, but close."

"One quick note. If your lead guitarist is going to join you, she needs to make up her mind now."

"I'll call her. If I don't get back to you, you'll know Snow in the Hollow is a trio." Crystal clicked off and rolled down the passenger window as the cop approached.

He squinted across the passenger seat at her. "Everything okay?"

Crystal's smile had to have told him absolutely perfect.

Back in traffic, she dialed Danica. Her friend—former friend—disconnected the call on the second ring.

Crystal shook her head. *If you don't believe, you don't receive.*

Chapter 23

On Friday, Crystal left Bass-Line's studios and drove down Music Row. The iconic street didn't look like an industry-dominated neighborhood. Sears Craftsman cottages or stone-fronted homes lined the road making the music business district homey, a Hollywood screenshot depicting middle-America. She imagined parents cooking in the kitchen and kids in front of the TV. These lovely homes didn't house families but the music industry. Funny how looks deceived.

Navigating traffic and tourists and trolleys, she clenched the steering wheel until she pulled into Vanderbilt's parking garage. Once more, she stepped into a surgical waiting room and found a middle-aged nurse at the reception.

"I'm here for Jesse Maxwell."

"Your name?"

She gave the lady her name, and the nurse tapped her keyboard. "Dr. Bernstein took Jesse in for surgery around noon. No update." She handed Crystal Jesse's case number so she could check his progress on the LED board.

Crystal's leg jiggled as she sat on the edge of the seat. The time inched toward three. Every passing minute, the time slowed even more. Within an hour, only a few people lingered in the waiting room. No one she recognized entered or left which meant no one but her waited on Jesse. His mom, a nurse in Blount Memorial, still hadn't made the trip to see her son. Joyce claimed her hospital hours and the welding shop kept the family away. More than likely, his father's issues tied her to Townsend.

Waiting on Jesse without her sister felt odd, like Mario without Luigi. Bert and no Ernie. Roxie, resigned to the truth about Jesse and her, stayed at UT.

Plugging in her earbuds, Crystal listened to the final take of the song that had to replace "Barefoot in the Hollow." Because Danica threatened copyright infringement, they had to come up with a last-minute replacement.

After an hour, she paced the room and studied the surgery LED board. To fill the time more than keep awake, she drank lots of coffee from the stand in the corner of the room. Sipping coffee, she stared out the window which offered one view—the parking lot. She counted cars, checked her phone for the time, drank more coffee. Three hours after she arrived, Jesse was wheeled into his room.

With directions from the nurse at reception, she scrambled through the maze of the hospital. Up one wing, down another until she found his room. She halted and stared at the room number. The door stood ajar. Did she dare step inside? She had to, but to see Jesse alone and in pain? Did she have the nerve?

Her legs ached, and her stomach churned like Mama making butter.

She forced herself to move forward. A tiny step took her into the room. She halted. There he was. Jesse lay in the hospital bed, hooked up to monitors, with an IV needle inserted into his hand. He looked so small and fragile. Tears welled up in her eyes, and she bit her lip to keep from crying out.

He slept—or appeared to. She stole toward the bed, not wanting to wake him. As she neared, she saw the pain etched on his face. He was far from resting peacefully.

Her heart ached, and she fought back the tears. She didn't want him to see her crying. The sight of him in so much pain caused her to sink onto the chair next to his bed. She reached out her hand. Afraid to touch him, to add to his hurt, she pulled her arm back and rested her hands in her lap.

Jesse's right arm still rested in the sling from UT. Aside from the concussion, the broken humerus, collarbone, and ribs were the least of his injuries. His left leg lay outside the thin white covers. A large metal hoop encircled his thigh. Supports traveled to two smaller circles surrounding the lower leg which was bent a few degrees at the knee. Pillows supported the apparatus. Rods bored through his red skin, swollen and so tight, she thought his skin would burst like a balloon.

Every axon in her body fired into her nerves like electrical shock tossing her stomach and tightening her breathing. Seeing Jesse screwed together like an erector set revolted her. The contraption holding Jesse's leg together had the makings of a medieval torture device. So much pain in order to heal.

"Crystal. Hi." Jesse sounded small and weak. The effects of the anesthesia sounded in the soft volume.

She ran her hands along her jeans and wriggled tension out of her fingers. The vision of Jesse, the understanding of the pain he was under, made her palms sweat.

His left hand snaked through the rails and reached for her. When she lay her fingers in his, he gripped them with surprising strength, warm and full of life. "Thanks for coming."

"Of course. Your mom called me. She said work tied them up, or they'd be here."

He didn't let go of her, but he tipped the fingers of his right hand in a drinking motion. "Dad's working on his hobby. Why Bradley lives at home is beyond me."

How indeed? Mama and Daddy would have to be dying not to show up at a time like this. How do I answer? "Your father's gotten worse since I've known him."

Jesse closed his eyes. "Glad you're here." He squeezed her hand, and a comfortable silence filled the room. Along with the scent of food.

The smell of meatloaf or chicken or something yummy wafted down the hall. Dinner time. A few minutes later, a worker placed a tray on the bedtable next to Jesse. Her stomach growled, and she wrapped her arm around her middle to quiet the noise. "Want me to help you with your dinner?" *Eat the meal for you?* Her blueberry yogurt gulped down during her noontime break had long been digested.

"Sure."

Crystal lifted the heavy brown plastic lid covering a plate taking up most of the dinner tray. Beneath the cover sat tepid water in two brown, plastic mugs, and a tea bag. Jell-O. Bouillon. "A big brouhaha for lukewarm, flavored water. Trays, delivery, heavy covers. Should've been filet mignon."

"Not hungry. You eat."

"Not me. I'll never be hungry enough for gelled sugar and salty bouillon." Crystal maneuvered the table over the bed and fixed Jesse's tea with a little sugar. She pressed the button to raise the head of the bed.

Jesse groaned as the bed rose.

She cringed. "Sorry."

"On pain meds. Not so bad." Jesse pushed the tray away.

"You need something to eat. If you don't, they'll never let you out of this joint."

"The way I feel now? Sounds good."

Crystal stood and supported herself against the bed, letting the bar hold her weight. She lifted the cup, but her braces and balancing against the bed bars made her feel like a marionette balanced clumsily with strings and ready to collapse. She'd dump the tea all over him. She chuckled.

Jesse shifted his gaze toward her. "What's so funny?"

"With my balance issues, I figured out why the tea water isn't hot."

He raised his eyebrows.

"I won't scald you when I fall on top of you with the tea."

"Sit." He patted the mattress.

"I don't want to hurt you."

"You'll take my mind off my leg." He winked.

Her face heated, but she lowered the rails and sat on the mattress. "Am I hurting you?"

He smiled. "Never."

The thought of sitting so close to feed him nagged her. So intimate. Too soon after his breakup. *Maybe I didn't heed Vernita's advice about men after all. Still looking for one.* She glanced at Jesse and looked away.

Not intimate. If I don't sit, I topple on him—definitely too cozy.

Although their relationship had ended, Roxie loved him. Would always love him. Crystal could never hurt her sister. Would never date Jesse.

Wait. She wasn't dating. Jesse needed help. The heat of his body mingled with her old crush. His father's domineering nature—not to mention his alcoholism—kept Jesse's family away when they should be by his side. He, like her sister, roiled in pain. Emotional anguish. She held the cup to his lips. "Sip."

Jesse did. He didn't even grimace as he swallowed the nasty tea.

"How about the green goop?"

"I love Jell-O."

"No wonder the Snow girls ditched you. We eat nothing made from horses' hooves." Crystal lifted a spoonful of lime gelatin.

"Roxie will. Well, she'd devour gelatin made from moose hooves or whale blubber."

"Frozen seal fat sweetened with birch syrup."

"In an igloo." Jesse took the offered Jell-O. "I prefer the real thing."

After three bites and a drop of bullion, Jesse pushed away her hand holding the Jell-O.

Crystal shifted back to the chair as darkness crept through the windows. Jesse's IV monitor beeped as the solution emptied. "I'll get a nurse."

"No." He gripped her arm. "Stay."

Crystal glanced at the IV bag.

"They always come. Sooner or later. Stay." He patted the bed. "Sit here."

Crystal blinked. Her body said 'run to Jesse.' Thoughts of him and Roxie begged her to keep her distance.

"Please?" Jesse whispered. He closed his eyes. "Pretty please. Sugar on top."

Crystal eased herself next to him. After a few minutes, soft breathing said he slept. She watched. The night nurse entered and replaced the IV bag. Crystal lingered another half hour. Her head nodded in sleep. She jerked her head up and popped her eyes open. She'd been in Jesse's room for almost three hours—unlike the waiting room, the time flew. Climbing to her feet, she bent and kissed Jesse's forehead. With care, she lifted the bed rails and gazed at his face, peaceful in sleep.

On the drive home, the feel of his skin on her lips loitered. Her body betrayed her determination. Every part of her skin wanted to press against him. Her breathing quickened. She eased onto Route 65. *Think of "Tangled Tango." Instead of Danica in my song, I'll imagine Jesse as part of the snarled, hopeless trio. Roxie, me.*

Her heart churned. *And Jesse.*

Drive, Snow. Drive. No music. No love. No heart palpitations except from traffic crazies. Crystal concentrated on the drive, and before long she sat at the counter eating cold cereal and scrolling through TikTok. For several hours, no thoughts of Jesse floated through her brain. She yawned. Eleven p.m. She showered and climbed into bed.

Why had she delayed in updating Roxie? Her sister would be yearning to hear how the surgery went.

Roxie wouldn't phone. She needed to keep her distance and the hurt at bay. Although midnight in Knoxville, Roxie would be up.

Crystal called.

Roxie picked up on the first ring.

A smile lifted Crystal's mood, smiling always did. Her sister must've had her phone in her hand waiting to hear from Crystal. "Jesse's resting. Dr. Bernstein said the surgery went well. We need to wait a day or two and check for complications."

"I'm so happy—both for his health and for you."

"Me?" What was Roxie thinking?

"You love him. He loves you." Roxie scoffed. "Madison understood Jesse's attraction to you long before I did." She paused. "At least, she understood before I accepted the fact."

"No—"

"Yes. I want you—" Again a laugh cut off Roxie's thoughts. "You marry him. Keep him away from Madison."

"Will do. Come to our wedding this weekend."

"I dance first with Jesse. Afterward, he's all yours."

They laughed together.

"How are you really doing?" Crystal asked. "This has to be hard with your breakup and all."

"I hurt, but he was right. If we stayed together, we'd kill our dreams. We are too alike and too different at the same time. Anyway." Roxie's voice brightened. The subject would change. "When do you open for Washbasin Gentry?"

"We open for the opening act, you remember?"

"Who cares how many opening acts you perform before? You'll play on the stage at *the* Ryman Auditorium. Now answer my question."

"The concert's on May fifth."

"What are you going to sing?"

"'Tangled Tango.' Turns out Bass-Line likes that song for our first release."

"My sister, the superstar." Silence filled the line.

Crystal thought of saying goodnight, but something in the silence urged her to hang on.

"One last thing before I say goodnight."

Crystal waited.

"All joking aside. You and Jesse need to date."

"No!" Even as she protested, the warmth of Jesse next to her, the intimacy of feeding him, told Crystal this was the permission she'd wanted from her sister since she was sixteen. "I could never inflict that kind of pain on you. Ever."

Silence.

"I love you, Sissy-Crissy. Good night," Roxie whispered. The line went dead.

Crystal shook her head, but something shifted inside. Friends. The three of them would always be friends. Nothing more.

Chapter 24

Roxie sat in Stearns's class and stifled a yawn. *Perfect class for April Fool's Day. What a fool I was to retake Biopolitics. And whatever fool scheduled this slog for eight a.m. ought to be fired.* Her head nodded. She jerked upright.
Focus.

Three minutes later, she pictured Jesse, who'd been transferred to the rehab clinic several days ago. Instead of her ministering to him, she saw Crystal sitting in his room, talking, touching ... The image hurt a little, but like exercise, the hurt was good. It spoke of healing and gaining strength.

Strength. Crystal said Jesse would have a hard time using his leg for running, but Dr. Bernstein prevented an amputation. Once more her heart constricted, and she bit back tears. Roxie glanced at Stearns fussing with the Smartboard, trying to recalibrate the computerized whiteboard. Keeping his back to the class, the prof lost himself in technology. Roxie stared out the window her heart heavy. The Stearns's monotone droned on about government policies. She tapped a note into her laptop, then thought of Jesse again. Her pain wasn't for herself. Jesse loved to move. A crippled phys. ed teacher had a tough job. As tough as a dancing musician.

Crystal.

Jesse.

She shook her head once more and stared at her monitor. Maybe swimming could replace running. Jesse had competed in triathlons. Of the three activities— swimming, biking, running—the swim was his least favorite. Still, he was skilled in the water.

Skilled at everything.

She glanced at Stearns. *Got to focus on Biopolitics. Not Jesse in Speedos.* She tapped on her computer, but foremost in her mind was Jesse in a skimpy bathing suit. She loved Speedos. Shouldn't if she were going to be a modest Christian woman.

Stearns moaned on. "In the west, water ..."

Water. Crystal, her mermaid sister, loved lakes and rivers, oceans, and pools. Since she was a baby, she'd swum like a seal.

Roxie sighed and stared out the window once more. Instead of the students strolling past, she saw Crystal and Jesse swimming laps, laughing.

Kissing.

She shook her head and tapped out a few notes. Stearns followed the same syllabus as last semester. He used the same phrasing in his lectures. *What a jerk I am to inflict this on myself all for an A. Pride. Stupid pride.* What difference did an A make? The University of Maine already had accepted her. She had a job waiting for her there as a TA. Who needed this course? She smiled.

Poor Jesse. He'd have to finish his degree next semester. He'd already turned down his dream job at Knoxville Academy.

"Ms. Snow, can you tell me how the linguistic and discursive give way to the event-driven, and post-political in the politics of water?"

Roxie jolted to attention. She slapped her laptop shut and stood. "I can't. Excuse me, I ... I need to leave." She hurried out of the room.

Her pace didn't slacken until she found a cubicle in Hodges Library. With notes set out and ready to work, she felt ... free? If luck were on her side, Stearns would think she darted from class because she was sick.

No. Who cared? Why did she spend so much of her life caring about her status? Would a straight 4.0 make her parents love her more? She knew the answer. What did she care about? Failing Stearns's course had no consequence. She had a B-minus in her transcript already. The low grade would hold if she garnered an F this semester. She never had to step foot in Stearns's room again. She opened her computer and worked on her other courses. *Six weeks and I'm out of here.*

At four-thirty, she arrived at her apartment. Her roommates boiled boxed mac and cheese—their standard fare—for dinner, and after five minutes of chitchat, she stepped into her room and rummaged through her drawers for clean clothes. With her shower supplies in hand, Roxie headed for the bathroom. Within two steps, her cell rang with an unknown number from California. Spam. She didn't bother to disconnect the call.

Fifteen minutes later, she'd scrubbed off the grit from the day. Roxie returned to her room. She lifted her cell to check for texts. A voice mail? Spam never left voice mails. She hit the play button.

"Congratulations." The first words of a real human, not a computerized voice, sounded cheerful. Real.

Congrats? Yeah, right. I'm a Publisher's Clearing House Sweepstakes Winner.

"This is *Wild World Magazine*. You've placed third in our wildlife photo contest. Your photographs will appear

279

in our magazine due out next month. Your five-hundred-dollar cash award will be mailed out to you once you confirm our call."

Roxie stopped the recording. She couldn't have heard right. She rewound the message. The same words in the same cheerful, human voice replayed. She continued the message.

"With a third-place win, you can join us on our Alaska photoshoot leaving on May 6 in Anchorage. Second- and third-place winners must pay a portion of the trip. Your fee, as a third-place winner, will be $4,000—half the price. Contact us at this number to confirm your spot for our premier photo expedition. Once again, congratulations."

Roxie's head spun. The timing for the contest announcement was right. April 1.

Wait. Could this be an April Fool's joke?

No. Only her family and Jesse knew about the contest. They never teased her if they thought she'd melt down. And any failure had her melting down.

She smiled.

Never again will I doubt who I am. Stearns can drone, and Jesse can leave me. I'm perfect the way that I am.

She sat on her bed and reveled in her revelation. She, Roxie Star Snow, was fearfully and wonderfully made, created from the womb to be who she was. Being best was nothing but pride. Placing third, though? *Forgive me, Lord. I'm going to brag.*

Her trembling fingers tapped in the website for *Wild World* headquarters on her phone. Her foot patted the floor as she waited for the site to load. She scrolled to the contest page. Read the news.

No!

"Yes!" Leaping off the bed, Roxie danced across her floor, called to her roommates. *To tarnation with avoiding pride. I'm a winner!* "Guess who won third-place in a major photo contest?"

"When?"

"I didn't know."

"Fantastic."

The words swirled around Roxie as delight filled her roommates' faces. All three of them whooped with glee and grinned and danced around the kitchen.

"I need to call Jes—I mean, I need to call Crystal." Roxie hurried back into her bedroom.

Wait.

Wild World was located in California—three hours earlier than here. Only two p.m. in LA. She'd contact them first. Once she finalized all the details, she'd drop the news to her family.

The contest director confirmed the details. She sounded more excited than Roxie. *How can she be happier than I? I'm a winner!*

The woman continued. "You have until April 15 to—"

"No need to wait. I'm going on the trip." Roxie took down the Venmo information the woman from *Wild World* gave her. She had a credit card. Paid off the balance each month. She hesitated. Couldn't pay off four grand in one swoop. She clicked her teeth together for a moment. She had one reasonable thing to do.

With trembling fingers, she opened her laptop, tapped into the Venmo site. Her credit card shook in clenched fingers. Roxie copied the number, the expiration date and the CV-something code into the payment information. Within seconds, her confirmation email popped up.

I'm third. Tears sprung to her eyes. She grinned and hugged herself. In January, she'd reenrolled in Stearns's class because she wasn't good enough and had earned her lowest grade ever. Today? All she felt was a giddy joy making her unable to breathe or stand. Every muscle trembled, except for her mouth. With her cheeks so taut, she had to be grinning like a circus clown.

Wait. She plopped on the bed as her bubbling joy popped, spitting drops of despair over her. Finals would start on the eighth of May, three days *after* she had to leave for Alaska. On the eighteenth, she was supposed to graduate, but she'd be in Alaska. She glanced at the screensaver dancing across her monitor hiding the website. She tapped the computer to life. On the eighteenth she'd be in Barrow, Alaska, on the Arctic Ocean. How she dreamed of dipping her toes into the Arctic Ocean. They'd return to Fairbanks on the twenty-first and fly home. *What do I do now?*

Cancel.

Her head drooped as despair weighted her. She had to. Four years of hard work couldn't be thrown away. She picked up her phone. Her finger hovered over the *Wild World* number.

When God opens doors, he makes a path through. Mama's mantra flitted through her consciousness. She tossed her phone aside.

The next day she stood outside Stearns's office, her hand poised to knock. She hesitated. She had allowed this man to ruin her life in so many ways. No. Never had her life been ruined by the pontificating bore. Her unbelief destroyed her joy. Her pride alone created drama and drudgery. She rapped on the door.

"Come in." Even during office hours, time carved out to meet students' needs, the officious professor sounded like his name. Stern.

She stepped inside, but the prof didn't look up from the writing pad in front of him.

"What do you want?" He scribbled away on the paper.

"I have an opportunity for a photoshoot with *Wild World Magazine*. I won third-place in a contest, and this award is one of the most prestigious in the United States."

At last, Stearns peered at her. He actually smiled as he lay down his pen. "Congratulations, Snow. And why are you sharing this information with me?" He leaned back and steepled his hands. "You and I don't see eye to eye. I'm not your favorite professor, so I gather you need something from me?"

"We fly to Alaska on May 5."

He tapped the tips of his fingers still steepled together. "Finals begin on the eighth."

"I understand. Two of my profs will let me take an early exam. The other will give me an incomplete until I return."

Stearns, still leaning back in his chair, stared at her. "What do you want?"

He can't deduce my wish? She swallowed hard. "Can I take your exam early?"

He didn't answer. His face registered no emotion.

"Or take an incomplete and finish the course when I return?" Roxie rubbed sweaty fingers together. She wished she'd taken a seat because she was going to keel over in a minute. "I won a once in a lifetime chance. Third-place."

Seconds ticked away. Had to be seconds but felt like minutes. Hours. Roxie ground her teeth and composed her face. Hoped she looked mature—not the anxious child she felt like.

Stearns leaned forward. "I cannot make an exception for one student without everyone looking for special arrangements to be created so they can take an early vacation."

"This isn't a vacation, sir. Winning third-place is an honor few attain. The trip will help my career, and—"

"If memory serves me, you plan on being a wildlife biologist specializing in trophic effects on moose. Running around Alaska taking pictures of mountains and whales breeching has nothing to do with trophic deterioration."

"This isn't—"

"Excuse me." Stearns picked up his pen. "You have my answer. Good day."

She stood staring for a minute while the prof continued his scribbling. At last, she exited. In the hallway, she considered slamming the door behind her. No. Immature. She eased the door shut.

One thing stood in her way.

One thing ruined everything.

Snow in the Hollow jammed in Centennial Park. A photographer snapped shots as fans blew toward them. Leanne's hair, freed from her braid, swirled around as she pounded drums. Crystal's hair, held back in a flowered headband, tangled in the breeze. Abilene's spiked locks stayed put, but her shirt caught the breeze and exposed her belly button ring. Snow in the Hollow improvised as their bare feet tapped.

"I think we have what we need." The photographer laid his camera aside.

The Bass-Line publicist handed Crystal her shoes. "Next stop, the Ryman. Our album will be out in September."

"You have the date?" Leanne joined Crystal.

"We do." The publicist grinned. "You can announce it to the world. September first."

Abilene joined them. "What?"

Crystal and Leanne jabbered the news together.

"September first. Good news." Leanne hopped as she slipped on her shoes. "Vacation tomorrow. When we return to Music City, we start our routine."

tangled lives

"No routine at the Ryman," Crystal reminded her. "We're the opening act."

"Need to get ready, because next year, we'll be the headliners." Abilene zipped her bass into her gig bag.

"Richie showed me what they want to do," Leanne said. "His company designed avatars acting out our movements on his computer. I can't wait until you see how they reposition you on stage, Ms. Snow in the Hollow."

Crystal lifted her crutches and stood. She shook her right leg. "Going to make me a reverse Transformer and turn the machine into a human? Only way to make this contraption dance."

"Nope. They plan to have a rotating section of the stage. For now, they'll substitute buff, gorgeous stagehands for the rotating stage. These dreamboats will cart you around like a 1950s' musical starlet."

Crystal bit her cuticle as she pictured herself in the arms of good-looking guys. She figured who Leanne had in mind. "Who might these studs be?"

"Conner, Richie, and Kenji will carry you around the stage." Leanne pointed and grinned. "Look how beet red she turns." Leanne's laughter started the other two chuckling.

"Conner and I are destined to Destin," Abilene smiled. "A week on a Florida beach."

"April's pretty cold, even in Florida. How'll you and Conner stay warm?" Crystal winked.

"Conner and I have some physical therapy to catch up on."

Crystal blushed again imagining Abilene and Conner's therapy.

"You're no longer a beet, Crystal. You've turned into a strawberry." Abilene laughed. "You pale blondes, your sister included, have complexion issues." She and Leanne waved as they hurried off.

An afternoon free. *I know how I'm spending the afternoon. Genuine PT.*

At the rehab center, she found Jesse lying on a padded table. His therapist lifted Jesse's leg. He turned his head and groaned. Then a smile split his face. The room brightened with his grin. "Afternoon, Crystal Joy. You're here early."

"We wrapped up our photoshoot for the debut album." She nodded to the table. "What he's doing to you doesn't look fun."

"Brutus here says I need to work on flexibility. Even if he kills me." He glanced at his therapist. "Is what you're doing legal?"

"Nope. One more rep, and I'll give you an early release." The therapist lifted Jesse's leg. Pressed the limb toward his chest, then lowered it.

Jesse grimaced. Sweat popped out on his forehead.

Again, the therapist lifted.

"You said one last rep."

"I lied. This one's the last." The therapist lowered Jesse's leg and stepped back to pick up his clipboard.

"Help me to my chair, Brutus."

The therapist smiled and hung the clipboard back on the peg. "You call me Brutus one more time, I may have to execute another rep of leg lifts." Brutus placed his arm behind Jesse's back and helped him into a sitting position.

Jesse stretched his arms against the therapy table. "Dizzy."

"Take your time."

After a few seconds, Jesse nodded, and the therapist looped Jesse's left arm around his shoulder.

With a few hops, Jesse collapsed into the wheelchair breathing hard.

"Excellent job today. You are way ahead of schedule in the rehab."

"I'm going to be sick."

Brutus handed Jesse a basin.

He lifted the basin to his mouth and gagged, but his stomach settled. Jesse waved a hand. "Better now. Are you torturing me tomorrow at the same time?"

The therapist cracked his knuckles. "I wouldn't miss the session. Going to afflict you good." He gave an evil laugh. "You want me to wheel you to your room or will Crystal?"

"I'll wheel him back." Crystal gripped the handles and used them as her crutches and pushed him toward the elevator.

"I registered for the Knoxville marathon next year." Using his good arm, Jesse gave the wheels a shove.

The wheelchair veered right, and Crystal stumbled. "Watch it."

Jesse tilted his head back and closed his eyes. "Not ready to train for the run yet."

"How will you race twenty-six point two miles?"

"Wheelchair division if I can't use my legs."

"Motorized wheelchair?"

Jesse laughed. "A guaranteed way to win."

They walked in silence, the feeling natural. Normal.

Back in his room, Crystal helped hoist his legs onto his bed. "You're a sweaty mess."

"Brutus doesn't let me rest."

"Wait here."

"Where else would I be?" Jesse blew her a kiss.

Crystal feigned wiping the smooch from her lips and stepped to the bathroom. She dampened a washcloth and returned to Jesse's bedside. She ran the wet cloth over his face and neck.

Jesse, with eyes closed, wore an expression that looked like he was in heaven.

"Enjoying this?" Crystal laid the cloth on the bedside table.

He opened his eyes and winked.

Her face heated.

"So, my pretty little nurse, how'd the session go?"

"We have an album cover. The shots are now in the hands of the graphic artists. Going to make us gorgeous babes cover girls."

"Give me five." Jesse raised his left hand.

Crystal swiped his palm.

"I'm hungry. Brutus makes me burn calories."

"The cafeteria's closed."

"The snack bar has fabulous, calorie-laden burgers and fries. I burned off a day's worth of calories. My money—"

"Nope. No money. I'm on my way to being a billionaire. Remember? We're opening for Washbasin Gentry next month."

"I want front row seats. What mere mortal knows performers at *the* Ryman?"

Crystal smirked. "Despite your tease, I'll treat you. No burger, though. You need something healthy." She threw Jesse a smile over her shoulder and hobbled toward the elevator.

Roxie worked her way down the hallway in Jesse's rehab center checking room numbers. She hadn't seen him since he'd been transferred from Vanderbilt, but she had to share the news of her win with him. Only he, even more than her sister, knew the raging desire she'd had to nab this prize. After telling Jesse, she'd drive to her sister's. Once they learned she was heading to Alaska *before* the semester ended, she would worry about her folks.

The easy stuff first.

Room 212.

"Hey, Jesse."

He beamed at her. "Two Snows in one day. God's blessing me." Jesse waved her in. "Have a seat. Crystal went to fetch me a something healthy even though I'm craving a burger. Brutus, my therapist, worked me over and burned a thousand calories. At least, one K worth of energy expended."

"What therapy are you doing?"

"Leg lifts."

Roxie raised her brows. "Your right leg?"

"Nope. My angelic, haloed one." He tapped his braces. "He does the lifting. I groan. Recovery will be a long haul."

"Do you think you'll run again?"

Jesse grimaced. "Who knows? Maybe I'll turn to swimming—a wimp's sport, but hey, your sister loves the water."

Roxie took the chair near the bed.

"What brings you out here today?"

"My true love for you."

"And besides your undying adoration?"

"Let's wait until my sister returns."

As though mentioning her beckoned Crystal, she returned with a bag clutched in her hand. "You won. Burger. With lettuce, tomato, and onion topping the greasy meat—we'll make believe the meal is healthy. No fries." She smiled at Roxie. "A wonderful surprise to see you here."

"Guess what?" Roxie clamped her teeth together. *I sound like a kid getting a pony for Christmas.*

Jesse laid his bag of food aside.

Crystal's gaze riveted on Roxie.

"You are looking at an award-winning photographer."

Crystal clapped. "You won *Wild World?*"

"If third-place is winning, yes." Roxie's cheeks tightened as her smile grew.

"Congratulations. Come here." Jesse held out his arms.

Roxie's heart stuttered. To hold Jesse. Did she dare?

Obviously, she did. She stretched beside him on the hospital bed, and he wrapped his arms around her. A soft kiss on the top of her head felt so ... normal.

"Forgive me for my Valentine's Day massacre of your photoshoot." He laughed. "Get my joke?"

Roxie rolled her eyes.

"I knew you had talent, but wow." Jesse let go, and Roxie rose to sit near her sister once more. "What's the prize for third?"

"Half price on the $8,000 Alaskan shoot and the five-hundred-dollar award. Better yet, Patrick St. Mary's leading the event."

"Who's Patrick St. Mary?" Crystal asked.

"The Ansel Adams of the twenty-first century. His photography's been in *Nat Geo*, *Wild World*, *Outdoor Photography*, *and* he's had his own show at Livingston Galleries in Soho."

"Oh, that Patrick St. Mary." Crystal rolled her eyes and chuckled.

Jesse laughed, the sound a duet with her sister's mirth. "When do you leave?"

Roxie ducked her head and raised her shoulders. *Now they yell.*

Crystal lifted Roxie's chin with her fingers. "Spit out your news."

"May fifth from McGhee Tyson. Leave Anchorage on the sixth."

Crystal frowned.

Jesse sat up straight.

The lecture would come.

"Finals start the eighth." Jesse frowned. "You'll leave two weeks before the semester ends. You'll be gone for graduation to boot. Are you going to throw away your whole career?"

Roxie gazed at the ceiling, silently counted. By the time she got to four, she glared at Jesse. "What about you? You're skipping—"

Jesse waved his hand over the hardware repairing his arm and his leg. "Like I have a choice?"

"You shouldn't have been kayaking—"

"Roxie." Crystal scowled. "You have six weeks left until graduation."

"You have no right to talk. You quit school—"

"Not with six weeks until the end. What about grad school? The debt you accrued?"

Roxie's lip trembled. She bit down to hide her anger. "I thought both of you would be happy. I need another think." She stood. "Good luck with therapy. See you when I come home from Alaska, Crystal." She strode out of the room.

The sun hinted at setting as rose tinted the sky. Roxie drove toward Jacksboro, another three-hour drive due east. The phone rang, and Crystal's name appeared on the monitor. Roxie hit the disconnect on the steering wheel. Crystal rang again, and Roxie ignored the phone. Finally, she drove into a rural cutoff from the interstate. Her sister would phone and text a hundred more times. The spotty cell service on the back road gave Roxie a legitimate excuse to ignore Crystal's nagging. Crystal quit school and followed her dreams. *How could she find fault with me? Why is she betraying me?* Roxie's resolved hardened, and despite being conflicted about Crystal's lack of support, she became more determined. No way would she lose this gift from God. Worst-case scenario? Finish her degree next semester. Alaska wouldn't wait.

The sky darkened as she drove. She'd arrive home near her folks' bedtime, but she had planned to stay overnight with her sister. Crystal proved to be a Brutus bigger than Jesse's therapist. Roxie'd call her tomorrow and apologize for ignoring her, but she'd made up her mind. Arrangements had been made. She'd graduate summa cum laude even with Stearns's B-minus. Even if she graduated a year from now.

Crystal and Jesse would accept her decision. However, Mama and Daddy? How they bragged on her. The first of their daughters to complete a four-year degree. Off to earn a masters and a PhD. They'd nag about ending her undergrad career early, but all of Roxie's studies would follow the prearranged plan. In August, she'd go to Maine. After two years, she'd start her PhD. in Fairbanks. With this trip, she'd know more about where in Alaska she'd want to live and study. She'd see lynx and wolverines and caribou and moose and brown bear.

Grizzlies. Needed to buy bear spray.

Nothing would change in Mama and Daddy's plans for her, except sitting through a tedious graduation ceremony listening to a boring speech from some low-level famous person. With over five-thousand graduates, no one would be signaled out for an honor. No one would walk to the stage and receive a diploma. They should be happy they didn't have to attend.

Roxie pulled into her familiar gravel driveway. A soft glow lit the living room. Now well after eleven—the twins would be asleep. A blue light flickering from the living room window said Mama and Daddy watched the news. She mounted the front porch, tried the door, which opened to the cozy living room.

Her folks sat on the couch. Daddy had wrapped his arm around her mother. Mama's head lay on Daddy's shoulder.

"Roxie?" Daddy leaped off the couch. "What are you doing here?"

Roxie winked. "Did I catch you in the act?"

Mama groaned and stepped over to Roxie. Gave her a hug. "Is everything okay? Is Jesse ...? She left the question unspoken.

"Jesse's good. I saw him and Crystal at the rehab center earlier this evening. Dumb sister still hasn't allowed him to date her. I'm going to have to work on her."

"What brings you home?" Daddy asked.

Roxie slanted her eyes toward the ceiling and exhaled. "Let's have tea—not any of Grandma Cora's herbal glop— maybe fresh ginger tea? We'll talk."

"Is something wrong?" Mama frowned. She reached to Roxie and caressed her hair. "I'm worried. Late Friday, tea, been with Jesse, and now here."

"Nothing's wrong." *For me. For you, I'm sure, but not for me.*

At the kitchen table, Roxie sat across from her parents. She dunked her tea bag. Up and down. Up again. "I've got great news." She riveted her eyes on the tea bag.

"Praise God."

Roxie, her head still bowed over the tea, peeked through her eyelashes to see Mama's hand pressed to her heart.

Roxie, focused on the cup in front of her, stirred honey into her tea. The spoon clinked against the mug. She lifted the fragrant tea and sniffed the steaming ginger scent.

"Enough stalling. Spit it out." Daddy laughed. "Not literally. Swallow the tea, then give us the news. Seeing your excitement and you coming here so late, has to be big news."

The tale of her win spilled out.

Without a smile, Daddy leaned across the table. "You leave two weeks before graduation. You will not throw away your senior year."

Resolution hardened Roxie's voice. She would leave for Alaska—with or without her folks' blessing. "Nothing will be thrown off schedule. The sole issue I have is Biopolitics. Stearns won't make any exceptions for taking his final. When I miss the exam, I'll get a zero."

"No." Mama's eyebrows slammed together. She frowned. "You'll not graduate."

Roxie put her tea down on the table and studied the cup. If she spoke, she'd say the wrong thing, make matters worse. Even with her head bowed, she could feel her folks' eyes on her. She looked up. "Yes, I'll have my degree. I already have a B-minus in Stearns's course. Last semester's grade will hold if he gives me an F—which he will."

"What about your other classes?" Daddy asked.

"I'll take two exams early and one when I return at the end of May." She smiled. "In time for your anniversary."

"This is too sudden." Mama got up and grabbed a washcloth. She wiped the clean counter. A sure sign of her distress. "I want to see you receive your diploma."

Mama sounded, what? Not sad. Not regretful. Selfish?

"I'll graduate. I told you. All arrangements are in place."

"But the ceremony?"

"Graduation will be a lot of jabbering overloaded with clichés of us being the future. No individual accolades will be announced. Not with five-thousand students."

Mama moved on to the stovetop and scrubbed harder. "Pearl dropped out of school."

"And now runs a successful bakery and is expecting your second grandchild."

Daddy crossed his arms. "Don't backtalk your mother."

"I'm not." She swallowed and softened her voice. "I'm not arguing. I need to explain. She glanced at her mother who sank back into her chair. She blinked as though holding back tears.

"Crystal quit school. You didn't fret about her." Why couldn't her folks see, the only thing they'd miss out on was a stupid ceremony?

"She wasn't ready to graduate. You? You're my chance to have a—"

Roxie stood and glared at her mother. "I'm *your* chance? *I want* to see? You say *I'm* selfish?" She turned back to her father. "I'd hoped someone would celebrate my victory. Crystal and Jesse called me stupid. You're more concerned about your desires." Roxie squared her shoulders. For once, she didn't want to hide. No tears threatened. "I'm sorry I've been a disappointment to you. But I'm not to God. Or to me. Alaska and photography are my dream. You regaled us all the time about how you lived your own lives."

"We did compromise. Made everyone happy."

"Which I've done my whole life. Jesse, you, Crystal, Aunt Sunny. When I agreed, you loved me."

"We've always—"

"Not the way I've seen things." Roxie closed her eyes as her thoughts scrambled. *Speak the truth.* "Not the way I understood your actions. I've been wrong a lot in my life. I'm young and have time to change. I'm starting with Alaska. I'll call you later." She strode across the kitchen to the living room and gathered up her purse. She opened the front door and marched to her car. Would her folks follow her? See how selfish they were. They nagged all the time about her need to believe in herself. When she did? A tear slipped when she started the engine." She dashed it away. "You will not cry. Never again."

Roxie pulled into the road. Within five minutes, the sobs engulfed her. Everyone mattered but her. But they were wrong. Unable to see the dark road with her eyes clouded with tears and pain, Roxie pulled to the shoulder and wiped her eyes and blew her nose. She was done running away. Of thinking she wasn't good enough.

Everyone else had to realize she and her dreams mattered.

Chapter 25

Roxie lay in bed. She shifted and faced the window. The moon inched toward the western horizon. *Never going to sleep.*

The next thing she knew, she opened her eyes to bright sunshine. The cheery light reminded her of her two failures. First her B-minus in Biopolitics—a subject more suited for nerds than her.

More important. Her family didn't celebrate her victory. The honor she earned. A ceremony they wanted to attend was the only thing they cared about. She brushed hair out of her eyes and fingered the scar on her forehead. The welt healed well, but evidence of her night terrors ran along her hairline in a slight, raised ridge. A permanent reminder of how she allowed her past to define her future. The wound would fade like the lies she once believed.

If a person believed the truth, the truth freed her.

Crystal, Jesse, Mama, Daddy all saw the old Roxie, the frightened girl afraid to hurt anyone, always sure she'd be shunned. Someday they'd see the change in her. She, Roxie Star Snow—soon to be Dr. Roxie Star Snow—was a winner. She'd graduate summa cum laude. Not first in the class. Being first didn't matter. She was the bronze medalist of the premier photography contest.

And her family? The Snows always came around. Always believed in her and her decisions. Especially once Grandma Cora got a hold of her family.

She had one more person to celebrate with. A guaranteed supporter who'd champion her cause. The thought popped her out of bed. She slipped on leggings and a comfortable tunic and jogged out to her car. She sang old hymns as she drove back to Jacksboro.

She hadn't pulled the key out of the ignition before Grandma Cora came running down the porch steps. Grandma yanked the door handle, and Roxie stepped out of her car. Warm arms pulled her tight. In the softness of Grandma Cora's bosom, Roxie smelled lavender, a scent reminiscent of her childhood, long baths with her sisters, weeding the garden.

"Roxie Star. I'm so glad you came to see me." Grandma released her and held her at arm's length. "You're as beautiful as ever."

"You flatter like always." Roxie kissed her cheek.

"I hear you have news."

Roxie stepped back. "Mama called you already?"

"We're Crabtrees. What can I tell you? Those lovely fools heard *my* take on things. Come in." Grandma grabbed her hand and tugged. "I made avocado chocolate pudding. You eat and tell me your side of things."

"Avocado in chocolate pudding?" She wanted to gag. Did revulsion sound in Roxie's voice? "Grandma, this is a new low, even for you."

Grandma Cora looped her arm through Roxie's and pulled her up the porch, chattering all the way. "Pshaw, don't knock what you haven't tried. Even Grandpa devours the dessert."

"Is the pudding green?"

"Don't be a pudding head." Grandma's hand gripped Roxie's harder. They stepped into the house.

Roxie sneezed. "How many cats do you have now?"

"I'm downsizing. Only seven."

I should've remembered my Claritin. When she was little, Grandma Cora had given her a kitty. Olaf always made her sneeze and her eyes water. Grandma's exposure therapy never worked, but Olaf had been her lifeline back then.

They sat at the kitchen table, and Grandma scooped out what looked like ordinary chocolate pudding. "This is made with avocado, of course, chocolate, dates and almond milk."

"Dates?" Roxie grimaced.

"Eat."

She lifted the spoon to her lips then licked the chocolate with the tip of her tongue. "I *love* this."

"Told you."

Roxie spooned pudding into her mouth. "Better with a full spoonful. So, how did you persuade my folks?"

Grandma shifted from her spot across from Roxie. Settling adjacent to her, Grandma edged the chair so she leaned in toward Roxie. "I didn't say or do a thing."

"Right."

"Your folks love you as much as they adore Pearl and Crystal. Those two had so many issues—you know the cliché about squeaky wheels." She took Roxie's face in her hands and turned it, so Roxie's nose nearly touched hers. "You are loved. Unconditionally."

Grandma's warm hands erased all caution Roxie felt.

"Your problem—"

"My?" Roxie ducked her head and shoved pudding into her mouth to hide her smile.

"Don't smirk."

She failed to hide a thing.

"Your problem is you expect others to see your point the moment you make it. You react before others have time to assess your needs. From your own experiences, have you always agreed with Jesse or Crystal immediately?"

Roxie glanced away.

"What aggravates us the most is our bad traits exhibited in others. Your mama called me by six this morning. She bragged on you so bad. Her famous photographer."

"Then why didn't she call me?"

"That's a surprise."

"What surprise?"

Grandma ran her hand down Roxie's cheek. "Let's go see Grandpa. He's in the garage tinkering on his 1956 Ford. One last thing before Grandpa begins his boring rundown on the glories of a broken-down Crown Vic—on Saturday, at seven, act surprised when you come here."

"I'm coming here?"

Grandma put a finger over her lips. "Shh. Remember? Surprise."

Crystal sat near Jesse as he waited for Brutus to bring him to the gym. She fished out her cell. Still no return call from her sister. "If Roxie doesn't call soon, Jesse, I'm driving to Knoxville."

Jesse slipped the phone out of her hand. "Roxie always comes around. If you push, and I know this from experience, she'll do the opposite even if the opposite is something she doesn't like."

"Ready?" Jesse's therapist stepped into the room pushing a wheelchair.

"Hey, Brutus."

"Jesse, stop using the name Brutus." Crystal scowled. "He was a stab-in-the-back traitor."

"Exactly." Jesse hoisted his legs over the side of the bed and hopped onto his good leg.

"What is your real name?" Crystal asked as she gathered her crutches.

"Sasha."

"See why I call him Brutus? Sasha's a girl's name." Jesse, with Brutus's help, shifted into the wheelchair. "Or a poodle's moniker." The three walked toward the elevator.

"Nope, I'm not a poodle and not a girl, last I checked. Sasha's a nickname for Alexander."

"Are you Russian? Your last name's Jones. Doesn't sound Eastern European." Jesse said.

"Not Russian either. My grandparents were hippies. Grew up in the sixties and smoked too much dope. They rubbed off on my folks—philosophy-wise. My parents might drink a beer a year while Grandma brews artisan beer and uses CBD for every ailment. Mom liked Alexander because the name meant helper of mankind. I was lucky they picked Alexander and Sasha. They had considered Barnaby." Brutus made a face and pressed the elevator button.

Crystal laughed.

"I think I like Brutus better than any of my real monikers."

"I know about dumb parents and name choices," Crystal said.

"Crystal's a pretty name." The elevator door opened, and Brutus wiggled the chair in.

"My biological parents were addicts and overdosed. I'm probably named for crystal meth. Our theory says they name Roxie for Roxicodone. My sister Pearl had a different father. He insisted on a normal name."

"She made up for her pretty name by marrying a Malachi." Jesse hit the basement button for the gym, and the doors slid closed. "There's a name worse than Sasha."

"Be careful, Jesse. Remember we're heading *to* therapy." Brutus cracked his knuckles.

"Of course, the three of us will never give our babies silly names." Crystal glanced at Jesse, then looked away. Had dark-skinned Jesse blushed?

Saturday night, Roxie stepped into Grandma Cora's house and sneezed. Maybe thirty people jammed into the small living room. Every Crabtree and Snow in a fifty-mile radius had to be here. The entire troop screamed, "Surprise."

Roxie covered her mouth as though shocked.

"Come here, my girl." Grandma grabbed Roxie and hugged her to her bosom. She whispered, "Good thing you're not going into acting."

"I didn't pull off a look of shock?"

Grandma shook her head.

Roxie pulled away and leaned forward. They didn't? For real? She raced across the crowded room and swallowed Crystal in a hug. "You came?"

"You doubted? We wouldn't miss a Snow celebration."

We? Behind Crystal, perched on the couch, Jesse and Phoebe, Aunt Sunny's second girl, chatted. When they were younger, she and her cousin were inseparable. Her heart hammered. "What are you doing out of rehab?"

He held out his arms for a hug.

Roxie, forgetting to remain aloof, fell into the familiar arms. After what seemed like a lifetime, she released her hold on him. "I didn't think you could leave yet.

"Rehab's not a prison, but you better love me forever. Three hours in Crystal's little car could kill anyone with a broken limb, let alone an Ilizerov frame."

Phoebe stood. "I'll get you something to eat. What do you want?"

"What do we have?"

Phoebe gave her the look. "We're at Grandma's. Don't worry. I remember your favs." Phoebe threaded her way to the buffet table.

Roxie grabbed Crystal's hand and pulled her onto the couch. "I love you, Sis." She leaned in and whispered in her sister's ear.

Crystal blushed.

Roxie gave her a stern look and wagged her finger at her. "I'm serious."

"I believe you."

"I need to say hello to everyone else." Instead of immediately greeting her family, Roxie slipped into the bathroom. She closed the door and leaned against it. The headiness of knowledge that slipped inside of her like the voice of God nested in Roxie's heart. *I am perfect as I am.*

She lifted her eyes ceiling ward and whispered. "Lord, I'll slip up on this revelation. Please keep your truth real. Remind me when I forget." She stepped to the mirror and ran a comb through her hair. At twenty-two, she'd spent so much of her life feeling inferior. Middle child. Abandoned. Taken away from Mama. Their worries over Pearl and concern about Crystal's spina bifida made her feel like a second-class child.

But never, ever was she second in her family's life.

Chapter 26

On the first Saturday in May, Crystal took the stage at the Ryman Auditorium. She settled on her stool, her bare feet on the cool rungs of the chair. Leanne and Abilene, also barefooted, readied their instruments. Benches like church pews rose in a semicircle and spoke of their origins in a church. In the back of the highest tier, lancet windows sporting red, yellow, blue, and clear glass reflected shards of colored light against the walls like a kaleidoscope. She inhaled and felt the legacy from the likes of June Carter or Johnny Cash left to those who'd perform after them. Now, barely out of her teens, she stood on stage breathing in the scent of humanity. The walls glowed in the stage lights with a dim and glorious light.

The moment felt holy.

The audience applauded. The clapping like a splattering of rain. Light. Polite. They'd come for Washbasin Gentry, a group from Stinking Creek, who'd become megastars playing their Appalachian instruments. Shann McGuffrey made most of them. Cigar box guitars, washbasin basses, washboards, and drums from found containers. He was a whiz on all of them and made his guitar playing rival Segovia or Tommy Emmanuel. The others in the band used his jerry-rigged instruments along with saws, spoons, beer bottles, and even a vacuum cleaner.

The Ryman was about two-thirds full, but the place felt packed. Concert goers climbed through rows searching for seats. Most were indifferent to the opening act.

It didn't matter. Anticipation overflowed her soul.

With an inhale moments before she took the mic, she smiled at Jesse in the front row. He blew her a kiss as he stood on his good leg and propped himself up on one crutch. The cast had come off his arm a few days before. No sooner had he delivered the air-smooch, he whistled and hollered and clapped like a fool.

She loved him.

Never told him. She remembered the promise she made to Roxie during the celebration of her *Wild World* win.

Not now.

Later.

Crystal moved the mic closer. "Thank you for your warm welcome. You are in for a treat tonight. Washbasin Gentry blows me away every time I hear them. You won't be disappointed in their set." She surveyed the entire auditorium before she spoke again. "You won't be disappointed in ours, either. We call this one 'Tangled Tango'."

She hit the opening strings and began the sensual, traditional tango. The band joined, instrument by instrument.

The audience quieted.

The tangled bluegrass music heated up. Crystal's alto sang the opening lyrics. Abilene's soprano joined her. Finally, Leanne, her drum set quiet for the moment joined the band. The three sang in a tangled, intricate melody. Then Leanne hit the drums. Abilene wailed on the bass, and the fiddle took off. The moods in the music—anger to jealousy to rage. In the end, a slow, sensual peace settled into a tone of love.

tangled lives

Before the last notes, the audience whooped. Some stood, many clapped. The place electrified, and the entire auditorium jumped to their feet.

For five minutes, the applause rocked the Ryman like an old-fashioned revival. Snow in the Hollow took their bows over and over. Once offstage, Crystal leaned on her crutches and swung her feet off the floor.

Leanne and Abilene gripped each other and danced in circles around her.

Back in the auditorium, the audience clapped in rhythm. "More." "Encore." "Another."

Leanne looked at Crystal and Abilene. "Can you believe this?"

"No. I ..." Words failed Crystal. She pointed.

Shann McGuffrey approached—only McGuffrey and Billy Gibbons from ZZ Top could grow a beard so wild. Shann smiled. "I should fire you and have the guards escort you out."

Crystal's heart stuttered as the audience continued whooping and demanding more. *Wait. He's smiling.*

"Y'all upstaged us. We love when we find new talent, and you, ladies, are the real deal." He nodded toward the stage. "You have another song? They need an encore. Nobody ever asked for an encore from a warm-up group."

Crystal looked from McGuffrey to the stage to her girls of the band and back to Shann. "For real?"

"No time to waste. First rule of entertainment—make the audience think you won't give a little extra, but don't wait too long." He pointed to the stage. "Go."

Crystal's crutches wobbled as she made her way front and center. Her hands gripped her supports so tight, feeling in them fled. She climbed on to her stool. Picked up her fiddle. The audience quieted.

"What an honor you've given us. We do have one more, the song—" Crystal tuned her fiddle. "—'Aaron's Lament' is one of the favorites at Jack's by the River." She hit the first note, and the crowd went wild.

With the final note, the audience exploded. Crystal carried her fiddle off stage, and the sound followed her down the hallways to her dressing room. They silenced when the door closed behind them.

They sat in stunned disbelief, their voices frozen as they looked from one to the other.

Someone knocked.

Conner and Richie stormed in and swooped up their girls.

Jesse?

Through the open door, she saw him leaning against the wall, a bouquet of flowers in his hand. He motioned for her to join him.

"You amaze me." Jesse pulled her close.

Her crutches clattering to the floor, not needed in the embrace of his arms. She melted into him. Her blood heated, and her promise to Roxie kept time with her pulse.

"I'm so proud—"

She cut off his words with her mouth. She drank greedily as shock waves traveled up her spine. Jesse had to feel the pounding of her heart. *This is what Leanne and Abilene feel, why they're so obsessed with their men.* For four years, she longed for Jesse. Deferred to her sister. Even after Roxie told her time again to freely love this man, she held back. If her toes had feeling, they'd be curling from the electricity zapping every other part of her body. She pulled away. "I love you, Jesse Maxwell. Be my man?"

"I am. Body, soul, and mind." He stumbled and grimaced as he jiggled the Ilizarov frame. "I think, though, we may have to act like old folks. Help me into the dressing room."

Together they joined their friends and sank onto the couch.

tangled lives

Abilene raised a glass of champagne. "To us."

Leanne stood and lifted her glass. "Especially to Crystal, the girl who has moxie and character. One who loves us—even Danica—as we are. Thank you."

Jesse pulled Crystal closer. "I love you too."

How could life be better?

Sitting at the gate in McGhee Tyson airport, Roxie adjusted her earbuds and queued the video Jesse sent a minute ago. Today. Crystal's debut. At the Ryman, the spotlight shown on her. If only the audience would recognize the import of this moment.

The set began. After a few bars of music, Roxie no longer sat alone in an airport terminal. She found herself in Nashville, lost in her sister's talent. In "Tangled Tango," Roxie felt the conflict of her life. As the music ended, she was released. At peace. Reluctantly, her finger hovered over the stop button on her cell. *Wait. Another song? She only had one. I thought.*

Crystal made her way back onstage. "What an honor you've given us ..."

She got an encore?

Roxie listened to the second song. The crazy one where tragedy turned to God's glory in "Aaron's Lament." Once through the set wasn't enough for Roxie. She replayed the performance.

Roxie blinked hard as a regret seeped through her. She could've had Jesse. Had she the sense of a turkey, she'd be marrying him instead of running off to Alaska. A smile lifted her lips. *On the other hand, I'd be running because I would have strangled the stubborn boy who heard me but never listened to what I needed.*

Jesse and Crystal, though. Better paired than Cash and Carter.

Than her and Jesse. Their love—as love should be.

She looked at her gate. Ten minutes until she boarded her red eye. First leg flew to O'Hare, second to Seattle. Tomorrow morning, she'd land in Anchorage. A path she hadn't considered because she hadn't believed in herself. Even as Jesse and Crystal began a life together, tonight would start a new phase of her own life. One where lies wouldn't take root in her soul.

Someday, Jesse and Crystal would marry. Roxie would make sure they stayed on track.

Vernita said no one needed a man to be complete. Her biological grandmother was right.

An announcement over the PA called for first-class passengers to board the flight to Chicago. First class. Not her.

With her finances, first class as an airline passenger was out of the question.

As a child of God? Oh, she was classy.

Crystal's set played once more through her earbuds. Roxie looked at the phone, kissed her fingers and touched the face of the cell.

Life was good.

Epilogue

Crystal shivered in Jesse's arms as they sat in McGhee Tyson airport. The long ramp leading from the gates sported gaily decorated Christmas trees. Lights twinkled in the closed shops. The crowded airport shuttled passengers in to meet their families on Christmas morning.

Jesse pulled her tighter, his leg, freed of all steel and plaster and screws, pressed hard against her. "Will you tell her now or wait until we get to your parents?"

Crystal gave him the look.

"I suppose my question should be, will you wait until after you smother her in hugs?"

"Before." Crystal looked at her hands. Despite the drafty hallway, warmth filled her. When a surge of passengers left the departure terminal, Crystal clambered to her feet.

Jesse looped his arm around her. "There." He pointed.

"Where?"

"Next to the tall guy wearing the orange Vols' toboggan."

Crystal spied her sister. She waved, her heart pounding, wanting to run. So much had happened in the eight months her sister had been gone. *Wait.* "She's not passing the guy in the hat. Look how she gazes at him. Holding hands? Roxie has another boyfriend."

As though her sister heard her, Roxie lifted her head. A smile split her face, and she ran. Within seconds, she held

Crystal in a bear hug that would make a grizzly proud. "Crissy-Sissy, how I missed you." She broke away. "Jesse." Roxie pecked his cheek.

The tall stranger stood behind her. Roxie grasped his hand and pulled him into the group.

Jesse held out his hand. "I'm—"

The stranger let go of the handle to his roller bag and shook. "Jesse Maxwell. Roxie's told me a lot about you."

Jesse stared at the man, and his eyes seemed to question.

"In the winter, the weather's cold and dark, especially up north. What can we do but talk and—"

Roxie elbowed the man.

The stranger turned to Crystal. "And you are the love of my wife's life."

Crystal stumbled back and bumped into the bench. *Wife?* She looked from the man to her sister.

Roxie ducked her head. Her shoulders rose. "Surprise." Her voice sounded soft and apologetic.

"You're married?" Crystal's breaths became shallow. Why hadn't Roxie told her?

"I guess Roxie wanted to surprise you. I'm Patrick St. Mary. We married before we traveled to the tundra to search for arctic fox in October."

"No communication up there." Roxie shuffled her feet and studied the tiled hallway as though a fascinating image coated the floor. "When we returned to Anchorage, I thought I'd surprise everyone for Christmas."

Crystal looked from Patrick to Roxie. Her heart sank. *Why didn't she call me?*

"I should've called."

"You read my mind."

"Let's get our bags," Roxie took Crystal's hand and squeezed. "Wait. What are you wearing?" She held up Crystal's left hand and fingered the diamond ring and grinned. "I'm off the hook for my secret. When did you get engaged?"

"This morning." Crystal turned toward her dreamy fiancé. "We're getting married in May. I want you to be the maid of honor." Crystal giggled. "I guess I should say matron of honor."

Roxie glanced at Patrick.

"Absolutely. She'll be there."

"You have the Tibetan—"

"I have nothing that will interfere with a Snow wedding."

They arrived at the luggage carousel, and Jesse pulled Patrick and Roxie aside. "Let everyone scramble for their bags. "Fill us in now about your wedding. I'd take you out to eat, but the Waffle House is the only restaurant open on Christmas morning."

Patrick looped his arm over Roxie's shoulder. "When the *Wild World* shoot ended, I headed for a gig on the Circle. I needed to head north. Roxie wanted to come. We couldn't travel alone until we married, so we did."

Crystal looked from Roxie to Patrick and back again. "Do you and Patrick love each other?"

They didn't need to answer. The look on their faces as they gazed into each other's eyes told their love story.

Her sister was finally as happy as she.

about the author

Carol McClain is an award-winning author and a passionate Christian. Her stories show the redemption of the unredeemable. Although themes range from forgiving the unforgiveable to escaping the trauma of the past, all her stories are told with humor and compassion. They will make you laugh and cry.

McClain lives in Tennessee with her husband and tries to stay sane while creating stories, pottery or stained glass. She serves on the board of ACFW Knoxville and facilitates the local writers' group at Postmark Lafollette.

You can connect with her at www.carolmcclain.com.

treasured lives books

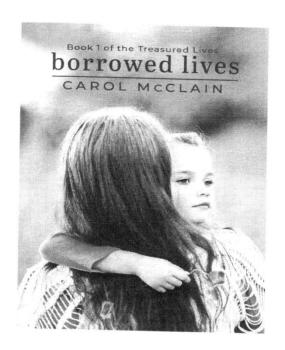

Book 1 of the Treasured Lives
borrowed lives
CAROL McCLAIN

Book 2 of the Treasured Lives
prodigal lives
CAROL McCLAIN

Made in the USA
Monee, IL
19 July 2023